A-166

THE BARRIER

[See p. 41

"GREAT LOVELY DOVE!" EJACULATED BURRELL, FERVENTLY ...
WONDERING IF THIS GLORIOUS THING COULD BE THE QUAINT
HALF-BREED GIRL OF YESTERDAY

The Barrier

By REX BEACH

AUTHOR OF
"The Spoilers," "The Silver Horde," Etc.

With Four Illustrations By
DENMAN FINK

A. L. BURT COMPANY
PUBLISHERS   NEW YORK

Published by arrangement with Harper & Brothers

BOOKS BY
REX BEACH

THE SILVER HORDE. Ill'd. Post 8vo. . $1.50
THE BARRIER. Illustrated. Post 8vo . . 1.50
THE SPOILERS. Illustrated. Post 8vo . . 1.50

HARPER & BROTHERS, PUBLISHERS, N. Y.

Copyright, 1908, by HARPER & BROTHERS.

Printed in the United States of America.

CONTENTS

CHAP.		PAGE
I.	THE LAST FRONTIER	1
II.	POLEON DORET'S HAND IS QUICKER THAN HIS TONGUE	15
III.	WITHOUT BENEFIT OF CLERGY	34
IV.	THE SOLDIER FINDS AN UNTRODDEN VALLEY	49
V.	A STORY IS BEGUN	67
VI.	THE BURRELL CODE	81
VII.	THE MAGIC OF BEN STARK	95
VIII.	THE KNIFE	107
IX.	THE AWAKENING	124
X.	MEADE BURRELL FINDS A PATH IN THE MOONLIGHT	141
XI.	WHERE THE PATH LED	158
XII.	A TANGLED SKEIN	174
XIII.	STARK TAKES A HAND IN THE GAME	190
XIV.	A MYSTERY IS UNRAVELLED	209
XV.	AND A KNOT TIGHTENED	229
XVI.	JOHN GALE'S HOUR	245
XVII.	THE LOVE OF POLEON DORET	259
XVIII.	RUNNION FINDS THE SINGING PEOPLE	283
XIX.	THE CALL OF THE OREADS	302

THE BARRIER

CHAPTER I

THE LAST FRONTIER

MANY men were in debt to the trader at Flambeau, and many counted him as a friend. The latter never reasoned why, except that he had done them favors, and in the North that counts for much. Perhaps they built likewise upon the fact that he was ever the same to all, and that, in days of plenty or in times of famine, his store was open to every man, and all received the same measure. Nor did he raise his prices when the boats were late. They recalled one bleak and blustery autumn when the steamer sank at the Lower Ramparts, taking with her all their winter's food, how he eked out his scanty stock, dealing to each and every one his portion, month by month. They remembered well the bitter winter that followed, when the spectre of famine haunted their cabins, and when for endless periods they cinched their belts, and cursed and went hungry to sleep, accepting, day by day, the rations doled out to them by the grim, gray man at the log store. Some of them had money-belts weighted low with gold washed from the bars at Forty Mile, and there were others who had wandered in from the

THE BARRIER

Koyukuk with the first frosts, foot-sore and dragging, the legs of their skin boots eaten to the ankle, and the taste of dog meat still in their mouths. Broken and dispirited, these had fared as well through that desperate winter as their brothers from up-river, and received pound for pound of musty flour, strip for strip of rusty bacon, lump for lump of precious sugar. Moreover, the price of no single thing had risen throughout the famine.

Some of them, to this day, owed bills at Old Man Gale's, of which they dared not think; but every fall and every spring they came again and told of their disappointment, and every time they fared back into the hills bearing another outfit, for which he rendered no account, not even when the debts grew year by year, not even to "No Creek" Lee, the most unlucky of them all, who said that a curse lay on him so that when a pay-streak heard him coming it got up and moved away and hid itself.

There were some who had purposely shirked a reckoning, in years past, but these were few, and their finish had been of a nature to discourage a similar practice on the part of others, and of a nature, moreover, to lead good men to care for the trader and for his methods. He mixed in no man's business, he took and paid his dues unfalteringly. He spoke in a level voice, and he smiled but rarely. He gazed at a stranger once and weighed him carefully, thereafter his eyes sought the distances again, as if in search of some visitor whom he knew or hoped or feared would come. Therefore, men judged he had lived as strong men live, and were glad to call him friend.

This day he stood in the door of his post staring up the sun-lit river, absorbing the warmth of the Arctic

THE LAST FRONTIER

afternoon. The Yukon swept down around the great bend beneath the high, cut banks and past the little town, disappearing behind the wooded point below, which masked the up-coming steamers till one heard the sighing labor of their stacks before he saw their smoke. It was a muddy, rushing giant, bearing a burden of sand and silt, so that one might hear it hiss and grind by stooping at its edge to listen; but the slanting sun this afternoon made it appear like a boiling flood of molten gold which issued silently out of a land of mystery and vanished into a valley of forgetfulness. At least so the trader fancied, and found himself wishing that it might carry away on its bosom the heavy trouble which weighed him down, and bring in its place forgetfulness of all that had gone before. Instead, however, it seemed to hurry with news of those strange doings "up-river," news that every downcoming steamboat verified. For years he had known that some day this thing would happen, that some day this isolation would be broken, that some day great hordes of men would overrun this unknown land, bringing with them that which he feared to meet, that which had made him what he was. And now that the time had come, he was unprepared.

The sound of shouting caused him to turn his head. Down-stream, a thousand yards away, men were raising a flag-staff made from the trunk of a slender fir, from which the bark had been stripped, heaving on their tackle as they sang in unison. They stood well out upon the river's bank before a group of well-made houses, the peeled timbers of which shone yellow in the sun. He noted the symmetrical arrangement of the buildings, noted the space about them that had been smoothed for a drill-ground, and from which the stumps

THE BARRIER

had been removed; noted that the men wore suits of blue; and noted, in particular, the figure of an officer commanding them.

The lines about the trader's mouth deepened, and his heavy brows contracted.

"That means the law," he murmured, half aloud, while in his voice was no trace of pleasure, nor of that interest which good men are wont to show at sight of the flag. "The last frontier is gone. The trail ends here!"

He stood so, meditating sombrely, till the fragment of a song hummed lightly by a girl fell pleasantly on his ears, whereupon the shadows vanished from his face, and he turned expectantly, the edges of his teeth showing beneath his mustache, the corners of his eyes wrinkling with pleasure.

The sight was good to him, for the girl approaching down the trail was like some wood sprite, light-footed, slender, and dark, with twin braids of hair to her waist framing an oval face colored by the wind and sun. She was very beautiful, and a great fever surged up through the old man's veins, till he gripped the boards at his side and bit sharply at the pipe between his teeth.

"The salmon-berries are ripe," she announced, "and the hills back of the village are pink with them. I took Constantine's squaw with me, and we picked quarts and quarts. I ate them all!"

Her laughter was like the tinkle of silver bells. Her head, thrown back as she laughed gayly, displayed a throat rounded and full and smooth, and tanned to the hue of her wind-beaten cheeks. Every move of her graceful body was unrestrained and flowing, with a hint of Indian freedom about it. Beaded and trimmed like a native princess, her garments manifested an ornature that spoke of savagery, yet they were neatly cut and held to the pattern of the whites.

"Constantine was drunk again last night, and I had to give him a talking to when we came back. Oh, but I laid him out! He's frightened to death of me when I'm angry."

She furrowed her brow in a scowl — the daintiest, most ridiculous pucker of a brow that ever man saw — and drew her red lips into an angry pout as she recounted her temperance talk till the trader broke in, his voice very soft, his gray-blue eyes as tender as those of a woman:

"It's good to have you home again, Necia. The old sun don't shine as bright when you're away, and when it rains it seems like the moss and the grass and the little trees was crying for you. I reckon everything weeps when you're gone, girl, everything except your old dad, and sometimes he feels like he'd have to bust out and join the rest of them."

He seated himself upon the worn spruce-log steps, and the girl settled beside him and snuggled against his knee.

"I missed you dreadfully, daddy," she said. "It seemed as if those days at the Mission would never end. Father Barnum and the others were very kind, and I studied hard, but there wasn't any fun in things without you."

"I reckon you know as much as a priest, now, don't you?"

"Oh, lots more," she said, gravely. "You see, I am a woman."

He nodded reflectively. "So you are! I keep forgetting that."

THE BARRIER

Their faces were set towards the west, where the low sun hung over a ragged range of hills topped with everlasting white. The great valley, dark with an untrodden wilderness of birch and spruce and alder, lay on this side, sombre and changeless, like a great, dark-green mat too large for its resting-place, its edges turned up towards the line of unmelting snow. Beyond were other ranges thrust skyward in a magnificent confusion, while still to the farther side lay the purple valley of the Koyukuk, a valley that called insistently to restless men, welcoming them in the spring, and sending them back in the late summer tired and haggard with the hunger of the North. Each year a tithe remained behind, the toll of the trackless places, but the rest went back again and again, and took new brothers with them.

"Did you like the books I sent you with Poleon when he went down to the coast? I borrowed them from Shakespeare George."

The girl laughed. "Of course I did—that is, all but one of them."

"Which one?"

"I think it was called *The Age of Reason*, or something like that. I didn't get a good look at it, for Father Barnum shrieked when he saw it, then snatched it as if it were afire. He carried it down to the river with the tongs."

"H'm! Now that I think of it," said the old man, "Shakespeare grinned when he gave it to me. You see, Poleon ain't much better on the read than I am, so we never noticed what kind of a book it was."

"When will Poleon get back, do you suppose?"

"Most any day now, unless the Dawson dance-halls

"I MISSED YOU DREADFULLY, DADDY," SAID NECIA. "THERE WASN'T ANY FUN IN THINGS WITHOUT YOU"

are too much for him. It won't take him long to sell our skins if what I hear is true."

"What is that?"

"About these Cheechakos. They say there are thousands of tenderfeet up there, and more coming in every day."

"Oh! If I had only been here in time to go with him!" breathed the girl. "I never saw a city. It must be just like Seattle, or New York."

Gale shook his head. "No. There's considerable difference. Some time I'll take you out to the States, and let you see the world—maybe." He uttered the last word in an undertone, as if in self-debate, but the girl was too excited to notice.

"You will take mother, too, and the kiddies, won't you?"

"Of course!"

"Oh! I—I—" The attempt to express what this prospect meant to her was beyond her girlish rapture, but her parted lips and shining eyes told the story to Gale. "And Poleon must go, too. We can't go anywhere without him." The old man smiled down upon her in reassurance. "I wonder what he'll say when he finds the soldiers have come. I wonder if he'll like it."

Gale turned his eyes down-stream to the barracks, and noted that the long flag-staff had at last been erected. Even as he looked he saw a bundle mounting towards its tip, and then beheld the Stars and Stripes flutter out in the air, while the men below cheered noisily. It was some time before he answered.

"Poleon Doret is like the rest of us men up here in the North. We have taken care of ourselves so far, and I guess we're able to keep it up without

THE BARRIER

the help of a smooth-faced Yankee kid for guardian."

"Lieutenant Burrell isn't a Yankee," said Necia. "He is a blue-grass man. He comes from Kentucky."

Her father grunted contemptuously. "I might have known it. Those rebels are a cultus, lazy lot. A regular male man with any ginger in him would shed his coat and go to work, instead of wearing his clothes buttoned up all day. It don't take much 'savvy' to run a handful of thirteen-dollar-a-month soldiers." Necia stirred a bit restlessly, and the trader continued: "It ain't man's work, it's—loafing. If he tries to boss us he'll get *quite* a surprise."

"He won't try to boss you. He has been sent here to build a military post, and to protect the miners in their own self-government. He won't take any part in their affairs as long as they are conducted peaceably."

Being at a loss for an answer to this unexpected defence, the old man grunted again, with added contempt, while his daughter continued:

"This rush to the upper country has brought in all sorts of people, good, bad—and worse; and the soldiers have been sent to prevent trouble, and to hold things steady till the law can be established. The Canadian Mounted Police are sending all their worst characters down-river, and our soldiers have been scattered among the American camps for our protection. I think it's fine."

"Where did you learn all this?"

"Lieutenant Burrell told me," she replied; at which her father regarded her keenly. She could not see the curious look in his eyes, nor did she turn when, a moment later, he resumed, in an altered tone:

THE LAST FRONTIER

"I reckon Poleon will bring you something pretty from Dawson, eh?"

"He has never failed to bring me presents, no matter where he came from. Dear old Poleon!" She smiled tenderly. "Do you remember that first day when he drifted, singing, into sight around the bend up yonder? He had paddled his birch-bark from the Chandelar without a thing to eat; hunger and hardship only made him the happier, and the closer he drew his belt the louder he sang."

"He was bound for his 'New Country'!"

"Yes. He didn't know where it lay, but the fret for travel was on him, and so he drifted and sang, as he had drifted and sung from the foot of Lake Le Barge."

"That was four years ago," mused Gale, "and he never found his 'New Country,' did he?"

"No. We tied him down and choked it out of him," Necia laughed. "Dear, funny old Poleon—he loves me like a brother."

The man opened his lips, then closed them, as if on second thought, and rose to his feet, for, coming towards them up the trail from the barracks, he beheld a trim, blue-coated figure. He peered at the approaching officer a moment, set his jaw more firmly, and disappeared into the store.

"Well, we have raised our flag-staff," said the Lieutenant as he took a seat below Necia. "It's like getting settled to keep house."

"Are you lazy?" inquired the girl.

"I dare say I am," he admitted. "I've never had time to find out. Why?"

"Are you going to boss our people around?" she continued, bent on her own investigation.

"No. Not as long as they behave. In fact, I hardly know what I am to do. Maybe you can tell me." His smile was peculiarly frank and winning. "You see, it's my first command, and my instructions, although comprehensive, are rather vague. I am supposed to see that mining rights are observed, to take any criminals who kindly offer themselves up to be arrested, and to sort of handle things that are too tough for the miners themselves."

"Why, you are a policeman!" said Necia, at which he made a wry face.

"The Department, in its wisdom, would have me, a tenderfoot, adjust those things that are too knotty for these men who have spent their lives along the frontier."

"I don't believe you will be very popular with our people," Necia announced, meditatively.

"No. I can see that already. I wasn't met with any brass-bands, and I haven't received any engraved silver from the admiring citizens of Flambeau. That leaves nothing but the women to like me, and, as you are the only one in camp, you will have to like me very much to make up for its shortcomings."

She approved of his unusual drawl; it gave him a kind of deliberation which every move of his long, lithe body belied and every glance of his eyes contradicted. Moreover, she liked his youth, so clean and fresh and strange in this land where old men are many and the young ones old with hardship and grave with the silence of the hills. Her life had been spent entirely among men who were her seniors, and, although she had ruled them like a spoiled queen, she knew as little of their sex as they did of hers. Unconsciously the strong young life within her had clam-

THE LAST FRONTIER

ored for companionship, and it was this that had drawn her to Poleon Doret—who would ever remain a boy—and it was this that drew her to the young Kentuckian; this, and something else in him, that the others lacked.

"Now that I think it over," he continued, "I'd rather have you like me than have the men do so."

"Of course," she nodded. "They do anything I want them to—all but father, and—"

"It isn't that," he interrupted, quickly. "It is because you *are* the only woman of the place, because you are such a surprise. To think that in the heart of this desolation I should find a girl like—like you, like the girls I know at home."

"Am I like other girls?" she inquired, eagerly. "I have often wondered."

"You are, and you are not. You are surprisingly conventional for these surroundings, and yet unconventionally surprising—for any place. Who are you? Where did you come from? How did you get here?"

"I am just what you see. I came from the States, and I was carried. That is all I can remember."

"Then you haven't lived here always?"

"Oh, dear, no! We came here while I was very little, but of late I have been away at school."

"Some seminary, eh?"

At this she laughed aloud. "Hardly that, either. I've been at the Mission. Father Barnum has been teaching me for five years. I came up-river a day ahead of you."

She asked no questions of him in return, for she had already learned all there was to know the day before from a grizzled corporal in whom was the hunger to talk. She had learned of a family of Burrells whose name was known throughout the South, and that Meade Burrell came from the Frankfort branch, the branch that had raised the soldiers. His father had fought with Lee, and an uncle was now in the service at Washington. On the mother's side the strain was equally militant, but the Meades had sought the sea. The old soldier had told her much more, of which she understood little; told her of the young man's sister, who had come all the way from Kentucky to see her brother off when he sailed from San Francisco; told her of the Lieutenant's many friends in Washington, and of his family name and honor. Meade Burrell was undoubtedly a fine young fellow in his corporal's eyes, and destined to reach great heights, as the other Burrells had before him. The old soldier, furthermore, had looked at her keenly and added that the Burrells were known as "divils among the weemen."

Resting thus on the steps of Old Man Gale's store, the two talked on till they were disturbed by the sound of shrill voices approaching, at which the man looked up. Coming down the trail from the town was a squaw and two children. At sight of Necia the little ones shouted gleefully and scampered forward, climbing over her like half-grown puppies. They were boy and girl, both brown as Siwashes, with eyes like jet beads and hair that was straight and coarse and black. At a glance Burrell knew them for "breeds," and evidently the darker half was closer to the surface now, for they choked, gurgled, stuttered, and coughed in their Indian tongue, while Necia answered them likewise. At a word from her they turned and saw him, then, abashed at the strange splendor of his uniform, fell silent, pressing close to her. The squaw, also, seemed to resent his presence, for, after a lowering glance,

THE LAST FRONTIER

she drew the shawl closer about her head, and, leaving the trail, slunk out of sight around the corner of the store.

Burrell looked up at his companion's clear-cut, delicate face, at the wind-tanned cheeks, against which her long braids lay like the blue-black locks of an Egyptian maid, then at her warm, dark eyes, in which was a hint of the golden light of the afternoon sun. He noted covertly the slender lines of her body and the dainty, firm, brown hands flung protectingly about the shoulders of her little friends, who were peering at him owlishly from their shelter.

The bitter revolt that had burned in him at the prospect of a long exile in this undiscovered spot died out suddenly. What a picture she made! How fresh and flower-like she looked, and yet the wisdom of her! He spoke impulsively:

"I am glad you are here, Miss Necia. I was glad the moment I saw you, and I have been growing gladder ever since, for I never imagined there would be anybody in this place but men and squaws—men who hate the law and squaws who slink about—like that." He nodded in the direction of the Indian woman's disappearance. "Either that, or, at best, a few 'breeds' like these little fellows."

She looked at him quickly.

"Well! What difference would that make?"

"Ugh! Squaws and half-breeds!" His tone conveyed in full his utter contempt.

The tiny hands of the boy and girl slid into her own as she arose. A curiously startled look lay in her eyes, and an inquiring, plaintive wrinkle came between her brows.

"I don't believe you understand," she said. "Lieutenant Burrell, this is my sister, Molly Gale, and this is my little brother John." Both round-eyed elfs made a ducking courtesy and blinked at the soldier, who gained his feet awkwardly, a flush rising into his cheeks.

From the regions at the rear of the store came the voice of an Indian woman calling:

"Necia! Necia!"

"Coming in a moment," the girl called back; then, turning to the young officer, she added, quietly: "Mother needs me now. Good-bye!"

CHAPTER II

POLEON DORET'S HAND IS QUICKER THAN HIS TONGUE

THE trader's house sat back of the post, farther up on the hill. It was a large, sleepy house, sprawling against the sunny side of the slope, as if it had sought the southern exposure for warmth, and had dozed off one sultry afternoon and never waked up from its slumber. It was of great, square-hewn timbers, built in the Russian style, the under side of each log hollowed to fit snugly over its fellow underneath, upon which dried moss had previously been spread, till in effect the foot-thick walls were tongued and grooved and, through years of seasoning, become so tinder dry that no frosts or heats could penetrate them. Many architects had worked on it as it grew, room by room, through the years, and every man had left behind the mark of his individuality, from Pretty Charlie the pilot, who swung an axe better than any Indian on the river, to Larsen the ship's carpenter, who worked with an adze and who starved the summer following on the Koyukuk. It had stretched a bit year by year, for the trader's family had been big in the early days when hunters and miners of both breeds came in to trade, to loaf, and to swap stories with him. Through the winter days, when the caribou were in the North and the moose were scarce, whole families of natives came and camped there, for Alluna, his squaw,

15

THE BARRIER

drew to her own blood, and they felt it their due to eat of the bounty of him who ruled them like an overlord; but when the first goose honked they slipped away until, by the time the salmon showed, the house was empty again and silent, save for Alluna and the youngsters. In return these people brought him many skins and much fresh meat, for which he paid no price, and, with the fall, his cache was filled with fish of which the bulk were dried king salmon as long as a grown man's leg and worth a dollar apiece to any traveller.

There are men whose wits are quick as light, and whose muscles have been so tempered and hardened by years of exercise that they are like those of a wild animal. Of such was John Gale; but with all his intelligence he was very slow at reading, hence he chose to spend his evenings with his pipe and his thoughts, rather than with a book, as lonesome men are supposed to do. He did with little sleep, and many nights he sat alone till Alluna and Necia would be awakened by his heavy step as he went to his bed. That he was a man who could really think, and that his thoughts were engrossing, no one doubted who saw him sitting enthralled at such a time, for he neither rocked, nor talked, nor moved a muscle hour after hour, and only his eyes were alive. To-night the spell was on him again, and he sat bulked up in his chair, rocklike and immovable.

From the open door of the next room he could hear Necia and the little ones. She had made them ready for bed, and was telling them the tale of the snowbird's spot.

"So when all the other birds had failed," he heard her say, "the little snowbird asked for a chance to

DORET'S HAND QUICKER THAN HIS TONGUE

try. He flew and flew, and just before he came to the edge of the world where the two Old Women lived he pulled out all of his feathers. When he came to them he said:

"'I am very cold. May I warm myself at your fire?'

"They saw how little and naked he was, and how he shivered, so they did not throw sticks at him, but allowed him to creep close. He watched his chance, and when they were not looking he picked up a red-hot coal in his beak and flew back home with it as fast as ever he could—and that is how fire came to the Indian people.

"Of course the coal was hot, and it burned his throat till a drop of blood came through, so ever since that day the snowbird has had a red spot on his throat."

The two children spoke out in their mother's tongue, clamoring for the story of the Good Beaver who saved the hunter's life, and she began, this time in the language of the Yukon people, while Gale listened to the low music of her voice, muffled and broken by the log partition.

His squaw came in, her arrival unannounced except by the scuff of her moccasins, and seated herself against the wall. She did not use a chair, of which there were several, but crouched upon a bear-skin, her knees beneath her chin, her toes a trifle drawn together. She sat thus for a long time, while Necia continued her stories and put the little ones to bed. Soon the girl came to say good-night.

John Gale had never kissed his daughter, and, as it was not a custom of her mother's race, she never missed the caresses. On rare occasions the old man romped with the little ones and took them in his arms and acted

THE BARRIER

as other fathers act, but he had never done these things with her. When she had gone he spoke without moving.

"She'll never marry Poleon Doret."

"Why?" inquired Alluna.

"He ain't her kind."

"Poleon is a good man."

"None better. But she'll marry some—some white man."

"Poleon is white," the squaw declared.

"He is and he ain't. I mean she'll marry an 'outside' man. He ain't good enough, and—well, he ain't her kind." Alluna's grunt of indignation was a sufficient answer to this, but he resumed, jerking his head in the direction of the barracks. "She's been talking a lot with this—this soldier."

"Him good man, too, I guess," said the wife.

"The hell he is!" cried the trader, fiercely. "He don't mean any good to her."

"Him got a woman, eh?" said the other.

"No, no! I reckon he's single all right, but you don't understand. He's different from us people. He's—he's—" Gale paused, at a loss for words to convey his meaning. "Well, he ain't the kind that would marry a half-breed."

Alluna pondered this cryptic remark unsuccessfully, and was still seeking its solution when her lord continued:

"If she really got to loving him it would be bad for all of us."

Evidently Alluna read some hidden meaning back of these words, for she spoke quickly, but in her own tongue now, as she was accustomed to do when excited or alarmed.

18

DORET'S HAND QUICKER THAN HIS TONGUE

"Then this thing must cease at once. The risk is too great. Better that you kill him before it is too late."

"Hardly that," said the trader.

"Think of the little ones and of me," the squaw insisted, and, encouraged by his silence, continued: "Why not? Soon the nights will grow dark. The river runs swiftly, and it never gives up its dead. I can do it if you dare not. No one would suspect me."

Gale rose and laid his big hand firmly on her shoulder.

"Don't talk like that. There has been too much blood let already. We'll allow things to run along a bit as they are. There's time enough to worry."

He rose, but instead of going to his room he strode out of the house and walked northward up the trail, passing through the town and out of sight. Alluna sat huddled up in the doorway, her shawl drawn close about her head, and waited for him until the late sun—which at this time of year revolves in a great circle overhead—dipped down below the distant mountains for the midnight hour, then rolled slanting out again a few points farther north, to begin its long journey anew; but he did not return. At last she crept stiffly in-doors, like an old and weary woman, the look of fright still staring in her eyes.

About nine o'clock the next morning a faint and long-drawn cry came from the farthest limits of the little camp. An instant later it was echoed closer, and then a dog began to howl. Before its voice had died away another took it up sadly, and within three breaths, from up and down the half-mile of scanty water-front, came the cry of "Steam-bo-o-a-t!" Cabin doors

THE BARRIER

opened and men came out, glanced up the stream and echoed the call, while from sleepy nooks and sun-warmed roofs wolf-dogs arose, yawning and stretching. Those who had slept late dressed as they hurried towards the landing-place, joining in the plaint, till men and malamutes united in the shrill, slow cry.

Down-stream came the faint-sighing *whoof-whoof* of a steamer, and then out from behind the bend she burst, running on the swift spring current with the speed of a deer. She blew hoarsely before the tardy ones had reached the bank, and when abreast of the town her bell clanged, the patter of her great wheel ceased, she reversed her engines and swung gracefully till her bow was up against the current, then ploughed back, inching in slowly until, with much shouting and the sound of many gongs, she slid her nose quietly into the bank beneath the trading-post and was made fast. Her cabin-deck was lined with passengers, most of whom were bound for the "outside," although still clad in mackinaw and overalls. They all gazed silently at the hundred men of Flambeau, who stared back at them till the gang-plank was placed, when they came ashore to stretch their legs. One of them, however, made sufficient noise to make up for the silence of the others. Before the steamer had grounded he appeared among the Siwash deck-hands, his head and shoulders towering above them, his white teeth gleaming from a face as dark as theirs, shouting to his friends ashore and pantomiming his delight to the two Gale children who had come with Alluna to welcome him.

"Who's dose beeg, tall people w'at stan' 'longside of you, Miz Gale?" he called to her; then, shading his eyes elaborately, he cried, in a great voice: "Wall!

DORET'S HAND QUICKER THAN HIS TONGUE

wal! I b'lieve dat's M'sieu Jean an' Mam'selle Mollee. Ba Gar! Dey get so beeg w'ile I'm gone I don' know dem no more!"

The youthful Gales wriggled at this delicious flattery and dug their tiny moccasined toes into the sand. Molly courtesied nervously and continuously as she clung to her mother, and the boy showed a gap where two front teeth had been and was now filled by a very pink tongue.

"W'en you goin' stop grow, anyhow, you two, eh?" continued the Frenchman, and then, in a tone of sadness: "If I t'ink you ack lak' dis, I don' buy all dese present. Dese t'ing ain' no good for ole folks. I guess I'll t'row dem away." He made as if to heave a bundle that he carried into the river, whereupon the children shrieked at him so shrilly that he laughed long and incontinently at the success of his sally.

Lieutenant Burrell had come with the others, for the arrival of a steamboat called for the presence of every soul in camp, and, spying Necia in the outskirts of the crowd, he took his place beside her. He felt constrained, after what had happened on the previous evening, but she seemed to have forgotten the episode, and greeted him with her usual frankness. Even had she remembered it, there was nothing he could say in explanation or in apology. He had lain awake for hours thinking of her, and had fallen asleep with her still in his mind, for the revelation of her blood had come as a shock to him, the full force of which he could not appreciate until he had given himself time to think of it calmly.

He had sprung from a race of slave-holders, from a land where birth and breed are more than any other thing, where a drop of impure blood effects an in-

THE BARRIER

eradicable stain; therefore the thought of this girl's ignoble parentage was so repugnant to him that the more he pondered it the more pitiful it seemed, the more monstrous. Lying awake and thinking of her in the stillness of his quarters, it had seemed a very unfortunate and a very terrible thing. During his morning duties the vision of her had been fresh before him again, and his constant contemplation of the matter had wrought a change in his attitude towards the girl, of which he was uncomfortably conscious and which he was glad to see she did not perceive.

"There are some of the lucky men from El Dorado Creek," she informed him, pointing out certain people on the deck. "They are going out to the States to get something to eat. They say that nothing like those mines have ever been heard of in the world. I wish father had gone up last year when the news came."

"Why didn't he?" asked the Lieutenant. "Surely he must have been among the first to learn of it."

"Yes. 'Stick' George sent him word a year ago last fall, when he made the first discovery, but for some reason father wouldn't go."

The men were pouring off the boat now, and through the crowd came the tall Frenchman, bearing in the hollow of each arm a child who clasped a bundle to its breast. His eyes grew brighter at sight of Necia, and he broke into a flood of patois; they fairly bombarded each other with quick questions and fragmentary answers till she remembered her companion, who had fallen back a pace and was studying the newcomer, whereupon she turned.

"Oh, I forgot my manners. Lieutenant Burrell,

DORET'S HAND QUICKER THAN HIS TONGUE

this is Napoleon Doret—our Poleon!" she added, with proud emphasis."

Doret checked his volubility and stared at the soldier, whom he appeared to see for the first time. The little brown people in his arms stared likewise, and it seemed to Burrell that a certain distrust was in each of the three pairs of eyes, only in those of the man there was no shyness. Instead, the Canadian looked him over gravely from head to heel, seeming to note each point of the unfamiliar attire; then he inquired, without removing his glance:

"W'ere'bouts you live, eh?"

"I live at the post yonder," said the Lieutenant.

"W'at biznesse you work at?"

"I am a soldier."

"W'at for you come 'ere? Dere's nobody fightin' roun' dis place."

"The Lieutenant has been stationed here, foolish," said Necia. "Come up to the store quick and tell me what it's like at Dawson." With a farewell nod to Burrell, she went off with Doret, whose speech was immediately released again.

In spite of the man's unfriendliness, Burrell watched him with admiration. There were no heels to his tufted fur boots, and yet he stood a good six feet two, as straight as a pine sapling, and it needed no second glance to tell of what metal he was made. His spirit showed in his whole body, in the set of his head, and, above all, in his dark, warm face, which glowed with eagerness when he talked, and that was ever—when he was not singing.

"I never see so many people since I lef' Quebec," he was saying. "She's jus' lak' beeg city—mus' be t'ree, four t'ousan' people. Every day some more

THE BARRIER

dey come, an' all night dey dance an' sing an' drink w'iskee. Ba gosh, dat's fine place!"

"Are there lots of white women?" asked the girl.

"Yes, two, t'ree hondred. Mos' of dem is work in dance-halls. Dere's one fine gal I see, name' Marie Bourgette. I tell you 'bout her by-an'-by."

"Oh, Poleon, you're in love!" cried Necia.

"No, siree!" he denied. "Dere's none of dem gal look half so purty lak' you." He would have said more, but spying the trader at the entrance of the store, he went to him, straightway launching into the details of their commercial enterprise, which, happily, had been most successful. Before they could finish, the crowd from the boat began to drift in, some of them buying drinks at the bar and others making purchases of tobacco and so forth, but for the main part merely idling about curiously.

Among the merchandise of the Post there were for sale a scanty assortment of fire-arms, cheap shot-guns, and a Winchester or two, displayed in a rack behind the counter in a manner to attract the eye of such native hunters as might need them, and with the rest hung a pair of Colt's revolvers. One of the new arrivals, who had separated from the others at the front, now called to Gale:

"Are those Colts for sale? Mine was stolen the other day." Evidently he was accustomed to Yukon prices, for he showed no surprise at the figure the trader named, but took the guns and tested each of them, whereupon the old man knew that here was no "Cheechako," as tenderfeet are known in the North, although the man's garb had deceived him at first glance. The stranger balanced the weapons, one in either hand, then he did the "double roll" neatly.

DORET'S HAND QUICKER THAN HIS TONGUE

following which he executed a move that Gale had not witnessed for many years. He extended one of the guns, butt foremost, as if surrendering it, the action being free and open, save for the fact that his forefinger was crooked and thrust through the triggerguard; then, with the slightest jerk of the wrist, the gun spun about, the handle jumped into his palm, and instantly there was a click as his thumb flipped the hammer. It was the old "road-agent spin," which Gale as a boy had practised hours at a time; but that this man was in earnest he showed by glancing upward sharply when the trader laughed.

"This one hangs all right," he said; "give me a box of cartridges."

He emptied his gold-sack in payment for the gun and ammunition, then remarked:

"That pretty nearly cleans me. If I had the price I'd take them both."

Gale wondered what need induced this fellow to spend his last few dollars on a fire-arm, but he said nothing until the man had loosened the bottom buttons of his vest and slipped the weapon inside the band of his trousers, concealing its handle beneath the edge of his waistcoat. Then he inquired:

"Bound for the outside?"

"No. I'm locating here."

The trader darted a quick glance at him. He did not like this man.

"There ain't much doing in this camp; it's a pretty poor place," he said, guardedly.

"I'll put in with you, from its looks," agreed the other. "It's got too many soldiers to be worth a damn." He snarled this bitterly, with a peculiar leering lift of his lip, as if his words tasted badly.

THE BARRIER

"Most of the boys are going up-river," said Gale.

"Well, those hills look as if they had gold in them," said the stranger, pointing vaguely. "I'm going to prospect."

Gale knew instinctively that the fellow was lying, for his hands were not those of a miner; but there was nothing to be said. His judgment was verified, however, when Poleon drew him aside later and said:

"You know dat feller?"

"No."

"He's bad man."

"How do you know?"

"She's leave Dawson damn queeck. Dose Mounted Police t'row 'im on de boat jus' before we lef'." Then he told a story that he had heard. The man, it seemed, had left Skagway between two suns, upon the disruption of Soapy Smith's band of desperadoes, and had made for the interior, but had been intercepted at the Pass by two members of the Citizens' Committee who came upon him suddenly. Pretending to yield, he had executed some unexpected coup as he delivered his gun, for both men fell, shot through the body. No one knew just what it was he did, nor cared to question him overmuch. The next heard of him was at Lake Bennett, over the line, where the Mounted Police recognized him and sent him on. They marked him well, however, and passed him on from post to post as they had driven others whose records were known; but he had lost himself in the confusion at Dawson for a few weeks, until the scarlet-coated riders searched him out, disarmed him, and forced him sullenly aboard this steamer. The offscourings of the Canadian frontier were drifting back into their native country to settle.

DORET'S HAND QUICKER THAN HIS TONGUE

Old Man Gale cared little for this, for he had spent his life among such men, but as he watched the fellow a scheme outlined itself in his head. Evidently the man dared not go farther down the river, for there was nothing save Indian camps and a Mission or two this side of St. Michael's, and at that point there was a court and many soldiers, where one was liable to meet the penalty of past misdeeds, hence he was probably resolved to stop here, and, judging by his record, he was a man of settled convictions. Continued persecution is wont to stir certain natures to such reckless desperation that interference is dangerous, and Gale, recalling his sullen look and ill-concealed contempt for the soldiers, put the stranger down as a man of this type. Furthermore, he had been impressed by the fellow's remarkable dexterity of wrist.

The trader stepped to the door, and, seeing Burrell on the deck of the steamer, went down towards him. It was a long chance, but the stakes were big and worth the risk. He had thought much during the night previous—in fact, for many hours—and the morning had found him still undecided, wherefore he took this course.

"Necia tells me that you aim to keep law and order here," he began, abruptly, having drawn the young man aside.

"Those are my instructions," said Burrell, "but they are so vague—"

"Well! This camp is bigger than it was an hour ago, and it 'ain't improved any in the growth. Yonder goes the new citizen." He pointed to the stranger, who had returned to the steamer for his baggage and was descending the gang-plank beneath them, a valise in each hand. "He's a thief and a murderer, and we don't want him here. Now, it's up to you."

THE BARRIER

"I don't understand," said the Lieutenant, whereupon the trader told him Doret's tale. "You and your men were sent here to keep things peaceable," he concluded, "and I reckon when a man is too tough for the Canuck police he is tough enough for you to tackle. There ain't a lock and key in the camp, and we ain't had a killing or a stealing in ten years. We'd like to keep it that way."

"Well—you see—I know nothing of that shooting affray, so I doubt if my authority would permit me to interfere," the soldier mused, half to himself.

"I allowed you were to use your own judgment," said the elder man.

"So I am, I suppose. There is one chance, Mr. Gale. If you'll back me up I'll send him on down to St. Michael's. That is the most I can do."

The Lieutenant outlined his plan, and as he went on the trader nodded approval.

The young man gazed back at him so squarely, his eyes were so pleasant and friendly, his whole person breathed such straight-up honesty and freshness, that shame arose in the old man, and he had hard shift to keep his glance from wavering. Without forethought he answered, impulsively:

"He's desperate and he's dangerous. I sold him a '45' just now." He was about to tell him where the man wore it, and to add a word concerning his dexterity with the gun, when the very fearless deliberation of the youth deterred him. On second thought, Gale yielded to an impulse to wait and see how Meade Burrell would act under fire. If the soldier emerged scathless, it would give him a line on his character; if he did not—well, that would be even better. The sight of his blue and brass awoke in the elder man

DORET'S HAND QUICKER THAN HIS TONGUE

dread and cowardice, emotions he had never experienced before. Anyhow, he owed it to himself, to Necia, and to the others to find out what kind of man this soldier was.

The crowd was coming back to the steamer, which had discharged her few bundles of freight, and there was no one inside the log post as they entered except Doret and the stranger, who had deposited his baggage at the rear and was talking with the Frenchman at the bar. At sight of the Lieutenant he became silent, and turned carelessly, although with a distrustful stare. Burrell wasted no time.

"Are you going to locate here?" he began.

"Yes."

"I notice you go skeleton-rigged," the soldier continued, indicating the man's baggage. "Pretty small outfit for a miner, isn't it?"

"It's plenty for me."

"Have you enough money to buy your season's grub?"

"I guess that's my business."

"Pardon me, it is my business also."

"What is this—a hold-up?" The man laughed harshly, at the same time swinging around till he faced his questioner. Gale noted that his right hand now hung directly over the spot where his suspenders buttoned on the right side. The trader moved aside and took up a position at some distance.

"My orders are to see that all new-comers either have an outfit or are able to buy one," said Burrell. "Those that are not equipped properly are to be sent down-river to St. Michael's, where there is plenty of everything and where they will be taken care of by the government. Mr. Gale has only sufficient provisions to winter the men already in this district."

THE BARRIER

"I can take care of myself," said the man, angrily, "whether I'm broke or not, and I don't want any of your interference." He shot a quick glance at Poleon Doret, but the Frenchman's face was like wood, and his hand still held the neck of the whiskey bottle he had set out for the stranger before the others entered. Gale leaned against the opposite counter, his countenance inert but for the eyes, which were fixed upon the Lieutenant.

"Come," said the officer, peremptorily, "I have heard all about you, and you are not the kind of citizen we want here, but if you have enough money for an outfit I can't send you away. If you haven't—"

"I'm broke," said the man, but at the note in his voice Poleon Doret's muscles tightened, and Burrell, who also read a sinister message in the tone, slid his heavy service revolver from its holster beneath his coat.

He had never done this thing before, and it galled him. He had never drawn a weapon on a man, and this playing at policeman became suddenly most repugnant, stirring in him the uncomfortable feeling that he was doing a mean thing, and not only a mean thing, but one of which he ought to be heartily ashamed. He felt decidedly amateurish, especially when he saw that the man apparently intended no resistance and made no move. However, he was in for it now, and must end as he had begun.

"Give me your gun," he said; "I'll unload it and give it back to you at the gang-plank."

"All right, you've got the upper hand," said the man through lips that had gone white. Drawing his weapon from beneath his vest, he presented it to the officer, butt foremost, hammer underneath. The cylinder reposed naturally in the palm of his hand,

DORET'S HAND QUICKER THAN HIS TONGUE

and the tip of his forefinger was thrust through the trigger-guard.

Burrell lowered the barrel of his revolver and put out his left hand for the other's weapon. Suddenly the man's wrist jerked, the soldier saw a blue flicker of sunlight on the steel as it whirled, saw the arm of Poleon Doret fling itself across the bar with the speed of a striking serpent, heard a smash of breaking glass, felt the shock of a concussion, and the spatter of some liquid in his face. Then he saw the man's revolver on the floor half-way across the room, saw fragments of glass with it, and saw the fellow step backward, snatching at the fingers of his right hand. A smell of powder-smoke and rank whiskey was in the air.

There are times when a man's hand will act more swiftly than his tongue. Napoleon Doret had seen the manner of the stranger's surrender of his gun, and, realizing too late what it meant, had acted. At the very instant of the fellow's treachery, Doret struck with his bottle just in time to knock the weapon from his hand, but not in time to prevent its discharge. The bullet was lodged in the wall a foot from where Gale stood. As the stranger staggered back, the Frenchman vaulted the bar, but, though swift as a cat, the soldier, who had also leaped, was before him. Aiming a sweeping downward blow with his Colt, Burrell clipped the Skagway man just above the ear, and he reeled; then as he fell the officer struck wickedly again at his opponent's skull, but Doret seized him by the arm.

"Ba Gar, don't kill 'im twice!"

Burrell wrenched his arm free and turned on Doret a face that remained long in the Frenchman's memory, a face suffused with fury and convulsed like that of a sprinter at the finish of a race. The two men stared at each other over the fallen figure for a brief moment, until the soldier gained mastery of himself and sheathed his weapon, when Poleon smiled.

"I spoil' a quart of good w'iskee on you. Dat's wort' five dollar."

The Lieutenant wiped the liquor from his face.

"Quick work, Doret," he said. "I owe you one."

Gale's face was hidden as he bent over the prostrate man, fingering a long and ragged cut which laid the fellow's scalp open from back of the ear to the temple, but he mumbled something unintelligible.

"Is he hurt badly?"

"No, you chipped him too low," said the trader. "I told you he was bad."

"He's goin' have nice birt'-mark, anyhow," said Doret, going back of the bar for some water. They revived the man, then bound up his injury hastily, and as the steamer cast off they led him to the bank and passed his grip-sacks to a roustabout. He said no word as he walked unsteadily up the plank, but turned and stared malignantly at them from the deck; then, as the craft swung outward into the stream, he grinned through the trickle of blood that stole down from beneath his wide hat, if the convulsive grimace he made could be termed a grin, and cried:

"I'd like to introduce myself, for I'm coming back to winter with you, Lieutenant! My name is Runnion." And until the steamer was hidden behind the bend below they saw him standing there gazing back at them fixedly.

As Burrell left the two men at the store, he gave his hand frankly to the French-Canadian, and said, while his cheeks flushed:

DORET'S HAND QUICKER THAN HIS TONGUE

"I want to thank you for saving me from my own awkwardness."

Doret became even more embarrassed than the Lieutenant at this show of gratitude, and grunted churlishly. But when the young man had gone he turned to Gale, who had watched them silently, and said:

"He's nice young feller, ole man. Sapre! W'en he's mad his eye got so red lak' my ondershirt."

But the trader made no reply.

CHAPTER III

WITHOUT BENEFIT OF CLERGY

WHEN the steamer had gone Napoleon Doret went to look for Necia, and found her playing with the younger Gales, who revelled in the gifts he had brought. Never had there been such a surprise. Never had there been such gorgeous presents for little folks. This was a land in which there were no toys, a country too young for babes; and any one whose youth had been like that of other children would have seen a pathos in the joy of these two. Poleon had been hard put to it to find anything suitable for his little friends, for although there was all manner of merchandise coming into Dawson, none of it was designed for tiny people, not even clothes.

It was evident that he had pleased them, for when he appeared they ran at his legs like twin cubs, incoherent and noisy, the pleasure within them too turbulent for expression. They had never played with a toy that Poleon had not built for them, nor worn a garment that Alluna had not made. This, then, was a day of revelations, for the first thing they beheld upon opening their packs was a pair of rubber boots for each. They were ladies' knee-boots, the smallest size in stock, but the Gales entered them bodily, so to speak, moccasins and all, clear to their hips, like the waders that duck-hunters use. When they ran they fell down and out of them, but their pride remained upright and serene, for were not these like the boots that Poleon wore, and not of Indian make, with foolish beads on them? Next, the youthful heir had found a straw hat of strange and wondrous fashion, with a brim like a board and a band of blue, which Poleon had bought from a college man who had retained this emblem of his past to the final moment. Like the boots, it was much too large for little John, and hard to master, but it made a brave display, as did a red cravat, which covered his front like a baseball catcher's harness. Molly had also two sets of side-combs, gorgeously ornamented with glass diamonds, and a silver-handled tooth-brush, with which she scrubbed the lame puppy. This puppy had three legs and the mange, and he was her particular pride.

There were certain other things, the use of which they did not understand, like queer-smelling, soft, yellow balls which Necia said were oranges and good to eat, although the skins were leathery and very bitter, nor were they nearly so pleasant to the nose as the toilet soap, which Necia would not allow them even to taste. Then there was a box of chocolate candies such as the superintendent at St. Michael's sent them every spring, and an atomizer, which Necia had filled with Florida Water. This worked on the puppy even better than the tooth-brush.

The elder girl laughed gladly as Poleon entered, though her eyes were wet with the pity of it.

"You seem to bring sunshine wherever you go," she said. "They have never had things to play with like other children, and it makes me cry to watch them."

"Ho, ho!" he chuckled, "dis ain' no time for cryin'. Ba gosh! I guess you don' have so much present w'en you was li'l' gal you'se'f, w'at? Mebbe you t'ink I forget you. Wal, I didn't."

He began to undo the fastenings of a parcel he carried in his arms, for Napoleon Doret had brought other things from Dawson besides his gifts to the children. Necia snatched at the package.

"Don't you dare open it! Why, that's half the fun." She was a child herself now, her face flushed and her hands a-tremble. Taking the package to the table, she hurriedly untied the knots while he stood watching her, his teeth showing white against his dark face, and his eyes half shut as if dazzled by the sight of her.

"Oh, why didn't you tie more knots in it?" she breathed as she undid the last, and then, opening the wrappings slowly, she gasped in astonishment. She shook it out gently, reverently—a clinging black lace gown of Paris make. Next she opened a box and took from it a picture hat, with long jet plumes, which she stroked and pressed fondly against her face. There were other garments also—a silken petticoat, silk stockings, and a pair of high-heeled shoes to match, with certain other delicate and dainty things which she modestly forbore to inspect before the Frenchman, who said no word, but only gazed at her, and for whom she had no eyes as yet. Finally she laid her presents aside, and, turning to him, said, in a hushed, awe-stricken voice:

"It's all there, everything complete! Oh, Poleon— you dear, dear Poleon!" She took his two big hands by the thumbs, as had been her custom ever since she was a child, and looked up at him, her eyes wet with emotion. But she could not keep away from the dress for long, and returned to feast her eyes upon it, the two children standing beside her, sprouting out of their rubber boots, with eyes and mouths round and protruding.

"You lak' it, eh?" pressed Poleon, hungry for more demonstrative expression.

"Oh-h," she sighed, "can't you *see*? Where on earth did you get it?" Then suddenly realizing its value, she cried, "Why, it must have cost a fortune!" A quick reproach leaped into her face, but he only laughed again.

"Wan night I gamble in beeg saloon. Yes, sir! I gamble good dat night, too. For w'ile I play roulette, den I dance, den I play some more, an' by-an'-by I see a new dance gal. She's Franche gal, from Montreal. Dat's de one I tol' you 'bout. Ba Gar! She's swell dress', too. She's name' Marie Bourgette."

"Oh, I've heard about her," said Necia. "She owns a claim on Bonanza Creek."

"Sure, she's frien's wit' Charlie McCormack, dat riche feller, but I don' know it dis tam', so I ask her for dance wit' me. Den we drink a bottle of champagne— twenty dollar.

"'Mamselle,' I say, 'how much you charge for sell me dat dress?'

"'For w'y shall I sell im,' she say; 'I don' wear 'im before till to-night, an' I don' get no more dress lak' dis for t'ousan' dollar.'"

Necia exclaimed excitedly.

"'For w'y you sell 'im?' I say. 'Biccause I'll tak' 'im down to Flambeau for Necia Gale, w'at never had no dress lak' dat in all her life.' Wal, sir, dat Marie Bourgette, she's hear of you before, an' your dad, too —mos' all dose Cheechakos know 'bout Old Man Gale— so she say:

37

THE BARRIER

"'W'at lookin' kind of gal is dis Necia?' An' I tell her all 'bout you. W'en I'm t'rough she say:

"'But maybe your little frien' is more bigger as I am. Maybe de dress won't fit.'

"'Ha! You don' know me, mamselle,' I say. 'I can guess de weight of a caribou to five poun'. She'll be same size la'kin' one inch 'roun' de wais'.'

"'Poleon Doret,' she say, 'you ain' no Franchemans to talk lak' dat. Look here! I can sell dis dress for t'ousan' dollar to-night, or I can trade 'im for gol'-mine on El Dorado Creek to some dose Swede w'at want to catch a gal, but I'm goin' sell 'im to you for t'ree hondred dollar, jus' w'at I pay for 'im. You wait here till I come back.'

"'No, no, Mamselle Marie, I'll go 'long, too, for so you don' change your min',' I say; an' I stan' outside her door till she pass me de whole dam' works.

"'Don' forget de little shoes,' I say—an' dat's how it come!"

"And you paid three hundred dollars for it!" Necia said, aghast. The Canadian shrugged.

"Only for de good heart of Marie Bourgette I pay wan t'ousan'," said he. "I mak' seven hondred dollar clean profit!"

"It was very nice of both of you, but—I can't wear it. I've never seen a dress like it, except in pictures, and I couldn't—" She saw his face fall, and said, impulsively:

"I'll wear it once, anyhow, Poleon, just for you. Go away quick, now, and let me put it on."

"Dat's good," he nodded, as he moved away. "I bet you mak' dose dance-hall women look lak' sucker."

No man may understand the girl's feelings as she set about clothing herself in her first fine dress. Time

38

and again she had studied pictures from the "outside" showing women arrayed in the newest styles, and had closed her eyes to fancy herself dressed in like manner. She had always had an instinctive feeling that some day she would leave the North and see the wonderful world of which men spoke so much, and mingle with the fine ladies of her picture-books, but she never dreamed to possess an evening-gown while she lived in Alaska. And now, even while she recognized the grotesqueness of the situation, she burned to wear it and see herself in the garb of other women. So, with the morning sun streaming brightly into her room, lighting up the moss-chinked walls, the rough barbarism of fur and head and trophy, she donned the beautiful garments.

Poleon's eye had been amazingly correct, for it fitted her neatly, save at the waist, which was even more than an inch too large, notwithstanding the fact that she had never worn such a corset as the well-formed Marie Bourgette was accustomed to.

She pondered long and hesitated modestly when she saw its low cut, which exposed her neck and shoulders in a totally unaccustomed manner, for it struck her as amazingly indecent until she scurried through her magazines again and saw that its construction, as compared with others, was most conservative. Even so she shrank at sight of herself below the line of sunburn, for she was ringed about like a blue-winged teal, the demarcation being more pronounced because of the natural whiteness of her skin. The year previous Doret had brought her from the coast a Spanish shawl, which a salt-water sailor had sold him, and which had lain folded away ever since. She brought it forth now and arranged it about her shoulders, but in spite of

THE BARRIER

this covering the fair flesh beneath peeped through its wide interstices most brazenly. She had never paid marked attention to the fairness of her skin till now, and all at once this difference between herself and her little brother and sister struck her. She had been a mother to them ever since they came, and had often laughed when she saw how brown their little bodies were, rejoicing in blushing quietude at her own whiteness, but to-day she neither laughed nor felt any joy, rather a dim wonder. She sat down, dress and all, in the thick softness of a great brown bear-skin and thought it over.

How odd it was, now that she considered it, that she needed no aid with these alien garments, that she knew instinctively their every feature, that there was no intricacy to cause her more than an instant's trouble. This knowledge must be a piece with the intuitive wit that had been the wonder of Father Barnum and had enabled her to absorb his teachings as fast as he gave them forth.

She was interrupted in her reverie by the passing of a shadow across her window and the stamp of a man's feet on the planks at the door. Of course, it was Poleon, who had come back to see her; so she rose hastily, gave one quick glance at the mirror above her washstand, choosing the side that distorted her image the least, and, hearing him still stamping, perfunctorily called:

"Come in! I'll be right out."

She kicked the train into place behind her, looped the shawl carelessly about her in a way to veil her modesty effectively, and, with an expectant smile at his extravagance of admiration, swept out into the big room, very self-conscious and very pleasing to the eye. She crossed proudly to the reading-table to give him a fair view of her splendor, and was into the middle of the room before she looked up. Taken aback, she uttered a little strangled cry and made a quick movement of retreat, only to check herself and stand with her chin high in the air, while wave after wave of color swept over her face.

"Great lovely dove!" ejaculated Burrell, fervently, staring at her.

"Oh, I—I thought you were Poleon. He—" In spite of herself she glanced towards her room as if to flee; she writhed at the utter absurdity of her appearance, and knew the Lieutenant must be laughing at her. But flight would only make it worse, so she stood as she was, having drawn back as far as she could, till the table checked her. Burrell, however, was not laughing, nor smiling even, for his embarrassment rivalled hers.

"I was looking for your father," he said, wondering if this glorious thing could be the quaint half-breed girl of yesterday. There was nothing of the native about her now, for her lithe young figure was drawn up to its height, and her head, upon which the long, black braids were coiled, was tipped back in a haughty poise. She had flung her hands out to grasp the table edge behind her, forgetful of her shawl, which drooped traitorously and showed such rounded lines as her ordinary dress scarce hinted at. This was no Indian maid, the soldier vowed; no blood but the purest could pulse in such veins, no spirit save the highest could flash in such eyes as these. A jealous rancor irked him at the thought of this beauty intended for the Frenchman's eyes.

"Can't you show yourself to me as well as to Poleon?" he said.

"Certainly not!" she declared. "He bought this dress for me, and I put it on to please him." Now she was herself again, for some note in the Lieutenant's voice gave her dominance over him. "After he sees it I will take it off, and—"

"Don't—don't take it off—ever," said Burrell. "I thought you were beautiful before, because of your quaintness and simplicity, but now—" his chest swelled —"why, this is a breath from home. You're like my sister and the girls back in Kentucky, only more wonderful."

"Am I?" she cried, eagerly. "Am I like other girls? Do I really look as if I'd always worn clothes like these?"

"Born to them," said he.

A smile broke over her grave face, assuming a hundred different shades of pleasure and making a child of her on the instant; all her reserve and hauteur vanished. Her warmth and unaffected frankness suffused him, as she stood out, turning to show the beauties of her gown, her brown hands fluttering tremulously as she talked.

"It's my first party-dress, you know, and I'm as proud of it as Molly is of her rubber boots. It's too big in here and too small right there; that girl must have had a bad chest; but otherwise it fits me as if it had been made for me, doesn't it? And the shoes! Aren't they the dearest things? See." She held her skirts back, showing her two feet side by side, her dainty ankles slim and shapely in their silk.

"They won't shed water," he said.

"I know; and look at the heels. I couldn't walk a mile to save my life."

"And they will come off if they get wet."

WITHOUT BENEFIT OF CLERGY

"But they make me very tall."

"They don't wear as well as moccasins." Both laughed delightedly till he broke in, impulsively:

"Oh, girl, don't you know how beautiful you are?"

"Of course I do!" she cried, imitating his change of voice; then added, naïvely, "That's why I hate to take it off."

"Where did you learn to wear things like that?" he questioned. "Where did you get that — well — that air?"

"It seems to me I've always known. There's nothing strange about it. The buttons and the hooks and the eyes are all where they belong. It's instinct, I suppose, from father's side—"

"Probably. I dare say I should understand the mechanism of a dress-suit, even if I'd never seen one," said the man, amused, yet impressed by her argument.

"I've always had visions of women dressed in this kind of clothing, white women—never natives—not dressed like this exactly, but in dainty, soft things, not at all like the ones I wear. I seem to have a memory, although it's hardly that, either—it's more like a dream—as if I were somebody else. Father says it is from reading too much."

"A memory of what?"

"It's too vague and tantalizing to tell what it is, except that I should be called Merridy."

"Merridy? Why that?"

"I'll show you. See." She slipped her hand inside the shawl and drew from her breast a thin gold chain on which was strung a band ring. "It was grandmother's—that's where I got the fancy for the name of Merridy, I suppose."

"May I look?"

THE BARRIER

"Of course. But I daren't take it off. I haven't had it off my neck since I was a baby." She held it out for him to examine, and, although it brought his head close to hers, there was no trace of coquetry in the invitation. He read the inscription, "From Dan to Merridy," but had no realization of what it meant, for he glimpsed the milk-white flesh almost at his lips, and felt her breath stirring his hair, while the delicate scent of her person seemed to loose every strong emotion in him. She was so dainty and yet so virile, so innocent and yet so wise, so cold and yet so pulsating.

"It is very pretty," he said, inanely.

At the look in his eyes as he raised his head her own widened, and she withdrew from him imperceptibly, dismissing him with a mere inflection.

"I wish you would send Poleon here. It's time he saw his present."

As Burrell walked out into the air he shut his jaws grimly and muttered: "Hold tight, young man. She's not your kind—she's not your kind."

Inside the store he found Doret and the trader in conversation with a man he had not met before, a ragged nondescript whose overalls were blue and faded and patched, particularly on the front of the legs above the knees, where a shovel-handle wears hardest; whose coat was of yellow mackinaw, the sleeves worn thin below the elbows, where they had rubbed against his legs in his work. As the soldier entered, the man turned on him a small, shrewd, weather-beaten face with one eye, while he went on talking to Gale.

"It ain't nothin' to git excited over, but it's wuth follerin'. If I wasn't so cussed unlucky I'd know there was a pay streak som'ere close by."

"Your luck is bound to change, Lee," said the

WITHOUT BENEFIT OF CLERGY

trader, who helped him to roll up a pack of provisions.

"Mebbe so. Who's the dressmaker?" He jerked his bushy head towards Burrell, who had stopped at the front door with Poleon to examine some yellow grains in a folded paper.

"He's the boss soldier."

"Purty, ain't he?"

"If you ain't good he'll get you," said Gale, a trifle cynically, at which Lee chuckled.

"I reckon there's several of us in camp that ain't been a whole lot too good," said he. "Has he tried to git anybody yet?"

"No, but he's liable to. What would happen if he did? Suppose, for instance, he went after you—or me?"

The one-eyed man snorted derisively. "It ain't wuth considerin'!"

"Why not?" insisted Gale, guardedly. "Maybe I've got a record—you don't know."

"If you have, don't tell me nothin' about it," hastily observed Lee. "I'm a God-fearin' citizen myself, leanin' ever towards peace and quietudes, but what's past is dead and gone, and I'd hate to see a lispin' child like that blue-and-yeller party try to reezureck it."

"He's got the American army to back him up—at least five of them."

"Five agin a hundred. He aims to overawe us, don't he?" snickered the unregenerate Lee, but his wrinkles changed and deepened as he leaned across the counter confidentially.

"You say the word, John, and I'll take some feller along to help me, and we'll transfer this military post. There's plenty that would like the job if you give the wink."

"Pshaw! I'm just supposing," said the trader. "As long as they play around and drill and toot that horn, and don't bother anybody, I allow they're not in the way."

"All right! It's up to you. However, if I happen to leap down on this pay streak before it sees me comin', I'm goin' to put my friends in first and foremost, and shut out these dressmakers complete. So long!" He thrust his arms beneath the legs of a new pair of blue overalls that formed his pack-straps, wriggled the burden comfortably into place between his shoulders, and slouched out past Doret, to whom he nodded, ignoring the "dressmaker."

Having given Necia's message to Poleon, the Lieutenant took up his business with the trader. It concerned the purchase of certain supplies that had been omitted from the military outfit, and when this was concluded he referred to the encounter of that morning.

"I don't want you to think I bungle everything in that manner," he said, "for I don't. I want to work with you, and I want to be friends with you."

"I'm willing," said Gale.

"Nobody dislikes playing policeman more than I do, but it's a part of my duty, and I'll have to do it," continued the young man.

"I reckon you simply aim to keep peace, eh? You ain't lookin' for nobody in particular?"

"Of course not—outside of certain notorious criminals who have escaped justice and worked north."

"Then there *is* a few that you want, eh?"

"Yes, certain old-timers. The officers at every post have descriptions of a few such, and if they show up we will take them in and hold them till courts are established."

WITHOUT BENEFIT OF CLERGY

"If you've got their names and descriptions, mebbe I could help you," said the trader, carelessly.

"Thank you, I'll bring up the list and we'll go over it together. You must have been here a good while."

"About ten years."

"Then Miss Necia was born out in the States?"

Gale shot a startled glance at the soldier before he answered in the affirmative, but Burrell was studying a pattern of sunlight on the floor and did not observe him. A moment later he inquired, hesitatingly:

"Is this your first marriage, Mr. Gale?" When the other did not answer, he looked up and quickly added:

"I beg your pardon, sir. What led me to ask was Miss Necia—she is so—well—she is such a remarkable girl."

Gale's face had undergone a change, but he answered, quietly:

"I 'ain't never been married."

"What?"

"When I took Alluna it wasn't the style, and neither one of us has thought much about it since."

"Oh, I see," exclaimed Burrell, hurriedly. "I'll bring that list with me the first time I think about it," and, nodding amiably, he sauntered out But his mind was in a whirl, and even after he had reached his quarters he found himself repeating:

"The other was bad enough. Poor little girl! Poor little girl!"

Gale likewise left the store and went into his house, the odd look still strong in his eyes, to find Necia posing in her new regalia for Poleon's benefit. At sight of her he fell into a strange and unexpected humor, and to their amazement commanded her roughly to take the things off. His voice and manner were harsh and at utter variance with any mood he had ever displayed before; nor would he explain his unreasoning fury, but strode out again, leaving her in tears and the Frenchman staring.

CHAPTER IV

THE SOLDIER FINDS AN UNTRODDEN VALLEY

DURING the weeks that followed Meade Burrell saw much of Necia. At first he had leaned on the excuse that he wanted to study the curious freak of heredity she presented; but that wore out quickly, and he let himself drift, content with the pleasure of her company and happy in the music of her laughter. Her quick wit and keen humor delighted him, and the mystery of her dark eyes seemed to hold the poetry and beauty of all the red races that lay behind her on the maternal side. At times he thought of her as he had seen her that morning in the dance-girl's dress, and remembered the purity of neck and breast it had displayed, but he attributed that to the same prank of heritage that had endowed her with other traits alien to her mother's race.

He had experienced a profound sense of pity for her upon learning her father's relation to Alluna, but this also largely vanished when he found that the girl was entirely oblivious to its significance. He had tried her in many subtle ways, and found that she regarded the matter innocently, as customary, and therefore in the light of an accepted convention; nor did she seem to see anything in her blood or station to render her inferior to other women. She questioned him tirelessly about his sister, and he was glad of this, for it placed no constraint between them. So that, as he explored her many quaint beliefs and pagan superstitions, the delight of being with her grew, and he ceased to reason whither it might lead him.

As for her, each day brought a keener delight. She unfolded before the Kentuckian like some beautiful woodland flower, and through innumerable, unnoticed familiarities took him into her innermost confidence, sharing with him those girlish hopes and beliefs and aspirations she had never voiced till now.

A month of this went by, and then Runnion returned. He came on an up-going steamer which panted in for a rest from its thousand-mile climb, and for breath to continue its fight against the never-tiring sweep of waters. The manner of his coming was bold, for he stood fairly upon the ship's deck, staring at the growing picture of the town, as he had watched it recede a month before, and his smile was evil now, as it had been then. With him was a stranger. When the boat was at rest Runnion sauntered down the gang-plank and up to the Lieutenant, who stood above the landing-place, and who noted that the scar, close up against his hat-band, was scarce healed. He accosted the officer with an insolent assurance.

"Well, I'm back again, you see, and I'm back to stay."

"Very well, Runnion; did you bring an outfit with you?" The young man addressed him civilly, although he felt that the fellow's presence was a menace and would lead to trouble.

"Yes, and I'm pretty fat besides." He shook a well-laden gold-sack at the officer. "I reckon I can rustle thirteen dollars a month most anywhere, if I'm left alone."

AN UNTRODDEN VALLEY

"What do you want in this place, anyhow?" demanded Burrell, curiously.

"None of your damned business," the man answered, grinning.

"Be sure it isn't," retorted the Lieutenant, "because it would please me right down to the ground if it were. I'd like to get you."

"I'm glad we understand each other," Runnion said, and turned to oversee the unloading of his freight, falling into conversation with the stranger, who had been surveying the town without leaving the boat. Evidently this man had a voice in Runnion's affairs, for he not only gave him instructions, but bossed the crew who handled his merchandise, and Meade Burrell concluded that he must be some incoming tenderfoot who had grub-staked the desperado to prospect in the hills back of Flambeau. As the two came up past him he saw that he was mistaken—this man was no more of a tenderfoot than Runnion; on the contrary, he had the bearing of one to whom new countries are old, who had trod the edge of things all his life. There was a hint of the meat-eating animal about him; his nose was keen and hawklike, his walk and movements those of the predatory beast, and as he passed by, Burrell observed that his eyes were of a peculiar cruelty that went well with his thin lips. He was older by far than Runnion, but, while the latter was mean-visaged and swaggering, the stranger's manner was noticeable for its repression.

Impelled by an irresistible desire to learn something about the man, the Lieutenant loitered after Runnion and his companion, and entered the store in time to see the latter greet "No Creek" Lee, the prospector, who had come into town for more food. Both men spoke with quiet restraint.

"Nine years since I saw you, Stark," said the miner. "Where you bound?"

"The diggings," replied Stark, as Lee addressed the stranger.

"Mining now?"

"No, same old thing, but I'm grub-staking a few men, as usual. One of them stays here. I may open a house in Dawson if the camp is as good as they say it is."

"This here's a good place for you."

Stark laughed noiselessly and without mirth. "Fine! There must be a hundred people living here."

"Never mind, you take it from me," said the miner, positively, "and get in now on the quiet. There's something doing." His one sharp eye detected the Lieutenant close by, so he drew his friend aside and began talking to him earnestly and with such evident effect as to alter Stark's plans on the moment; for when Runnion entered the store shortly Stark spoke to him quickly, following which they both hurried back to the steamer and saw to the unloading of much additional freight and baggage. From the volume and variety of this merchandise, it was evident that Mr. Stark would in no wise be a burden to the community.

Burrell was not sufficiently versed in the ways of mining-camps to know exactly what this abrupt change of policy meant, but that there was something in the air he knew from the mysterious manner of "No Creek" Lee and from the suppressed excitement of Doret and the trader. His curiosity got the better of him finally, and he fell into talk with Lee, inquiring about the stranger by way of an opening.

AN UNTRODDEN VALLEY

"That's Ben Stark. I knew him back in the Cassiar country," said Lee.

"Is he a mining man?"

"Well, summat. He's made and lost a bank-roll that a greyhound couldn't leap over in the mining business, but it ain't his reg'lar graft. He run one of the biggest places in the Northwest for years."

"Saloon, eh?"

"Saloon and variety house—seven bartenders, that's all. He's the feller that killed the gold-commissioner. Of course, that put him on the hike again."

"How do you mean?"

"Well, he had a record as long as a sick man's drug bill before he went into that country, and when he put the commissioner away them Canadian officials went after him like they was killin' snakes, and it cost him all he had made to get clear. If it had happened across the line, the coroner's jury would have freed him, 'cause the commissioner was drunk and started the row; but it happened right in Stark's saloon, and you know Canucks is stronger than vitriol for law and order. Not bein' his first offence, it went hard with him."

"He looks like a killer," said Burrell.

"Yes, but he ain't the common kind. He always lets the other man begin, and therefore he ain't never done time."

"Come, now," argued the Lieutenant, "if it were the other man who invariably shot first, Stark would have been killed long ago."

"I don't care what *would* have happened, it *'ain't* happened, and he's got notches on his gun till it looks like a cub bear had chawed it. If you was a Western man you'd know what they say about him.

THE BARRIER

'The bullet 'ain't been run to kill him.' That's the sayin'. You needn't grin, there's many a better man than you believes it."

"Who is it that the bullet hasn't been run to kill?" said the trader's deep voice behind them. He had finished with his duties, and now sauntered forward.

"Ben Stark," said Lee, turning. "You know him, John?"

"No, I never saw him, but I know who he is—used to hear of him in the Cœur d'Alenes."

"That's him I was talking to," said the miner. "He's an old friend of mine, and he's going to locate here."

Burrell thought he saw Lee wink at the trader, but he was not sure, for at that moment the man of whom they were speaking re-entered. Lee introduced him, and the three men shook hands. While the soldier fell into easy conversation with the new-comer, Gale gazed at him narrowly, studying him as he studied all men who came as strangers. As he was doing so Alluna entered, followed by Johnny and Molly. She had come for sugar, and asked for it in her native tongue. Upon her exit Stark broke off talking to the Lieutenant and turned to the trader.

"Your squaw, Mr. Gale?"

The old man nodded.

"Pah-Ute, eh?"

"Yes. Why, do you savvy the talk?"

"Some. I lived in California once."

"Where?" The question came like a shot.

"Oh, here and there; I followed the Mother Lode for a spell."

"I don't recall the name," said the trader, after a bit.

AN UNTRODDEN VALLEY

"Possibly. Where were you located?"

"I never lit on any one place long enough to call it home."

It seemed to Burrell that both men were sparring cautiously in an indirect, impersonal manner.

"Those your kids, too, eh?" Stark continued.

"Yes, and I got another one besides — older. A girl."

"She's a 'pip,' too," said "No Creek" Lee, fervently. "She's plumb beautiful."

"All of them half-breeds?" questioned Stark.

"Sure." The trader's answer was short, and when the other showed no intention of pressing the subject further he sauntered away; but no sooner was he out of hearing than Stark said: "Humph! They're all alike."

"Who?"

"Squaw-men."

"This one ain't," Lee declared. "He's different; ain't he, Lieutenant?"

"He certainly is," agreed Burrell. This was the first criticism he had heard of Necia's father, and although Stark volunteered no argument, it was plain that his opinion remained unaffected.

The old man went through the store at the rear and straightway sought Alluna. Speaking to her with unwonted severity in the Pah-Ute language, he said:

"I have told you never to use your native tongue before strangers. That man in the store understands."

"I only asked for sugar to cook the berries with," she replied.

"True, but another time you might say more, therefore the less you speak it the better. He is the kind who sees much and talks little. Address me in Siwash or in English unless we are alone."

"I do not like that man," said the woman. "His eyes are bad, like a fish eagle's, and he has no heart."

Suddenly she dropped her work and came close up to him. "Can he be the one?"

"I don't know. Stark is not the name, but he might have changed it; he had reasons enough."

"Who is this man Stark?"

"I don't know that, either. I used to hear of him when I was in British Columbia."

"But surely you must know if he is the same—she must have told you how he looked—others must have told you—"

Gale shook his head. "Very little. I could not ask her, and others knew him so well they never doubted that I had seen him; but this much I do know, he was dark—"

"This man is dark—"

"—and his spirit was like that of a mad horse—"

"This man's temper is black—"

"—and his eyes were cruel."

"This man has evil eyes."

"He lacked five years of my age," said the trader.

"This man is forty years old. It must be he," said the squaw.

Even Necia would have marvelled had she heard this revelation of her father's age, for his hair and brows were grizzled, and his face had the look of a man of sixty, while only those who knew him well, like Doret, were aware of his great strength and the endurance that belied his appearance.

"We will send Necia down to the Mission to-night,

AN UNTRODDEN VALLEY

and let Father Barnum keep her there till this man goes," said the squaw, after some deliberation.

"No, she must stay here," Gale replied, with decision. "The man has come here to live, so it won't do any good to send her away, and, after all, what is to be will be. But she must never be seen in that dance-girl's dress again, at least, not till I learn more about this Stark. It makes no difference whether this one is the man or not; he will come and I shall know him. For a year I have felt that the time was growing short, and now I know it."

"No, no!" Alluna cried; "we have no strangers here. No white men except the soldiers and this one have come in a year. This is but a little trading-post."

"It was yesterday, but it isn't to-day. Lee has made a strike—like the one George Carmack made on the Klondike. He came to tell me and Poleon, and we are going back with him to-night, but you must say nothing or it will start a stampede."

"Other men will come—a great many of them?" interrogated Alluna, fearfully, ignoring utterly the momentous news.

"Yes. Flambeau will be another Dawson if this find is what Lee thinks it is. I stayed away from the Upper Country because I knew crowds of men would come from the States, and I feared that he might be among them; but it's no use hiding any longer, there's no other place for us to go. If Lee has got a mine, I'll have the one next to it, for we will be the first ones on the ground. What happens after that won't matter much, you four will be provided for. We are to leave in an hour, one at a time, to avoid comment."

"But why did this man stop here?" insisted the

THE BARRIER

woman. "Why did he not stay on the steamboat and go to Dawson?"

"He's a friend of Lee's. He is going with us." Then he added, almost in a whisper, "Before we return I shall know."

Alluna seized his arm. "Promise to come back, John! Promise that you will come back even if this should be the man."

"I promise. Don't worry, little woman; I'm not ready for a reckoning yet."

He gave her certain instructions about the store, charging her in particular to observe the utmost secrecy regarding the strike, else she might precipitate a premature excitement which would go far towards ruining his and Poleon's chances. All of which she noted; then, as he turned away, she laid her hand on his arm and said:

"If you do not know him he will not know you. Is it not so?."

"Yes."

"Then the rest is easy—"

But he only shook his head doubtfully and answered, "Perhaps—I am not sure," and went inside, where he made up a light pack of bacon, flour and tea, a pail or two, a coffee-pot and a frying-pan, which he rolled inside a robe of rabbit-skin and bound about in turn with a light tarpaulin. It did not weigh thirty pounds in all. Selecting a new pair of water-boots, he stuffed dry grass inside them, oiled up his six-shooter, then slipped out the back way, and in five minutes was hidden in the thickets. Half an hour later, having completed a détour of the town, he struck the trail to the interior, where he found Poleon Doret, equipped in a similar manner, resting beside a stream, singing the songs of his people.

AN UNTRODDEN VALLEY

When Burrell returned to his quarters he tried to mitigate the feeling of lonesomeness that oppressed him by tackling his neglected correspondence. Somehow, to-day, the sense of his isolation had come over him stronger than ever. His rank forbade any intimacy with his miserable handful of men, who had already fallen into the monotony of routine, while every friendly overture he made towards the citizens of Flambeau was met with distrust and coldness, his stripes of office seeming to erect a barrier and induce an ostracism stronger and more complete than if they had been emblems of the penitentiary. He began to resent it keenly. Even Doret and the trader seemed to share the general feeling, hence the thought of the long, lonesome winter approaching reduced the Lieutenant to a state of black despondency, deepened by the knowledge that he now had an open enemy in camp in the person of Runnion. Then, too, he had taken a morbid dislike to the new man, Stark. So that, all in all, the youth felt he had good reason to be in the dumps this afternoon. There was nothing desirable in this place—everything undesirable—except Necia. Her presence in Flambeau went far towards making his humdrum existence bearable, but of late he had found himself dwelling with growing seriousness on the unhappy circumstances of her birth, and had almost made up his mind that it would be wise not to see her any more. The tempting vision of her in the ball-dress remained vividly in his imagination, causing him hours of sweet torment. There was a sparkle, a fineness, a gentleness about her that seemed to make the few women he had known well dull and commonplace, and even his sister, whom till now he had held as the perfection of all things feminine, suffered by comparison with this maiden of the frontier.

He was steeped in this sweet, grave melancholy, when a knock came at his door, and he arose to find Necia herself there, excited and radiant. She came in without sign of embarrassment or slightest consciousness of the possible impropriety of her act.

"The most wonderful thing has happened," she began at once, when she found they were alone. "You'll faint for joy."

"What is it?"

"Nobody knows except father and Poleon and the two new men—"

"What is it?"

"I teased the news out of mother, and then came right here."

He laughed. "But what—may I ask—"

"Lee has made a strike—a wonderful strike—richer than the Klondike."

"So? The old man's luck has changed. I'm right glad of that," said the soldier.

"I came as fast as I could, because to-morrow everybody will know about it, and it will be too late."

"Too late for what?"

"For us to get in on it, of course. Oh, but won't there be a stampede! Why, all the people bound for Dawson on the next boat will pile off here, then the news will go up-river and down-river, and thousands of others will come pouring in from everywhere, and this will be a city. Then we will stake our town lots and sell them for ever so much money, and go around with our noses in the air, and they will say to each other:

AN UNTRODDEN VALLEY

"'Who is that beautiful lady with the fine clothes?' and somebody will answer:

"'Why, that is Miss Necia Gale, the mine-owner.' And then *you* will come along, and they will say:

"'That is Lieutenant Burrell, the millionaire, and—'"

"Hold on! hold on!" said the soldier, stopping her breathless patter. "Tell me all about this."

"Well, 'No Creek' came in this morning to tell dad and Poleon. Then the boat arrived with an old friend of Lee's, a Mr. Stark, so Lee told him, too, and now they've all gone back to his creek to stake more claims. They slipped away quietly to prevent suspicion, but I knew there was something up from the way Poleon acted, so I made Alluna tell me all about it. They haven't more than two hours start of us, and we can overtake them easily."

"We! Why, we are not going?"

"Yes, we are," she insisted, impatiently—"you and I. That's why I came, so you can get a mine for yourself and be a rich man, and so you can help me get one. I know the way. Hurry up!"

"No," said he, in as firm a tone as he could command. "In the first place, these men don't like me, and they don't want me to share in this."

"What do you care?"

"In the second place, I'm not a miner. I don't know how to proceed."

"Never mind; I do. I've heard nothing but mining all my life."

"In the third place, I don't think I have the right, for I'm a soldier. I'm working for Uncle Sam, and I don't believe I ought to take up mining claims. I'm not sure there is anything to prevent it, but neither am I sure it would be quite the square thing—are you?"

"Why, of course it's all right," said Necia, her eager face clouding with the look of a hurt child. "If you don't do it, somebody else will."

But the Lieutenant shook his head. "Maybe I'm foolish, but I can't see my way clear, much as I would like to."

"Oh, dear! Oh, dear!" she exclaimed, brokenly. "I do so want to go. I want you to be rich, and I want to be rich myself. I want to be a fine lady, and go outside and live like other girls. It's—the only chance —I ever had—and I'll never have another. Oh, it means so much to me; it means life, future, everything! Why, it means heaven to a girl like me!" Her eyes were wet with the sudden dashing of her hopes, and her chin quivered in a sweet, girlish way that made the youth almost surrender on the instant. But she turned to the window and gazed out over the river, continuing, after a moment's pause: "Please don't—mind me—but you can't understand what a difference this would make to me."

"We couldn't possibly overtake them if we tried," he said, as if willing to treat with his conscience.

"No, but we could beat them in. I know where Lee is working, for I went up last winter with Constantine and his dog-team, over a short cut by way of Black Bear Creek. We took it coming back, and I could find it again, but Lee doesn't know that route, so he will follow the summer trail, which is fifteen miles farther. You see, his creek makes a great bend to the southward, and heads back towards the river, so by crossing the divide at the source of Black Bear you drop into it a few miles above his cabin."

While she made this appeal Burrell fought with himself. There were reasons why he longed to take this

AN UNTRODDEN VALLEY

trip, more than he had longed for anything since boyhood. These men of Flambeau had disregarded him, and insisted on treating him with contemptuous distrust, despite his repeated friendly overtures; wherefore he was hungry to beat them at their own game, hungry to thrust himself ahead of them and compel them to reckon with him as an equal, preferring a state of open enmity, if necessary, to this condition of indifferent toleration. Moreover, he knew that Necia was coveted by half of them, and if he spent a night in the woods alone with her it would stir them up a bit, he fancied. By Heaven! That would make them sit up and notice him! But then—it might work a wrong upon her; and yet, would it? He was not so sure that it would. She had come to him; she was old enough to know her mind, and she was but a half-breed girl, after all, who doubtless was not so simple as she seemed. Other men had no such scruples in this or any other land, and yet the young man hesitated until, encouraged by his silence, the girl came forward and spoke again, impulsively:

"Don't be silly, Mr. Burrell. Come! Please come with me, won't you?"

She took him by the edges of his coat and drew him to her coaxingly. It may have been partly the spirit of revolt that had been growing in him all day, or it may have been wholly the sense of her there beside him, warm and pleading, but something caused a great wave to surge up through his veins, caused him to take her in his arms, fiercely kissing her upturned face again and again, crying softly, deep down in his throat:

"Yes! Yes! Yes! You little witch! I'll go anywhere with you! Anywhere! Anywhere!" The impulse was blind and ungovernable, and it grew as his lips met hers, while, strangely enough, she made no resistance, yielding herself quietly, till he found her arms wound softly about his neck and her face nestling close to his. Neither of them knew how long they stood thus blended together, but soon he grew conscious of the beating of her heart against his breast, as she lay there like a little fluttering bird, and felt the throbbing of his own heart swaying him. Her arms, her lips, and her whole body clung to his in a sweet surrender, and yet there was nothing immodest or unmaidenly about it, for his strength and ardor had lifted her and drawn her to him as on the sweep of a great wave.

She drew her face free and hid it against his neck, breathing softly and with shy timidity, as if the sound of the words she whispered half frightened her.

"I love you. I love you, Meade."

It may happen that a man will spend months in friendly and charming intimacy with a woman and never feel the violence or tenderness of passion till there comes a psychic moment or a physical touch that suddenly enwraps them like a flame. So it was with Burrell. The sweet burden of this girl in his arms, the sense of her yielding lips, the warmth of her caressing hands, momentarily unleashed a leaping pack of mad desires, and it was she who finally drew herself away to remind him smilingly that he was wasting time.

"My lips will be here when those mines are worked out," she said. "No, no!" and she held him off as he came towards her again, insisting that if they were going they must be off at once, and that he could have no more kisses for the present. "But, of

AN UNTRODDEN VALLEY

course, it is a long trip, and we will have to sit down now and then to rest," she added, shyly; at which he vowed that he was far from strong, and could not walk but a little way at a time, yet even so, he declared, the trail would be too short, even though it led to Canada.

"Then get your pack made up," she ordered, "for we must be well up towards the head of Black Bear Creek before it grows dark enough to camp."

Swiftly he made his preparations; a madness was upon him now, and he took no pains to check or analyze the reasons for his decision. The thought of her loveliness in his arms once more, far up among the perfumed wooded heights, as the silent darkness stole upon them, stirred in him such a fret to be gone that it was like a fever. He slipped away to the barracks with instructions for his corporal, but was back again in a moment. Finally he took up his burden of blanket and food, then said to her:

"Well, are you ready, little one?"

"Yes, Meade," she answered, simply.

"And you are sure you won't regret it?"

"Not while you love me."

He kissed her again before they stepped out on the river trail that wound along the bank. A hundred yards beyond they were hidden by the groves of birch and fir.

Two hours later they paused where the foaming waters of Black Bear Creek rioted down across a gravelled bar and into the silent, sweeping river, standing at the entrance to a wooded, grass-grown valley, with rolling hills and domes displayed at its head, while back of them lay the town, six miles away, its low, squat buildings tiny and toylike, but distinctly silhouetted against the evening sky.

THE BARRIER

"Is it not time to rest?" said the soldier, laughingly, yet with a look of yearning in his misty eyes as he took the girlish figure in his arms. But she only smiled up at him and, releasing his hold, led the way into the forest.

He turned for a moment and shook his fist at the village and those in it, laughing loudly as if from the feel of the blood that leaped within him. Then he joined his companion, and, hand-in-hand, they left the broad reaches of the greater stream behind them and plunged into the untrodden valley.

CHAPTER V

A STORY IS BEGUN

> *"It's fonny t'ing how two brown eye*
> *Was changin' everyt'ing—*
> *De cloud she's no more on de sky,*
> *An' winter's jus' lak' spring.*
> *Dey mak' my pack so very light,*
> *De trail, she's not so long—*
> *I'd walk it t'orty mile to-night*
> *For hear her sing wan song.*
> *But now I'm busy mak' fortune*
> *For marry on dat girl,*
> *An' if she's tole me yass, dat's soon,*
> *Bonheur! I'm own de worl'!"*

POLEON DORET sang gayly as the trader came towards him through the open grove of birch, for he was happy this afternoon, and, being much of a dreamer, this fresh enterprise awoke in him a boyish pleasure. Then Necia had teased him as he came away, and begged him, as was always her custom, to take her with him, no matter whence or whither, so long as there was adventure afoot. Well, it would not be long now before he could say yes, and he would take her on a journey far longer than either of them had yet taken—a journey that would never end. Had not the gods looked with favor, at last, upon his long novitiate, and been pleased with the faith he had kept? Had not this discovery of "No Creek" Lee's been providentially arranged for his own especial benefit? A fool could see that this was a mark of celestial approbation, and none but a fool would question the wisdom of the gods. Had he not watched the girl grow from a slip of thirteen and spoken never a word of his love? Had he not served and guarded her with all the gentle chivalry of an olden knight? Of course! And here was his reward, a gift of wealth to crown his service, all for her. Now that she was a woman, and had seen him tried, and knew he was a man, he would bring his burden of prosperity and lay it at her feet, saying:

"Here is another offering, my Necia, and with it go the laughter and the music and the heart of Poleon Doret."

Sacré! It would not take her long to wake up after that! The world was very bright indeed this afternoon, and he burst again into song in company with the voices of the forest people:

> "*Chanté, rossignol, chanté!*
> *Toi qui à le cœur gai;*
> *Tu as le cœur à rire*
> *Mai j' l' ai-t-à pleurer,*
>   *Il y a longtemps que j' t'aime*
>   *Jamais je ne t'oublierai.*"[1]

"Whew!" said Gale, slipping out of his pack-straps "the skeeters is bad."

[1] "Sing, little bird, oh, sing away!
You with the voice so light and gay!
Yours is a heart that laughter cheers,
Mine is a heart that's full of tears.
   Long have I loved, I love her yet;
   Leave her I can, but not forget."

A STORY IS BEGUN

"You bet your gum boots," said Poleon. "Dey're mos' so t'ick as de summer dey kill Johnnie Platt on de Porcupine." Both men wore gauntleted gloves of caribou-skin and head harnesses of mosquito-netting stretched over globelike frames of thin steel bands, which they slipped on over their hats after the manner of divers' helmets, for without protection of some kind the insects would have made travel impossible once the Yukon breezes were left behind or once the trail dipped from the high divides where there was no moss.

"Let's see. It was you that found him, wasn't it?" said Gale.

"Sure t'ing! I'm comin' down for grub in my canoe, w'en I see dis feller on de bank, walkin' lak' he's in beeg horry. 'Ba Gar!' I say, 'dere's man goin' so fast he'll meet hese'f comin' home!' Den he turn roun' an' go tearin' back, wavin' hees arms lak' he's callin' me, till he fall down. W'en I paddle close up, I don' know 'im no more dan stranger, an' me an' Johnnie Platt is trap togeder wan winter. W'at you t'ink of dat?"

"I saw a fellow killed that way at Holy Cross," interpolated the trader.

"'Hello,' I say, 'w'at's de matter?' An' den I see somet'ing 'bout 'im dat look familiar. Hees face she's all swell' up an' bleedin' lak' raw meat." The Frenchman curled his upper lip back from his teeth and shook his head at the remembrance.

"Jesu, dat's 'orrible sight! Dem fly is drive 'im crazee. Hees nose an' ears is look lak' holes in beeg red sponge, an' hees eye are close up tight."

"He died before you got him in, didn't he?"

"Yes. He was good man, too. Some tam' if I ever

have bad enemy w'at I like to see catch hell I'm goin'
turn 'im loose 'mong dose skeeter-bug."

"Holy Mackinaw!" ejaculated Gale. "Who'd ever
think of that? Why, that's worse than dropping water
on his skull till he goes crazy, like them Chinamen do."

The Frenchman nodded. "It's de wors' t'ing I
know. Dat's w'y I lak' to geeve it to my enemy."

"Imagine fightin' the little devils till they stung you
crazy and pizened your eyes shut!"

Gale fell to considering this, while Poleon filled his
pipe, and, raising his veil, undertook to smoke. The
pests proved too numerous, however, and forced him
to give it up.

"Ba gosh! Dey're hongry!"

"It will be all right when we get out of the woods,"
said the elder man.

"I guess you been purty glad for havin' Necia
home again, eh?" ventured the other after a while,
unable to avoid any longer the subject uppermost in
his mind.

"Yes, I'm glad she's through with her schooling."

"She's gettin' purty beeg gal now."

"That's right."

"By-an'-by she's goin' marry on some feller—
w'at?"

"I suppose so. She ain't the kind to stay single."

"Ha! Dat's right, too. Mebbe you don' care if
she does get marry, eh?"

"Not if she gets a man that will treat her right."

"Wal! Wal! Dere's no trouble 'bout dat," exclaimed Doret, fervently. "No man w'at's livin' could
treat her bad. She's too good an' too purty for have
bad husban'."

"She is, is she?" Gale turned on him with a strange

A STORY IS BEGUN

glare in his eyes. "Them's the kind that get the he-devils. There's something about a good girl that attracts a bad man, particularly if she's pretty; and it goes double, too — the good men get the hellions. A fellow can't get so tough but what he can catch a good woman, and a decent man usually draws a critter that looks like a sled and acts like a timber wolf."

"Necia wouldn't marry on no bad man," said Doret, positively.

"No?" said Gale. "Let me tell you what I saw with my own eyes. I knew a girl once that was just as good and pure as Necia, and just as pretty, too — yes, and a thousand times prettier."

"Ho, ho!" laughed Doret, sceptically.

"She was an Eastern girl, and she come West where men were different to what she'd been used to. Those were early days, and it was a new country, where a person didn't know much about his neighbor's past and cared less; and, although there were a heap of girls thereabouts, they were the kind you'll always find in such communities, while this one was plumb different. Man! Man! But she was different. She was a *woman!* Two fellows fell in love with her. One of them lived in the same camp as her, and he was a good man, leastways everybody said he was, but he wasn't wise to all the fancy tricks that pretty women hanker after; and, it being his first affair, he was right down buffaloed at the very thought of her, so he just hung around and slept late so that he might dream about her and feel like he was her equal or that she loved back at him. You know! The other fellow came from a neighboring town, and he wasn't the same kind, for he'd knocked around more, and was a better liar but he wasn't right. No, sir! He was sure a wrong guy, as it came out, but he was handsomer and younger, and the very purity and innocence of the girl drew him, I reckon, being a change from what he had ever mixed up with."

"W'y don' dis good man tak' a shot at him?" asked Poleon, hotly.

"First, he didn't realize what was going on, being too tied up with dreaming, I reckon; and, second, neither man didn't know the other by sight, living as they did in different parts; third, he was an ordinary sort of fellow, and hadn't ever had any trouble, man to man, at that time. Anyhow, the girl up and took the bad one."

"W'at does de good man do, eh?"

"Well, he was all tore up about it, but he went away like a sick quail hides out."

"Dat's too bad."

"He heard about them now and then, and what he heard tore him up worse than the other had, for the girl's husband couldn't wear the harness long, and, having taken away what good there was in her, he made up in deviltry for the time he had lost. She stood it pretty well, and never whimpered, even when her eyes were open and she saw what a prize-package she had drawn. The fact that she was game enough to stand for him and yet keep herself clean without complaint made the man worse. He tried to break her spirit in a thousand ways, tried to make her the same as he was, tried to make her a bad woman, like the others he had known. It appeared like the one pleasure he got was to torture her."

"W'y don' she quit 'im?" said Doret. "Dat ain' wrong for quit a man lak' him."

"She couldn't quit on account of the kid. They had

A STORY IS BEGUN

a youngster. Then, too, she had ideas of her own; so she stood it for three years, living worse than a dog, till she saw it wasn't any use—till she saw that he would make a bad woman of her as sure as he would make one of the kid—till he got rough— "

"No! No! You don' mean dat? No man don' hurt no woman," interjected Doret.

"By God! That's just what I mean," the trader answered, while his face had grown so gray as to match his brows. "He beat her."

Poleon broke into French words that accorded well with the trader's harsh voice.

"The woman sent for the other man after that, for he had been living lonely, loving her all the time, and you'd better believe he went."

"Ha! Dat's fine! Dat's dam' fine!" said the other. "I'll bet dere's hell to pay den—w'at?"

"Yes, there was a kind of reckoning." The old man lapsed into moody silence, the younger one waiting eagerly for him to continue, but there came the sound of voices down the trail, and they looked up.

"Here comes Lee," said Gale.

"W'at happen' den? I'm got great interes' 'bout dis woman," insisted Poleon.

"It's a long story, and I just told you this much to show what I said was true about a good girl and a bad man, and to show why I want Necia to get a good one. The sooner it happens the better it will suit me."

Neither man had ever spoken thus openly to the other about Necia before, and although their language was indirect, each knew the other's thought. But there was no time for further talk now, for the others were close upon them. As they came into view, Gale exclaimed:

"Well, if he hasn't brought Runnion along!"

"Humph!" grunted Doret. "I don' t'ink much of dat feller. W'at's de matter wit' 'No Creek,' anyhow?"

The three new arrivals dropped down upon the moss to rest, for the up-trail was heavy and the air sultry inside the forest. Lee was the first to speak.

"Did you get away without bein' seen?" he asked.

"Sure," answered Gale. "Poleon has been here two hours."

"That's good; I don't want nobody taggin' along."

"We came right through the town boldly," announced Stark; "but if they had seen you two they would have suspected something, sure."

Runnion volunteered nothing except oaths at the mosquitoes and at his pack-straps, which were new and cut him already. As no explanation of his presence was offered, neither the trader nor Doret made any comment then, but it came out later, when the old miner dropped far enough behind the others to render conversation possible.

"You decided to take in another one, eh?" Gale asked Lee.

"It wasn't exactly my doin's," replied the miner. "Stark asked me to let Runnion come 'long, bein' as he had grub-staked him, and he seemed so set on it that I ackeressed. You see, it's the first chance I ever had to pay him back for a favor he done me in the Cassiar country. There's plenty of land to go around."

It was Lee's affair, thought the trader, and he might tell whom he liked, so he said no more, but fell to studying the back of the man next in front, who happened to be Stark, observing every move and trick of him, and, during the frequent pauses, making a point of listening and watching him guardedly.

A STORY IS BEGUN

All through the afternoon the five men wound up the valley, following one another's footsteps, emerging from sombre thickets of fir to flounder across wide pastures of "nigger-heads," that wobbled and wriggled and bowed beneath their feet, until at cost of much effort and profanity they gained the firmer footing of the forest. Occasionally they came upon the stream, and found easier going along its gravel bars, till a bend threw them again into the meadows and mesas on either hand. Their course led them far up the big valley to another stream that entered from the right, bearing backward in a great bow towards the Yukon, and always there were dense clouds of mosquitoes above their heads. At one point Stark, hot and irritable, remarked:

"There must be a shorter cut than this, Lee?"

"I reckon there is," the miner replied, "but I've always had a pack to carry, so I chose the level ground ruther than climb the divides."

"S'pose dose people at camp hear 'bout dis strike an' beat us in?" suggested Poleon.

"It wouldn't be easy going for them after they got there," Stark said, sourly. "I, for one, wouldn't stand for it."

"Nor I," agreed Runnion.

"I don't see how you'd help yourself," the trader remarked. "One man's got as good a right as another."

"I guess I'd help myself, all right," Stark laughed, significantly, as did Runnion, who added:

"Lee is entitled to put in anybody he wants on his own discovery, and if anybody tries to get ahead of us there's liable to be trouble."

"I reckon if I don't know no short-cut, nobody else

does," Lee remarked, whereupon Doret spoke up reassuringly:

"Dere's no use gettin' scare' lak' dat, biccause nobody knows w'ere Lee's creek she's locate' but John an' me, an' dere's nobody w'at knows he mak' de strike but us four."

"That's right," said Gale; "the only other way across is by Black Bear Creek, and there ain't a half-dozen men ever been up to the head of that stream, much less over the divide, so I don't allow there's any use to fret ourselves."

They went on their way, travelling leisurely until late evening, when they camped at the mouth of the valley up which the miner's cabin lay. They chose a long gravel bar, that curved like a scimitar, and made down upon its outer tip where the breeze tended to thin the plague of insects. They were all old-stagers in the ways of camplife, so there was no lost motion or bickering as to their respective duties. Their preparations were simple. First they built a circle of smudges out of wet driftwood, and inside this Lee kindled a camp-fire of dry sticks, upon which he cooked, protected by the smoke of the others, while Gale went back to the edge of the forest and felled a dozen small firs, the branches of which he clipped. These Poleon and Runnion bore down to the end of the spit for bedding, while Stark chopped a pile of dry wood for the night. Gale noted that the new man swung an axe with the free dexterity of one to whom its feel was familiar, also that he never made a slip nor dulled it on the gravel of the bar, displaying an all-round completeness and a knack of doing things efficiently that won reluctant approval from the trader despite the unreasoning dislike he had taken to him.

A STORY IS BEGUN

Lee was ready for them by the time they had finished their tasks, and, fanned by the breeze that sucked up the stream and lulled by the waters, they ate their scanty supper. Their one-eyed guide had lived so long among mosquitoes and had become so inoculated with their poison that he was in a measure impervious to their sting, hence the insects gathered on his wrinkled, hair-grown hide only to give up in melancholy disgust and fly to other and fuller-blooded feeding-grounds. Camp had been made early, at Gale's suggestion, instead of pushing on a few miles farther, as Lee had intended; and now, when the cool evening fell and the draught quickened, it became possible to lay off gloves and head-gear; so they sat about the fire, talking, smoking, and rubbing their tired feet.

It is at such hours and in the smoke of such fires that men hark backward and bring forth the sacred, time-worn memories they have treasured, to turn them over fondly by the glow of dying embers. It is at such times that men's garrulity asserts itself, for the barriers of caution are let down, as are the gates of remembrance, and it is then that friends and enemies are made, for there are those who cannot listen and others who cannot understand.

"No Creek" Lee, the one-eyed miner who had made this lucky strike, told in simple words of his long and solitary quest, when ill-luck had risen with him at the dawn and misfortune had stalked beside him as he drifted and drank from camp to camp, while the gloom of a settled pessimism soured him, and men began to shun him because of the evil that seemed to follow in his steps.

"I've been rainbow-chasin' forty years," he said, "and never caught nothin' but cramps and epidemics

THE BARRIER

and inflammations. I'm the only miner in Alaska that never made a discovery of gold and never had a creek named after him."

"Is that how you got your name?" asked Runnion.

"It is. I never was no good to myself nor nobody else. I just occupied space. I've been the vermifuge appendix of the body politic; yes, worse'n that—I've been an appendix with a seed in it. I made myself sore, and everybody around me, but I'm at the bat now, and don't you never let that fact escape you."

"How are you going to spend your money?" inquired Stark.

"I'm goin' to eat it up! I've fed on dried and desiccated and other disastrous and dissatisfactory diets till I'm all shrivelled up inside like a dead puff-ball; now it's me for the big feed and the long drink. I'm goin' to 'Frisco and get full of wasteful and exorbitant grub, of one kind and another, like tomatters and French vicious water."

Poleon Doret laughed with the others; he was bubbling with the spirits of a boy whose life is clean, for whom there are no eyes in the black dark that lies beyond a camp-fire, and for whom there are no unforgettable faces in its smoke. When Lee fell silent the trader and Stark resumed their talk, which was mainly of California, it seemed to the Frenchman, who also noted that it was his friend who subtly shaped the topics. In time their stories revived his memory of the conversation in the birch grove that morning, and when there occurred a lapse in the talk he said:

"Say, John, w'at happen' to dat gal we was talkin' 'bout dis mornin'?"

Gale shook his head and turned again to his com-

A STORY IS BEGUN

panion, but the young man's mind was bent on its quest, and he continued:

"Dat was strange tale, for sure."

"What was it?" questioned Runnion.

"John was tell 'bout a feller he knowed w'at marry a good gal jus' to mak' her bad lak' hese'f."

"How's that?" inquired Stark, turning curiously upon the old man; but Gale knocked the ashes from his pipe and replied:

"Oh, it's a long story—happened when I was in Washington State."

Poleon was about to correct him—it was California, he had said—when Gale arose, remarking sleepily that it was time to turn in if they wished to get any rest before the mosquitoes got bad again, then sauntered away from the fire and spread his blanket. The rest followed and made down their beds; then, drawing on gloves and hat-nets, and rolling themselves up in their coverings, fell to snoring. All except the trader, who lay for hours on his back staring up at the stars, as if trying to solve some riddle that baffled him.

They awoke early, and in half an hour had eaten, remade their packs, and were ready to resume their march. As they were about to start, Gale said:

"I reckon we'd better settle right now who has the choice of locations when we get up yonder. I've been on stampedes where it saved a heap of hard feeling."

"I'm agreeable," said Stark. "Then there won't be any misunderstanding."

The others, being likewise old at the game, acquiesced. They knew that in such cases grave trouble has often occurred when two men have cast eyes on the same claim, and have felt the miner's causeless "hunch" that gold lies here or there, or that the ground one of them covets is wanted by the other.

"I'll hold the straws," said Lee, "and every feller will have an even break." Turning his back on the others, he cut four splinters of varying lengths, and, arranging them so that the ends peeped evenly from his big hand, he held them out.

"The longest one has the first choice, and so on," he said, presenting them to Gale, who promptly drew the longest of the four. He turned to Doret, but the Frenchman waved him courteously to Stark, and, when both he and Runnion had made their choice, Lee handed him the remaining one, which was next in length to that of the trader. Stark and Runnion qualified in the order they drew, the latter cursing his evil luck.

"Never min', ole man," laughed Poleon, "de las' shot she's de sure wan."

They took up their burdens again, and filed towards the narrow valley that stretched away into the hazy distances.

CHAPTER VI

THE BURRELL CODE

NOT until his dying day will Burrell lose the memory of that march with Necia through the untrodden valley, and yet its incidents were never clearcut nor distinct when he looked back upon them, but blended into one dreamlike procession, as if he wandered through some calenture where every image was delightfully distorted and each act deliciously unreal, yet all the sweeter from its fleeting unreality. They talked and laughed and sang with a rush of spirits as untamed as the waters in the course they followed. They wandered, hand-in-hand, into a land of illusions, where there was nothing real but love and nothing tangible but joy. The touch of their lips had waked that delight which comes but once in a lifetime and then to but few; it was like the moon-madness of the tropics or the dementia of the forest folk in spring. A gentle frenzy possessed them, rendering them insensible to fatigue and causing them to hurry the more breathlessly that they might sooner rest and sit beside each other. At times they fell into sweet silences where the waters laughed with them and the trees whispered their secret, bowing and nodding in joyous surprise at this invasion; or, again, the breezes romped with them, withdrawing now and then to rush out and greet them at the bends in boisterous pleasure.

THE BARRIER

They held to the bed of the stream, for its volume was low and enabled them to ford it from bar to bar. Necia had been raised in the open, with the wild places for her playground, and her muscles were like those of a boy, hence the two swung merrily onward, as if in playful contest, while the youth had never occasion to wait for her or to moderate his gait. Indeed, her footing was more sure than his, as he found when she ventured out unhesitatingly upon felled logs that lay across swift, brawling depths. The wilderness had no mystery for her, and no terrors, so she was ever at his side, or in advance, while her eyes, schooled in the tints of the forest, and more active than those of a bird, saw every moving thing, from the flash of a camp-robber's wing through some hidden glade to the inquisitive nodding of a fool hen where it perched high up against the bole of a spruce. They surprised a marten fishing in a drift-wood dam, but she would not let the soldier shoot, and made him pass it by, where it sat amazed till it realized that these were lovers and resumed its fishing. Gradually the stream diminished, and its bowldered bed became more difficult to traverse, until, assuming the airs of a leader, the girl commanded him to lay off his pack, at which he pretended to obey mutinously, though thrilling with the keenest delight at his own submission.

"What are you going to do?" he inquired.

"Mind your own business, sir," she commanded, sternly.

From her belt she drew a little hunting-knife, with which she cut and trimmed a slender birch the thickness of his thumb, whereupon he pretended great fright, and said:

"Please! please! What have I done?"

THE BURRELL CODE

"A great deal! You are a most bold and stubborn creature."

"All pack animals are stubborn," he declared. "It's the only privilege they have."

"You are much too presumptuous, also, as I discovered in your quarters."

"My only presumption is in loving you."

"That was not presumption," she smiled; "it was pre-emption. You must be punished."

"I shall run away," he threatened. "I shall gallop right off through the woods and—begin to eat grass. I am very wild."

As she talked she drew from her pocket a spool of line, and took a fly-hook from her hat; then, in a trice, she had rigged a fishing-rod, and, creeping out upon a ledge, she whipped the pool below of a half-dozen rainbow trout, which she thrust into his coat while they were still wriggling. Then she as quickly put up her gear, and they resumed their journey, climbing more steeply now, until, when the sun was low, they quit the stream-bed and made through the forest towards the shoulder of an untimbered ridge that ran down into the valley. And there, high up on the edge of the spruce, they selected a mossy shelf and pitched their camp.

They had become so intimate by now as to fall into a whimsical mode of speech, and Necia reverted to a childish habit in her talk that brought many a smile to the youth's face. It had been her fancy as a little girl to speak in adjectives, ignoring many of her nouns, and its quaintness had so amused her father that on rare occasions, when the humor was on him, he also took it up. She now addressed herself to Burrell in the same manner.

"I think we are very smarts to come so far," she said.

"You travel like a deer," he declared, admiringly. "Why, you have tired me down." Removing his pack, he stretched his arms and shook out the ache in his shoulders.

"Which way does our course lie now, Pathfinder?"

"Right up the side of this big, and then along the ridge. In two hours we come to a gully running so"—she indicated an imaginary direction—"which we go down till it joins another stream so, and right there we'll find old 'No Creek's' cabin, so! Won't they be surprised to see us! I think we're very cunning to beat them in, don't you?" She laughed a glad little bubbling laugh, and he cried:

"Oh, girl! How wonderful you are!"

"It's getting very dark and fierce," she chided, "and all the housework must be done."

So he built a fire, then fetched a bucket of water from a rill that trickled down among the rocks near by. He made as if to prepare their meal, but she would have none of it.

"Bigs should never cook," she declared. "That work belongs to littles," then forced him to vacate her domain and turn himself to the manlier duties of chopping wood and boughs.

First, however, she showed him how to place two green foot-logs upon which the teapot and the frying-pan would sit without upsetting, and how long she wished the sticks of cooking-wood. Then she banished him, as it were, and he built a wickiup of spruce tops, under the shelter of which he piled thick, fragrant billows of "Yukon feathers."

Once while he was busy at his task he paused to

revel in the colors that lay against hill and valley, and to drink in the splendid isolation of it all. Below lay the bed of Black Bear Creek, silent and sombre in the creeping twilight; beyond, away beyond, across the westward brim of the Yukon basin, the peaks were blue and ivory and gold in the last rays of the sun; while the open slopes behind and all about wore a carpet of fragrant short-lived flowers, nodding as if towards sleep, and over all was the hush of the lonely hills. A gust blew a whiff of the camp smoke towards him, and he turned back to watch Necia kneeling beside the fire like some graceful virgin at her altar rites, while the peculiar acrid out-door odor of burning spruce was like an incense in his nostrils.

He filled his chest deeply and leaned on his axe, for he found himself shaking as if under the spell of some great expectancy.

"Your supper is getting cold," she called to him.

He took a seat beside her on a pile of boughs where the smoke was least troublesome; he had chosen a spot that was sheltered by a lichen-covered ledge, and this low wall behind, with the wickiup joining it, formed an enclosure that lent them a certain air of privacy. They ate ravenously, and drank deep cupfuls of the unflavored tea. By the time they were finished the night had fallen and the air was just cool enough to make the fire agreeable. Burrell heaped on more wood and stretched out beside her.

"This day has been so wonderful," said the girl, "that I shall never go to sleep. I can't bear to end it."

"But you must be weary, little maid," he said, gently; "I am."

"Wait, let me see." She stretched her limbs and moved slightly to try her muscles. "Yes, I am a very tired, but not the kind of tired that makes you want to go to bed. I want to talk, talk, talk, and not about ourselves either, but about sensibles. Tell me about your people—your sister."

He had expected her to ask this, for the subject seemed to have an inexhaustible charm for her. She would sit rapt and motionless as long as he cared to talk of his sister, in her wide, meditative eyes the shadow of a great unvoiced longing. It always seemed to make her grave and thoughtful, he had noticed, so he had tried lately to avoid the topic, and to-night in particular he wanted to do so, for this was no time for melancholy. He had not even allowed himself to think, as yet, and there were reasons why he did not wish her to do so; thought and realization and a readjustment of their relations would come after tonight, but this was the hour of illusion, and it must not be broken; therefore he began to tell her of other people and of his youth, making his tales as fanciful as possible, choosing deliberately to foster the merry humor in which they had been all day. He told her of his father, the crotchety old soldier, whose absurd sense of duty and whose elaborate Southern courtesy had become a byword in the South. He told her household tales that were prized like pieces of the Burrell plate, beautiful heirlooms of sentiment that mark the honor of high-blooded houses; following which there was much to recount of the Meades, from the admiral who fought as a boy in the Bay of Tripoli down to the cousin who was at Annapolis; the while his listener hung upon his words hungrily, her mind so quick in pursuit of his that it spurred him unconsciously, her great, dark eyes half closed in silent laughter or wide with wonder, and in them always the warmth of the leaping firelight blended with the trust of a new-born virginal love.

Without realizing it, the young man drifted further than he had intended, and further than he had ever allowed himself to go before, for in him was a clean and honest pride of birth, like his mother's glory in her forebears, the expression of which he had learned to repress, inasmuch as it was a Dixie-land conceit and had been misunderstood when he went North to the Academy. In some this would have seemed bigoted and feminine, this immoderate admiration for his own blood, this exaggerated appreciation of his family honor, but in this Southern youth it was merely the unconscious commendation of an upright manliness for an upright code. When he had finished, the girl remarked, with honest approval:

"What a fine you are. Those people of yours have all been good men and women, haven't they?"

"Most of them," he admitted, "and I think the reason is that we've been soldiers. The army discipline is good for a man. It narrows a fellow, I suppose, but it keeps him straight."

Then he began to laugh silently.

"What is it?" she said, curiously.

"Oh, nothing! I was just wondering what my strait-laced ancestors would say if they could see me now."

"What do you mean?" the girl asked, in open-eyed wonderment.

"I don't care," he went on, unheeding her question. "They did worse things in their time, from what I hear." He leaned forward to draw her to him.

"Worse things? But we are doing nothing bad," said Necia, holding him off. "There's no wrong in loving."

"Of course not," he assured her.

"I am proud of it," she declared. "It is the finest thing, the greatest thing that has ever come into my life. Why, I simply can't hold it; I want to sing it to the stars and cry it out to the whole world. Don't you?"

"I hardly think we'd better advertise," he said, dryly.

"Why not?"

"Well, I shouldn't care to publish the tale of this excursion of ours, would you?"

"I don't see any reason against it. I have often taken trips with Poleon, and been gone with him for days and days at a time."

"But you were not a woman then," he said, softly.

"No, not until to-day, that's true. Dear, dear! How I did grow all of a sudden! And yet I'm just the same as I was yesterday, and I'll always be the same, just a wild little. Please don't ever let me be a big tame. I don't want to be commonplace and ordinary. I want to be natural—and good."

"You couldn't be like other women," he declared, and there was more tenderness than hunger in his tone now, as she looked up at him trustingly from the shelter of his arms. "It would spoil you to grow up."

"It is so good to be alive and to love you like this!" she continued, dreamily, staring into the fire. "I seem to have come out of a gloomy house into the glory of a warm spring day, for my eyes are blinded and I can't see half the beautifuls I want to, there are so many about me."

"Those are my arms," interjected the soldier, lightly, in an effort to ward off her growing seriousness.

"I've never been afraid of anything, and yet I feel so safe inside them. Isn't it queer?"

THE BURRELL CODE

The young man became conscious of a vague discomfort, and realized dimly that for hours now he had been smothering with words and caresses a something that had striven with him to be heard, a something that instead of dying grew stronger the more utterly this innocent maid yielded to him. It was as if he had ridden impulse with rough spurs in a fierce desire to distance certain voices, and in the first mad gallop had lost them, but now far back heard them calling again more strongly every moment. A man's honor, if old, may travel feebly, but its pursuit is persistent. It was the talk about his people that had raised this damned uneasiness and indecision, he thought. Why had he ever started it?

"The marvellous part of it all," continued the girl, "is that it will never end. I know I shall love you always. Do you suppose I am really different from other girls?"

"Everything is different to-night—the whole world," he declared, impatiently. "I thought I knew myself, but suddenly I seem strange in my own eyes."

"I've had a big handicap," she said, "but you must help me to overcome it. I want to be like your sister."

He rose and piled more wood upon the fire. What possessed the girl? It was as if she knew each cunning joint of his armor, as if she had realized her peril and had set about the awakening of his conscience, deliberately and with a cautious wisdom beyond her years. Well, she had done it—and he swore to himself. Then he melted at the sight of her, crouched there against the shadows, following his every movement with her soul in her eyes, the tenderest trace of a smile upon her lips. He vowed he was a reprobate to wrong her so; it was her white soul and her woman's love that spoke.

When she beheld him gazing at her, she tilted her head sidewise daintily, like a little bird.

"Oh, my! What a fierce you are all at once!"

Her smile flashed up as if illumined by the leaping blaze, and he crossed quickly, kneeling beside her.

"Dear, wonderful girl," he said, "it is going to be my heart's work to see that you never change and that you remain just what you are. You can't understand what this means to me, for I, too, was blinded, but the darkness of the night has restored my vision. Now you must go to sleep; the hours are short and we must be going early."

He piled up a great, sweet-scented couch of springy boughs, and fashioned her a pillow out of a bundle of smaller ones, around which he wrapped his khaki coat; then he removed her high-laced boots, and, taking her tiny feet, one in the palm of either hand, bowed his head over them and kissed them with a sense of her gracious purity and his own unworthiness. He spread one of the big gray blankets over her, and tucked her in, while she sighed in delightful languor, looking up at him all the time.

"I'll sit here beside you for a while," he said. "I want to smoke a bit."

She stole a slim, brown hand out from beneath the cover and snuggled it in his, and he leaned forward, closing her lids down with his lips. Her utter weariness was manifest, for she fell asleep almost instantly, her fingers twined about his in a childlike grip.

At times a great desire to feel her in his arms, to have her on his breast, surged over him, for he had lived long apart from women, and the solitude of the night seemed to mock him. He was a strong man, and in his veins ran the blood of wayward forebears who were wont to possess that which they conquered in the lists of love, mingled with which was the blood of spirited Southern women who had on occasion loved not wisely, according to Kentucky rumor, but only too well. Nevertheless, they were honest men and women, if over-sentimental, and had transmitted to him a heritage of chivalry and a high sense of honor and courage. Strange to say, this little, simple half-breed girl had revived this honor and courage, even when he tried most stubbornly to smother it. If only her love was like her blood, he might have had no scruples; or if her blood were as pure as her love—even then it would be easier; but, as it was, he must give her up to-night, and for all time. Her love had placed a barrier between them greater and more insurmountable than her blood.

He sat for a long time with the dwindling firelight playing about him, his manhood and his desires locked in a grim struggle, wondering at the hold this forest elf had gained upon him, wondering how it was that she had stolen into his heart and head and taken such utter possession of him. It would be no easy task to shut her out of his mind and put her away from him. And she . . . ?

He gently withdrew his fingers from her grasp, and, seeking the other side of the wickiup, covered himself over without disturbing her, and fell asleep.

It was early dawn when Necia crept to him.

"I dreamed you had gone away," she said, shivering violently and drawing close. "Oh, it was a terrible awakening—"

"I was too tired to dream," he said.

"So I had to come and see if you were really here."

He quickly rekindled the fire, and they made a hasty breakfast. Before the warmth of the rising sun had penetrated the cold air they had climbed the ridge and obtained a wondrous view of broken country, the hills alight with the morning rays, the valleys misty and mystical. They made good progress on the summit, which was paved with barren rock and sparsely carpeted with short moss, while there was never a hint of insects to annoy them. Merrily they swung along, buoyed up by an unnatural exaltation; yet now and then, as they drew near their destination, the young man had a chilling premonition of evil to come, and wondered if he had not been foolhardy to undertake this rash enterprise.

"I wish Stark was not one of Lee's party," he said once. "He may misunderstand our being together this way."

"But when he learns that we love each other, that will explain everything."

"I'm not so sure. He doesn't know you as Lee and Poleon and your father do. I think we had better say nothing at all about—you and me—to any one."

"But why?" questioned the girl, stopping abruptly. "They will know it, anyhow, when they see us. I can't conceal it."

"I am wiser in this than you are," the soldier insisted, "and we mustn't act like lovers; trust this to me."

"Oh, I won't play that!" cried Necia, petulantly. "If all this is going to end when we get to Lee's cabin, we'll stay right here forever."

He was not sure of all the logic he advanced in convincing her, but she yielded finally, saying:

THE BURRELL CODE

"Well, I suppose you know best, and, anyhow, littles should always mind."

They clung to the divide for several hours, then descended into the bed of a stream, which they followed until it joined a larger one a couple of miles below, and there, sheltered in a grove of whispering firs, they found Lee's cabin nestling in a narrow, forked valley. Evidently the miner had selected a point on the main creek just below the confluence of the feeders as a place in which to prospect, and Burrell fell to wondering which one of these smaller streams supplied the run of gold.

"There's no one here," said Necia, gleefully. "We've beat them in! We've beat them in!"

They had been walking rapidly since dawn, and, although Burrell's watch showed two o'clock, she refused to halt for lunch, declaring that the others might arrive at any moment; so down they went to the lower end of " No Creek " Lee's location, where Burrell blazed a smooth spot on the down-stream side of a tree and wrote thereon at Necia's dictation. When he had finished, she signed her name, and he witnessed it, then paced off four hundred and forty steps, where he squared a spruce-tree, which she marked: "Lower centre end stake of No. 1 below discovery. Necia Gale, locator." She was vastly excited and immensely elated at her good-fortune in acquiring the claim next to Lee's, and chattered like a magpie, filling the glades with resounding echoes and dancing about in the bright sunlight that filtered through the branches.

"Now you stake the one below mine," she said. "It's just as good, and maybe better — nobody can tell." But he shook his head.

"I'm not going to stake anything," said he.

THE BARRIER

"You must!" she cried, quickly, the sparkle dying from her eyes. "You said you would, or I never would have brought you."

"I merely said I would come with you," he corrected. "I did not promise to take up a claim, for I don't think I ought to do so. If I were a civilian, it would be different, but this is government land, and I am a part of the government, as it were. Then, too, in addition to the question of my right to do it, there would be the certainty of making enemies of your people, old "No Creek" and the rest, and I can't afford that now. With you it is different, for you are entitled to this ground. After Lee's friends have shared in his discovery I may change my mind."

All arguments and pleading were in vain; he remained obdurate and insisted on her locating two other claims for herself, one on each of the smaller creeks where they came together above the house.

"But nobody ever stakes more than one claim on a gulch," objected the girl. "It's a custom of the miners."

"Then we'll call each one of these branches a different and separate creek," he said. "The gold was carried down one of those smaller streams, and we won't take any chances on which one it was. When a fellow plays a big game he should play to win, and, as this means such a great deal to you, we won't overlook any bets."

Necia consented, and when her three claims had been properly located the couple returned to the cabin to get lunch and to await with some foreboding the coming of the others and what of good or ill it might bring.

CHAPTER VII

THE MAGIC OF BEN STARK

BEFORE the party came in sight, the sound of their voices reached the cabin, and Burrell rose nervously and sauntered to the door. Uncertain how this affair might terminate, he chose to get first look at his enemies, if they should prove to be such, realizing the advantage that goes to a man who stands squarely on both feet.

The trail came through the brush at the rear, and he heard Lee say:

"This here's the place, boys—the shack ain't fifty yards away."

"Likely looking gulch," Gale was heard to reply, in his deep tones—there was a crackle of dead brush, a sound as of a man tripping and falling heavily, then oaths in a voice that made the Lieutenant start.

"Ha, ha!" laughed Doret. "You mus' be tired, Meestaire R-r-unnion. Better you pick up your feet. Dat's t'ree tam' you've—"

They emerged into the open behind the house to pause in line back of Lee, who was staring at the stovepipe of his cabin, from which came a wisp of smoke. It seemed to Burrell that they held their position for a long time. Then he heard Lee say:

"Well, I'll be damned! Somebody's here ahead of us."

"We've been beaten," growled Stark, angrily, pushing past him and coming round the corner, an ugly look in his eyes.

Burrell was standing at ease in the door, smoking, one forearm resting on the jamb, his wide shoulders nearly filling the entrance.

"Good-afternoon," he nodded, pleasantly.

Lee answered him unintelligibly; Stark said nothing, but Runnion's exclamation was plain.

"It's that damned blue-belly!"

"When did *you* get here?" said Stark, after a pause.

"A few hours ago."

"How did you come?" asked Lee.

"Black Bear Creek," said the soldier, curtly, at which Runnion broke into profanity.

"Better hush," Burrell admonished him; "there's a lady inside," and at that instant Necia showed her laughing face under his arm, while the trader uttered her name in amazement.

"Lunch is ready," she said. "We've been expecting you for quite a while."

"Ba Gar! Dat's fonny t'ing for sure," said Poleon. "Who tol' you 'bout dis strike—eh?"

"Mother; I made her," the girl answered.

"Take off your packs and come in," Burrell invited, but Stark strode forward.

"Hold on a minute. This don't look good to me. You say your mother told you. I suppose you're Old Man Gale's other daughter—eh?"

Necia nodded.

"What time of day was it when you learned about this?"

"Cut that out," roughly interjected Gale. "Do you think I double-crossed you?"

THE MAGIC OF BEN STARK

The other turned upon him.

"It looks that way, and I intend to find out. You said yesterday you hadn't told anybody—"

"I didn't think about the woman," said the trader, a trifle disconcerted, whereupon Runnion gave vent to an ironical sneer.

"But here's your girl and this man ahead of us. I suppose there's others on the way, too."

"Nonsense!" Burrell cut in. "Don't quarrel about this. Miss Gale got wind of your secret, and beat you at your own game, so that ends it; but there's plenty of ground left for all of you, and no harm done. Nobody knows of this strike from us, I can assure you."

"I call it dam' sleeck work," chuckled the Canadian, slipping out of his straps. "De nex' tam' I go stampedin' I tak' you 'long, Necia."

"Me, too," said Lee. "An' now I'm goin' to tear into some of them beans I smell a bilin' in yonder."

The others followed, although Stark and Runnion looked black and had little to say. It was an uncomfortable meal—every one was ill at ease; Gale, in particular, was quiet, and ate less than any of them. His eyes sought Stark's face frequently, and once the blood left his cheeks and his eyes blazed as he observed the gambler eying Necia, gazing at her with the same boldness he would have used in scanning a horse.

"You are a mighty good-looking girl for a 'blood,'" remarked Stark, at last.

"Thank you," she replied, simply, and the soldier's vague dislike of the man crystallized into hate on the instant. There was a tone back of his words that seemed aimed at the trader, Meade thought, but Gale showed no sign of it, so the meal was finished in silence, after which the five belated prospectors went out to make their locations, for the fear of interruption was upon them now.

First they went down-stream, and, according to their agreement, the trader staked first, followed by Poleon and Stark, thus throwing Runnion's claim more than a mile distant from Lee's discovery. From here they went up the creek to find the girl's other locations, one on each branch, at which Stark sneeringly remarked that she had pre-empted enough ground for a full-grown white woman.

Runnion's displeasure was even more open, and he fell into foul-mouthed mutterings, addressing himself to Poleon and Stark while the trader was out of ear-shot.

"This affair don't smell right, and I still think it's a frame-up."

"Bah!" exclaimed Doret.

"The old man sent the girl on ahead of us to blanket all the good ground. That's what he did!"

"Dat's fool talk," declared the Frenchman.

"I'm not so sure," Stark broke in. "You remember he hung back and wanted to go slow from the start; and didn't he ask us to camp early last night? Looks now as if he did it just to give her time to get in first. He admitted that he knew the Black Bear trail, and if he lied about keeping his mouth shut to the squaw, he'd lie about other—"

"Wait wan minnit," interrupted Poleon, his voice as soft as a woman's. "I tol' you dat *I* know all 'bout dis Black Bear Creek, too—you 'member, eh? Wal, mebbe you t'ink I'm traitor, too. W'at? W'y don' you spik out?"

The three of them were alone, and only the sound of Gale's axe came to them; but at the light in the Canadian's face Runnion hastily disclaimed any such thought on his part, and Stark shrugged his denial.

"I don' know you feller' at all," continued Poleon, "but Ole Man Gale, he's my frien', so I guess you don' better talk no more lak' dat."

"Don't get sore," said Stark. "I simply say it looks bad." But the other had turned his back and was walking on.

There are men quite devoid of the ability to read the human face, and Runnion was of this species. Moreover, malice was so bitter in his mouth that he must have it out, so when they paused to blaze the next stake he addressed himself to Stark loud enough for Poleon to hear.

"That Lieutenant is more of a man than I thought he was."

"How so?" inquired the older man.

"Well, it takes nerve to steal a girl for one night and then face the father; but the old man don't seem to mind it any more than she does. I guess he knows what it means, all right."

Stark laughed raucously. "I thought of that myself," he said.

"That's probably how Gale got *his* squaw," concluded Runnion, with a sneer.

It seemed a full minute before the Frenchman gave sign that he had heard, then a strange cry broke from his throat and he began to tremble as if with cold. He was no longer the singer of songs or the man who was forever a boy; the mocking anger of a moment ago was gone; in its place was a consuming fury that sucked the blood from beneath his tan, leaving him the pallor of ashes, while his mouth twitched and his head rolled slightly from side to side like a palsied old man's. The red of his lips was blanched, leaving two white streaks against a faded, muddy background, through which came strange and frightful oaths in a bastard tongue. Runnion drew back, fearful, and the older man ceased chopping and let his axe hang loosely in his hand. But evidently Poleon meant no violence, for he allowed the passion to run from him freely until it had spent its vigor, then said to Runnion:

"M'sieu, eider you are brave man or dam' fool."

"What do you mean, Frenchy?" said the man addressed, uneasily.

"Somebody goin' die for w'at you say jus' now. Mebbe it's goin' be you, m'sieu; mebbe it's goin' be him; I can't tell yet, but I'm hope an' pray it's goin' be you, biccause I t'ink w'at you say is a lie, an' nobody can spik dose kin' of lie 'bout Necia Gale."

He went crashing blindly through the underbrush, his head wagging, his shoulders slumped loosely forward like those of a drunken man, his lips framing words they could not understand.

When he had disappeared Runnion drew a deep breath.

"I guess I've framed something for Mister Burrell this time."

"You go about it queer," said Stark. "I'd rather tackle a gang-saw than a man like Poleon Doret. Your frame-up may work double."

"Huh! No chance. The soldier was out all night alone with that half-breed girl, and anybody can see she's crazy about him. What's the answer?"

"Well, she's mighty pretty," agreed the other, "most too pretty for a mixed blood, but you can't make that Frenchman believe she's wrong."

"Why, he believes it now," chuckled Runnion, "or

THE MAGIC OF BEN STARK

at least he's jealous, and that's just as good. Those two will have trouble before dark. I wish they would—then I'd have a chance."

"Have you got your eye on her, too?"

"Sure! Do you blame me?"

"No, but she's too good for you."

"Then she's too good for them. I think I'll enter the running."

"Better stay out," the gambler advised; "you'll have sore feet before you finish. As a matter of fact, I don't like her father any better than you like her lovers—"

"Well, it's mutual. I can see Gale hates you like poison."

"—and I don't intend to see him and his tribe hog all the best ground hereabouts."

"They've already done it. You can't stop them."

Before answering, Stark listened for the trader, but evidently Gale had finished his task and returned to the shack, for there was neither sign nor sound of him.

"Yes, I can stop them," said Stark. "I want the ground that girl has staked, and I'm going to get it. It lies next to Lee's, and it's sure to be rich; ours is so far away it may not be worth the recorder's fees. This creek may be as spotted as a coach-dog, so I don't intend to take any chances."

"She made her locations legally," said Runnion.

"You leave that to me. When will the other boys be here?"

"To-morrow morning. I told them to follow about four hours behind, and not to run in on us till we had finished. They'll camp a few miles down the creek, and be in early."

"You couldn't get but three, eh?"

"That's all I could find who would agree to give up half."

"Can we count on them?"

"Huh!" the other grunted. "They worked with me and Soapy on the Skagway trail."

"Good. Five against three, not counting the girl and the Lieutenant," Stark mused. "Well, that will do it." He outlined his plan, then the two returned to the cabin to find Lee cooking supper. Poleon was there with the others, but, except for his silence, he showed no sign of what had taken place that afternoon.

Stark developed a loquacious mood after supper, devoting himself entirely to Necia, in whom he seemed to take great interest. He was an engaging talker, with a peculiar knack of suggestion in story-telling—an unconscious halting and elusiveness that told more than words could express—and, knowing his West so well, he fascinated the girl, who hung upon his tales with flattering eagerness.

Poleon had finished several pipes, and now sat in the shadows in the open doorway, apparently tired and dejected, though his eyes shone like diamonds and roved from one to the other. Half unconsciously he heard Stark saying:

"This girl was about your size, but not so dark. However, you remind me of her in some ways—that's why it puts her in my mind, I suppose. She was about your age at the time—nineteen."

"Oh, I'm not eighteen yet," said Necia.

"Well, she was a fine woman, anyhow, the best that ever set foot in Chandon, and there was a great deal of talk when she chose young Bennett over the Gaylord man, for Bennett had been running second best from the start, and everybody thought it was settled between her and the other one. However, they were married quietly."

The story did not interest the Canadian; his mind was in too great agitation to care for dead tales; his heart burned within him too fiercely, and he felt too great a desire to put his hands to work. As he watched Burrell and Runnion bend over the table looking at a little can of gold-dust that Lee had taken from under his bunk, his eyes grew red and bloodshot beneath his hat-brim. Which one of the two would it be, he wondered. From the corner of his eye he saw Gale rise from Lee's bed, where he had stretched himself to smoke, and take his six-shooter from his belt, then remove the knotted bandanna from his neck, and begin to clean the gun, his head bowed over it earnestly, his face in the shadow. He had ever been a careful and methodical man, reflected Poleon, and evidently would not go to sleep with his fire-arm in bad condition.

"Nobody imagined that Gaylord would cause trouble," Stark was saying, "for he didn't seem to be a jealous sort, just stupid and kind of heavy-witted; but one night he took advantage of Bennett's absence and sneaked up to the house." The story-teller paused, and Necia, who was under the spell of his recital, urged him on:

"Yes, yes. What happened then? Go on." But Stark stared gloomily at his hands, and held his silence for a full minute, the tale appearing to have awakened more than a fleeting interest in him.

"It was one of the worst killings that ever happened in those parts," he continued. "Bennett came back to find his wife murdered and the kid gone."

"Oh!" said the girl, in a shocked voice.

"Yes, there was the deuce of a time. The town

rose up in a body, and we—you see, I happened to be there—we followed the man for weeks. We trailed him and the kid clear over into the Nevada desert where we lost them."

"Poor man!"

"Poor man?" The story-teller raised his eyes and laughed sinisterly. "I don't see where that comes in."

"And you never caught him?"

"No. Not yet."

"He died of thirst in the desert, maybe, he and the little one."

"That's what we thought at the time, but I don't believe it now."

"How so?"

"Well, I've crossed his trail since then. No. Gaylord is alive to-day, and so is the girl. Some time we'll meet—" His voice gave out, and he stared again at the floor.

"Couldn't the little girl be traced?" said Necia. "What was her name?"

Stark made to speak, but the word was never uttered, for there came a deafening roar that caused Lee's candle to leap and flicker and the air inside the cabin to strike the occupants like a blow. Instantly there was confusion, and each man sprang to his feet crying out affrightedly, for the noise had come with utter unexpectedness.

"My God, I've killed him!" cried Gale, and with one jump he cleared half the room and was beside Stark, while his revolver lay on the floor where he had been sitting.

"What is it?" exclaimed Burrell; but there was no need to ask, for powder-smoke was beginning to fill the room and the trader's face gave answer. It

THE MAGIC OF BEN STARK

was whiter than that of his daughter, who had crouched fearfully against the wall, and he shook like a man with ague. But Stark stood unhurt, and more composed than any of them; following the first bound from his chair, he had relapsed into his customary quiet. There had blazed up one momentary flash of suspicion and anger, but it died straightway, for no man could have beheld the trader and not felt contrition. His condition was pitiable, and the sight of a strong man overcome is not pleasant; when it was seen that no harm had been done the others strove to make light of the accident.

"Get together, all of you! It's nothing to be excited over," said Stark.

"How did it happen?" Runnion finally asked Gale, who had sunk limply upon the edge of the bunk; but when the old man undertook to answer his words were unintelligible, and he shook his head helplessly.

Stark laid his finger on the hole that the bullet had bored in the log close to where he was sitting, and laughed.

"Never mind, old man, it missed me by six inches. You know there never was a bullet that could kill me. I'm six-shooter proof."

"Wha'd I tell you?" triumphantly ejaculated Lee, turning his one eye upon the Lieutenant. "You laughed at me, didn't you?"

"I'm beginning to believe it myself," declared the soldier.

"It's a cinch," said Stark, positively.

Doret, of all in the cabin, had said nothing. Seated apart from the others, he had seen the affair from a distance, as it were, and now stepped to the bed to lay his hand on Gale's shoulder.

"Brace up, John! Sacré bleu! Your face look lak' flour. Come outside an' get li'l' air."

"It will do you good, father," urged Necia.

The trader silently rose, picked up his hat, and shambled out into the night behind the Frenchman.

"The old man takes it hard," said Lee, shaking his head, and Burrell remarked:

"I've seen things like that in army quarters, and the fellow who accidentally discharges his gun invariably gets a greater shock than his companion."

"I call it damned careless, begging your pardon, Miss Necia," said Runnion.

Poleon led his friend down the trail for half a mile without speaking, till Gale had regained a grip of himself and muttered, finally:

"I never did such a thing before, Poleon, never in all my life."

The young man turned squarely and faced him, the starlight illumining their faces dimly.

"Why?" said Doret.

"Why?" echoed Gale, with a start. "Well, because I'm careful, I suppose."

"Why?" insisted the Frenchman.

"I—I—I— What do you mean?"

"Don' lie wit' me, John. I'm happen to be watch you underneat' my hat w'en you turn roun' for see if anybody lookin'."

"You saw?"

"Yes."

"I thought you were asleep," said Gale.

CHAPTER VIII

THE KNIFE

IN every community, be it never so small, there are undesirable citizens; and, while the little party was still at breakfast on the following morning, three such members of society came around the cabin and let fall their packs, greeting the occupants boisterously.

"Well, well!" said Lee, coming to the door. "You're travellin' kind of early, ain't you?"

"Yes—early and late," one of them laughed, while the other two sprawled about as if to rest.

"How far are you goin'?"

"Not far," the spokesman answered.

Now in the North there is one formality that must be observed with friend or enemy, and, though Lee knew these men for what they were, he said:

"Better have some breakfast, anyhow."

"We just ate." There was an uncomfortable pause, then the speaker continued: "Look here. It's no use to flush around. We want a piece of this creek."

"What are you goin' to do with it?"

"Cut that out, Lee. We're on."

"Who wised you up to this?" inquired the miner, angrily, for he had other friends besides those present whom he wished to profit by this strike, and he had hoped to keep out this scum.

"Never mind who put us Jerry. We're here, ain't we?"

Stark spoke up. "You can't keep news of a gold strike when the wind blows, Lee. It travels on the breeze."

The harm was done, and there was no use in concealment, so Lee reluctantly told them of his discovery and warned them of the stakes already placed.

"And see here, you fellers," he concluded, "I've been forty years at this game and never had a creek named after me, but this one is goin' to be called ' " No Creek " Lee Creek ' or I fight. Does it go?"

"Sure, that's a good name, and we'll vote for it."

"Then go as far as you like," said the miner, dismissing them curtly.

"I'll step along with the boys and show them where our upper stakes are," volunteered Stark, and Runnion offered to do the same, adding that it were best to make sure of no conflict so early in the game. The five disappeared into the woods, leaving the others at the cabin to make preparations for the homeward trip.

"That man who did the talking is a tin-horn gambler who drifted in a month ago, the same as Runnion, and the others ain't much better," said Gale, when they had gone. "Seems like the crooks always beat the straight men in."

"Never knowed it to fail," Lee agreed. "There's a dozen good men in camp I'd like to see in on this find, but it 'll be too late 'gin we get back."

"Dose bum an' saloon feller got all de bes' claims at Klondike," said Poleon. "I guess it's goin' be de same here."

"I don't like the look of this," observed the Lieutenant, thoughtfully. "I'm afraid there's some kind of a job on foot."

"There's nothing they can do,' Gale answered.

THE KNIFE

"We've got our ground staked out, and it's up to them to choose what's left."

They were nearly ready to set out for Flambeau when the five men returned.

"Before you go," said Stark, "I think we'd better organize our mining district. There are enough present to do it."

"We can make the kind of laws we want before the gang comes along," Runnion chimed in, "and elect a recorder who will give us a square deal."

"I'll agree if we give Lee the job," said Gale. "It's coming to him as the discoverer, and I reckon the money will be handy, seeing the hard luck he's played in."

"That's agreeable to me," Stark replied, and proceeded forthwith to call a miners' meeting, being himself straightway nominated as chairman by one of the strangers. There was no objection, so he went in, as did Lee, who was made secretary, with instructions to write out the business of the meeting, together with the by-laws as they were passed.

The group assembled in the cleared space before the cabin to make rules and regulations governing the district, for it is a custom in all mining sections removed from authority for the property holders thus to make local laws governing the size of claims, the amount of assessment work, the size of the recorder's fees, the character of those who may hold mines, and such other questions as arise to affect their personal or property interests. In the days prior to the establishment of courts and the adoption of a code of laws for Alaska, the entire country was governed in this way, even to the adjudication of criminal actions. It was the primitive majority rule that prevails in every new land, and the courts later recognized and approved the laws so made and administered, even when they differed in every district, and even when these statutes were often grotesque and ridiculous. As a whole, however, they were direct in their effect and worked no hardship; in fact, government by miners' meeting is looked upon to this day, by those who lived under it, as vastly superior to the complicated machinery which later took its place.

The law permits six or more people to organize a mining district and adopt articles of government, so this instance was quite ordinary and proper.

Lee had come by his learning slowly, and he wrote after the fashion of a school-boy, who views his characters from every angle and follows their intricacies with corresponding movements of the tongue, hence the business of the meeting progressed slowly.

It was of wondrous interest to Necia to be an integral part of such important matters, and she took pride in voting on every question; but Burrell, who observed the proceedings from neutral ground, could not shake off the notion that all was not right. Things moved too smoothly. It looked as if there had been a rehearsal. Poleon and the trader, however, seemed not to notice it, and Lee was wallowing to the waist in his own troubles, so the young man kept his eyes open and waited.

The surprise came when they had completed the organization of the district and had nearly finished adopting by-laws. It was so boldly attempted and so crude in its working-out that it seemed almost laughable to the soldier, until he saw these men were in deadly earnest and animated by the cruelest of motives. Moreover, it showed the first glimpse of Stark's spite against the trader, which the Lieutenant had divined.

THE KNIFE

Runnion moved the adoption of a rule that no women be allowed to locate mining claims, and one of the strangers seconded it.

"What's that?" said Lee, raising his one eye from the note-book in which he was transcribing.

"It isn't right to let women in on a man's game," said Runnion.

"That's my idea," echoed the seconder.

"I s'pose this is aimed at my girl," said Gale, springing to his feet. "I might have known you bums were up to some crooked work."

Poleon likewise rose and ranged himself with the trader.

"Ba Gar! I don' stan' for dat," said he, excitedly. "You want for jump Necia's claims, eh?"

"As long as I'm chairman we'll have no rough work," declared Stark, glaring at them. "If you want trouble, you two, I reckon you can have it, but, whether you do or not, the majority is going to rule, and we'll make what laws we want to."

He took no pains now to mask his dislike of Gale, who began to move towards him in his dogged, resolute way. Necia, observing them, hastened to her father's side, for that which she sensed in the bearing of both men quite overcame her indignation at this blow against herself.

"No, no, don't have any trouble," she pleaded, as she clung to the trader. "For my sake, daddy, sit down." Then she whispered fiercely into his ear: "Can't you see he's trying to make you fight? There's too many of them. Wait! *Wait!*"

Burrell attempted to speak, but Stark, who was presiding, turned upon him fiercely:

"Now this is *one* time when you can't butt in,

THE BARRIER

Mr. Soldier Man. This is our business. Is that plain?"

The Lieutenant realized that he had no place in this discussion, and yet their move was so openly brazen that he could restrain himself with difficulty. A moment later he saw the futility of interference, when Stark continued, addressing the trader:

"This isn't aimed at you in particular, Gale, nor at your girl, for a motion to disqualify her isn't necessary. She isn't old enough to hold mining property."

"She's eighteen," declared the trader.

"Not according to *her* story."

"Well, I can keep her claims for her till she gets of age."

"We've just fixed it so you can't," grinned Runnion, cunningly. "No man can hold more than one claim on a creek. You voted for that yourself."

Too late, Gale saw the trick by which Stark had used him to rob his own daughter. If he and his two friends had declined to be a part of this meeting, the others could not have held it, and before another assembly could have been called the creek would have been staked from end to end, from rim to rim, by honest men, over whom no such action could pass; but, as it was, his own votes had been used to sew him up in a mesh of motions and resolutions.

"No Creek" Lee had the name of a man slow in speech and action, and one who roused himself to anger deliberately, much as a serpent stings itself into a painful fury; but now it was apparent that he was boiling over, for he stammered and halted and blurted explosively.

"You're a bunch of rascals, all of you, tryin' to down a pore girl and get her ground; but who put ye wise

THE KNIFE

to this thing, in the first place? Who found this gold? Just because there's enough of you to vote that motion through, that don't make it legal, not by a damned sight, and it won't hold, because I won't write it in the book. You—you—" He glared at them malevolently, searching his mind for an epithet sufficiently vile, and, finding it, spat it out — "dressmakers!"

So this was why both Stark and Runnion had gone up the creek with the three new men, thought Burrell. No doubt they had deliberately arranged the whole thing so that the new arrivals could immediately relocate each of Necia's claims—the pick of all the ground outside Lee's discovery, and the surest to be valuable—and that Stark would share in the robbery. He or Runnion, or both of them, had broken Lee's oath of secrecy even before leaving camp, which accounted for the presence of these thugs; and now, as he revolved the situation rapidly in his mind, the soldier looked up at a sudden thought. Poleon had begun to speak, and from his appearance it seemed possible that he might not cease with words; moreover, it was further evident that they were all intent on the excited Frenchman and had no eyes for the Lieutenant. Carefully slipping around the corner of the cabin, and keeping the house between him and the others, Burrell broke into a swift run, making the utmost possible speed for fear they should miss him and guess his purpose, or, worse yet, finish their discussion and adjourn before he could complete his task. He was a light man on his feet, and he dodged through the forest, running more carelessly the farther he went, visiting first the upper claims, then, making a wide détour of the cabin, he came back to the initial stake of Necia's lower claim, staggering from his exertions, his lungs bursting from the strain. He had covered nearly a mile, but, even so, he laughed grimly as he walked back towards the cabin, for it was a game worth playing, and he was glad to take a hand on the side of the trader and the girl. Coming within earshot, he heard the meeting vote to adjourn. It could not have terminated more opportunely had he held a stop-watch on it.

From the look of triumph on Runnion's face, the Lieutenant needed no glance at Gale or Poleon or Necia to know that the will of the majority had prevailed, and that the girl's importunities had restrained her advocates from a resort to violence. She looked very forlorn, like a little child just robbed and deceived, with the shock of its first great disillusionment still fresh in its eyes.

Runnion addressed the other conspirators loudly.

"Well, boys, there are three good claims open for relocation. I'm sorry I can't stake one of them."

"They won't lie open long," said one of the undesirable citizens, starting to turn down-stream while his two companions made for the opposite direction. But Burrell stopped them.

"Too late, boys. Your little game went wrong. Now! Now! Don't get excited. Whew! I had quite a run."

Gale paused in his tracks and looked at the young man queerly.

"What do you mean?"

"I've jumped those claims myself."

"*You* jumped them!" cried Necia.

"Sure! I changed my mind about staking."

"It's a lie!" cried Runnion, at which Burrell whirled on him.

THE KNIFE

"I've been waiting for this, Runnion—ever since you came back. Now—"

"I mean you haven't had time," the other temporized, hurriedly.

"Oh, that sounds better! If you don't believe me take a look for yourself; you'll find my notice just beneath Miss Gale's." Then to "No Creek" Lee he continued, "Kindly record them for me so there will be no question of priority."

"I'll be damned if I do!" said the belligerent recorder. "You're worse'n these crooks. That ground belongs to Necia Gale."

Up to this time Stark had remained silent, his impassive face betraying not a shadow of chagrin, for he was a good loser; but now he spoke at large.

"Anybody who thinks the American army is asleep is crazy." Then to Burrell, "You certainly are a nice young man to double-cross your friends like that."

"You're no friend of mine," Meade retorted.

"I? What do you mean?"

"I double-crossed you, Stark, nobody else."

The Kentuckian glared at him with a look like that which Runnion had seen in his face on that first day at the trading-post. The thought of these five men banded together to rob this little maid had caused a giddiness to rise up in him, and his passions were beginning to whirl and dance.

"There's no use mouthing words about it," said he. "These thugs are your tools, and you tried to steal that ground because it's sure to be rich."

Stark exclaimed angrily, but the other gave him no time to break in.

"Now, don't get rough, because *that* is my game, and I'd be pleased enough to take you back a prisoner."

Then turning to Lee, he said: "Don't make me force you to record my locations. I staked those claims for Miss Gale, and I'll deed them to her when she turns eighteen."

Poleon Doret called to Runnion: "M'sieu, you 'member w'at I tol' you yestidday? I'm begin for t'ink it's goin' be you."

The man paled in his anger, but said nothing. Necia clapped her hands gleefully.

Seeing that the game had gone against him, Stark got his feelings under control quickly, and shrugged his shoulders as he turned away.

"You're in the wrong, Lieutenant," he remarked; "but I don't want any trouble. You've got the law with you." Then to Runnion and the others he said, "Well, I'm ready to hit the trail."

When they had shouldered their packs and disappeared down the valley, Gale held out his hand to the soldier. "Young man, I reckon you and I will be friends."

"Thank you," said Burrell, taking the offer of friendship which he knew was genuine at last.

"I'm in on that!" said "No Creek" Lee; "you're all right!"

Poleon had been watching Stark's party disappear, but now he turned and addressed the young soldier.

"You mak' some enemies to-day, M'sieu."

"That's right," agreed Lee. "Ben Stark will never let up on you now."

"Very well, that is his privilege."

"You don't savvy what it means to get him down on you," insisted Lee. "He'll frame things up to suit himself, then pick a row with you. He's the quickest man on a trigger in the West, but he won't never

THE KNIFE

make no open play, only just devil the life out of you with little things till you flare up, then he'll down you. That's how he killed the gold commissioner back in British Columbia."

Necia had said little so far, but the look in her eyes repaid the soldier for his undertaking in her behalf, and for any mischief that might ensue from it.. She came forward and laid her hands upon his.

"Promise that you won't have trouble with him," she begged, anxiously, "for it's all my fault, and I'd—I'd always blame myself if any hurt came to you. Promise! Won't you?"

"Don't worry, daughter," reassured Gale. "There's nothing Stark can do, and whatever happens we're with the Lieutenant. He's our kind of people."

Burrell liked this grizzled old fellow with the watchful eyes, and was glad now that he could grip his hand and face him squarely with no guilt upon his conscience.

By this time Doret had finished with their blankets, and the four set out for town, but instead of following the others they accepted Necia as guide and chose the trail to Black Bear Creek. They had not gone far before she took occasion to lag behind with the Lieutenant.

"I couldn't thank you before all those people—they would have read our secret—but you know how I feel, don't you, Meade?"

"Why! It was a simple thing—"

"It was splendid when you defied them. My, what a fierce you are! Oh, boy! What if something should happen to you over this!"

"But there's no chance. It's all done, and you'll have your fine dresses and be able to hold your nose just as high as you want."

"Whatever I get I will owe to you. I—I've been thinking. Suppose—well, suppose you keep two of those claims; they are sure to be rich—"

"Why, Necia!" he exclaimed.

"They're yours, and I have no right to them under the law. Of course it would be very handsome of you to give me one—the poorest."

"You ought to have your ears boxed," he laughed at her.

"I don't see why. You—you—may be very poor, for all I know."

"I am," he declared, "but not poor enough to take payment for a favor."

"Well, then, if they are really mine to do with as I please, I'll sell one to you—"

"Thanks. I couldn't avail myself of the offer," he said, with mock hauteur.

"If you were a business man instead of a fighting person you would listen to my proposition before you declined it. I'll make the price right, and you may pay me when we get behind yonder clump of bushes." She pouted her lips invitingly, but he declared she was a minor and as such her bargain would not hold.

It was evidently her mood to re-enter the land of whims and travel again, as they had on the way from town, but he knew that for him such a thing could not be, for his eyes had cleared since then. He knew that he could never again wander through the happy valley, for he vowed this maid should be no plaything for him or for any other man, and as there could be no honorable end to this affair, it must terminate at once. Just how this was to be consummated he had not determined as yet, nor did he like to set about its

THE KNIFE

solution, it hurt him so to think of losing her. However, she was very young, only a child, and in time would come to count him but a memory, no doubt, while as for him—well, it would be hard to forget her, but he could and would. He reasoned glibly that this was the only honest course, and his reasoning convinced him; then, all of a sudden, the pressure of her warm lips came upon him and the remembrance upset every premise and process of his logic. Nevertheless, he was honest in his stubborn determination to conclude the affair, and finally decided to let time show him the way.

She seemed to be very happy, her mood being in marked contrast to that of Poleon and the trader, both of whom had fallen silent and gloomy, and in whom the hours wrought no change. The latter had tacitly acknowledged his treachery towards Stark on the previous night, but beyond that he would not go, offering no motive, excuse, or explanation, choosing to stand in the eyes of his friend as an intended murderer, notwithstanding which Poleon let the matter drop—for was not his friend a good man? Had he not been tried in a hundred ways? The young Frenchman knew there must have been strong reason for Gale's outburst, and was content to trust him without puzzling his mind to discover the cause of it.

Now, a secret must either grow or die—there is no fallow age for it—and this one had lived with Gale for fifteen years, until it had made an old man of him. It weighed him down until the desire to be rid of it almost became overpowering at times; but his caution was ingrained and powerful, and so it was that he resisted the temptation to confide in his partner, although the effort left him tired and inert. The only one to whom he could talk was Alluna — she understood, and though she might not help, the sound of his own voice at least always afforded him some relief.

As to Poleon, no one had ever seen him thus. Never in all his life of dream and song and romance had he known a heavy heart until now, for if at times he had wept like a girl, it was at the hurts of others. He had loved a bit and gambled much, with equal misfortune, and the next day he had forgotten. He had lived the free, clean life of a man who wins joyously or goes down with defiance in his throat, but this venomous thing that Runnion had planted in him had seeped and circulated through his being until every fibre was penetrated with a bitter poison. Most of his troubles could be grappled with bare hands, but here was one against which force would not avail, hence he was unhappy.

The party reached Flambeau on the following day, sufficiently ahead of Stark and his men for Lee to make known his find to his friends, and by sunset the place was depopulated, while a line of men could be seen creeping slowly up the valleys.

Gale found Alluna in charge of the store, but no opportunity of talking alone with her occurred until late in the evening, after Necia had put the two little ones to bed and had followed them wearily. Then he told his squaw. She took the news better than he expected, and showed no emotion such as other women would have displayed, even when he told her of the gunshot. Instead, she inquired:

"Why did you try it there before all those others?"

"Well, when I heard him talking, the wish to kill him was more than I could stand, and it came on me all at once, so that I was mad, I suppose. I never did the like before." He half shuddered at the memory.

"I am sorry," she said.

"Yes! So am I."

"Sorry that you failed, for you will never have as good a chance again. What was the matter with your aim? I have seen you hit a knot-hole, shooting from the hip."

"The man is charmed," declared Gale. "He's bullet-proof."

"There are people," she agreed, "that a gunshot will not injure. There was a man like that among my people—my father's enemy—but he was not proof against steel."

"Your old man knifed him, eh?"

She nodded.

"Ugh!" the man shivered. "I couldn't do that. A gun is a straight man's friend, but a knife is the weapon of traitors. I couldn't drive it home."

"Does this man suspect?"

"No."

"Then it is child's play. We will lay a trap."

"No, by God!" Gale interrupted her hotly. "I tried that kind of work, and it won't do. I'm no murderer."

"Those are only words," said the woman, quietly. "To kill your enemy is the law."

The only light in the room came from the stove, a great iron cylinder made from a coal-oil tank that lay on a rectangular bed of sand held inside of four timbers, with a door in one end to take whole lengths of cordwood, and which, being open, lit the space in front, throwing the sides and corners of the place into blacker mystery.

THE BARRIER

When he made no answer the squaw slipped out into the shadows, leaving him staring into the flames, to return a moment later bearing something in her hands, which she placed in his. It was a knife in a scabbard, old and worn.

"There is no magic that can turn bright steel," she said, then squatted again in the dimness outside of the firelight. Gale slid the case from the long blade and held it in his palm, letting the firelight flicker on it. He balanced it and tested the feel of its handle against his palm, then tried the edge of it with his thumb-nail, and found it honed like a razor.

"A child could kill with it," said Alluna. "Both edges of the blade are so thin that a finger's weight will bury it. One should hold the wrist firmly till it pierces through the coat, that is all—after that the flesh takes it easily, like butter."

The glancing, glinting light flashing from the deadly thing seemed to fascinate the man, for he held it a long while silently. Then he spoke.

"For fifteen years I've been a haunted man, with a soul like a dark and dismal garret peopled with bats and varmints that flap and flutter all the time. I used to figger that if I killed this man I'd kill that memory, too, and those flitting, noiseless things would leave me, but the thought of doing it made me afraid every time, so I ran away, which never did no good—you can't outfoot a memory—and I knew all the while that we'd meet sooner or later. Now that the day is here at last, I'm not ready for it. I'd like to run away again if there was any place to run to, but I've followed frontiers till I've seen them disappear one by one; I've retreated till my back is against the Circle, and there isn't any further land to go to. All the time I've

THE KNIFE

prayed and planned for this meeting, and yet—I'm undecided."

"Kill him!" said Alluna.

"God knows I've always hated trouble, whereas it's what he lives on. I've always wanted to die in bed, while he's been a killer all his life and the smoke hangs forever in his eyes. Only for an accident we might have lived here all our days and never had a 'run-in,' which makes me wonder if I hadn't better let things go on as they are."

"Kill him! It is the law," repeated Alluna, stubbornly, but he put her aside with a slow shake of the head and arose as if very tired.

"No! I don't think I can do it—not in cold blood, anyhow. Good-night! I'm going to sleep on it." He crossed to the door of his room, but as he went she noted that he slipped the knife and scabbard inside the bosom of his shirt.

CHAPTER IX

THE AWAKENING

EARLY the next morning Corporal Thomas came into the store and found Necia tending it while Gale was out. Ever since the day she had questioned him about Burrell, this old man had taken every occasion to talk with the girl, and when he asked her this morning about the reports concerning Lee's strike, she told him of her trip, and all that had occurred.

"You see, I'm a mine-owner now," she concluded. "If it hadn't been a secret I would have told you before I went so you could have been one of the first."

"I'm goin', anyhow," he said, "if the Lieutenant will let me and if it's not too late."

Then she told him of the trail by Black Bear Creek which would save him several hours.

"So that's how you and he made it?" he observed, gazing at her shrewdly. "I supposed you went with your father?"

"Oh, no! We beat him in," she said, and fell to musing at the memory of those hours passed alone with Meade, while her eyes shone and her cheeks glowed. The Corporal saw the look, and it bore out a theory he had formed during the past month, so, as he lingered, he set about a task that had lain in his mind for some time. As a rule he was not a careful man in his speech, and the delicacy of this manœuvre taxed his ingenuity to the utmost, for he loved the girl and feared to say too much.

"The Lieutenant is a smart young fellow," he began; "and it was slick work jumpin' all those claims. It's just like him to befriend a girl like you—I've seen him do it before—"

"What!" exclaimed Necia, "befriend other girls?"

"Or things just like it. He's always doing favors that get him into trouble."

"This couldn't cause him trouble, could it, outside of Stark's and Runnion's grudge?"

"No, I reckon not," assented the Corporal, groping blindly for some way of expressing what he wished to say. "Except, of course, it might cause a lot of talk at headquarters when it's known what he's done for you and how he done it. I heard something about it down the street this morning, so I'm afraid it will get to St. Michael's, and then to his folks." He realized that he was not getting on well, for the task was harder than he had imagined.

"I don't understand," said Necia. "He hasn't done anything that any man wouldn't do under the same circumstances."

"No man's got a right to make folks talk about a nice girl," said the Corporal; "and the feller that told me about it said he reckoned you two was in love." He hurried along now without offering her a chance to speak. "Of course, that had to be caught up quick; you're too fine a girl for that."

"Too fine?" Necia laughed.

"I mean you're too fine and good to let him put you in wrong, just as he's too fine a fellow and got too much ahead of him to make what his people would call a messy-alliance."

"Would his people object to — to such a thing?" questioned the girl. They were alone in the store, and so they could talk freely. "I'm just supposing, you know."

"Oh, Lord! *Would* they object?" Corporal Thomas laughed in a highly artificial manner that made Necia bridle and draw herself up indignantly.

"Why should they, I'd like to know? I'm just as pretty as other girls, and I'm just as good. I know just as much as they do, too, except—about certain things."

"You sure are all of that and more, too," the Corporal declared, heartily, "but if you knowed more about things outside you'd understand why it ain't possible. I can't tell you without hurtin' your feelin's, and I like you too much for that, Miss Necia. Seems as if I'm almost a daddy to you, and I've only knowed you for a few weeks—"

"Go ahead and tell me; I won't be offended," insisted the girl. "You *must*. I don't know much about such things, for I've lived all my life with men like father and Poleon, and the priests at the Mission, who treat me just like one of themselves. But somebody will want to marry me some day, I suppose, so I ought to know what is wrong with me." She flushed up darkly under her brown cheeks.

The feeling came over Corporal Thomas that he had hurt a helpless animal of some gentle kind; that he was bungling his work, and that he was not of the calibre to go into the social amenities. He began to perspire uncomfortably, but went on, doggedly:

"I'm goin' to tell you a story, not because it applies

THE AWAKENING

to Lieutenant Burrell, or because he's in love with you, which of course he ain't any more than you be with him—"

"Of course," said the girl.

"—but just to show you what I mean. It was a good long spell ago, when I was at Fort Supply, which was the frontier in them days like this is now. We freighted in from Dodge City with bull teams, and it was sure the fringe of the frontier; no women—no society—nothin' much except a fort, a lot of Injuns, and a few officials with their wives and families. Now them kind of places is all right for married men, but they're tough sleddin' for single ones, and after a while a feller gets awful careless about himself; he seems to go backward and run down mighty quick when he gets away from civilization and his people and restaurants and such things; he gets plumb reckless and forgetful of what's what. Well, there was a captain with us, a young feller that looked like the Lieutenant here, and a good deal the same sort—high-tempered and chivalrious and all that sort of thing; a West Pointer, too, good family and all that, and, what's more, a captain at twenty-five. Now, our head freighter was married to a squaw, or leastways he had been, but in them days nobody thought much of it any more than they do up here now, and particularly because he'd had a government contract for a long while, ran a big gang of men and critters, and had made a lot of money. Likewise he had a girl, who lived at the fort, and was mighty nice to look at, and restful to the eye after a year or so of cactus-trees and mesquite and buffalo-grass. She was twice as nice and twice as pretty as the women at the post, and as for money—well, her dad could have bought and sold all the officers in a

THE BARRIER

lump; but they and their wives looked down on her, and she didn't mix with them none whatever. To make it short, the captain married her. Seemed like he got disregardful of everything, and the hunger to have a woman just overpowered him. She'd been courted by every single man for four hundred miles around. She was pretty and full of fire, and they was both of an age to love hard, so Jefferson swore he'd make the other women take her; but soldierin' is a heap different from any other profession, and the army has got its own traditions. The plan wouldn't work. By-and-by the captain got tired of trying, and gave up the attempt—just devoted himself to her—and then we was transferred, all but him. We shifted to a better post, but Captain Jefferson was changed to another company and had to stay at Supply. Gee! it was a rotten hole! Influence had been used, and there he stuck, while the new officers cut him out completely, just like the others had done, so I was told, and it drifted on that way for a long time, him forever makin' an uphill fight to get his wife reco'nized and always quittin' loser. His folks back East was scandalized and froze him cold, callin' him a squaw-man; and the story went all through the army, till his brother officers had to treat him cold in order to keep enough warmth at home to live by, one thing leading to another till he finally resented it openly. After that he didn't last long. They made it so unpleasant that he quit the service—crowded him out, that's all. He was a born soldier, too, and didn't know nothing else nor care for nothing else; as fine a man as I ever served under, but it soured him so that a rattlesnake couldn't have lived with him. He tried to go into some kind of business after he quit the army, but he wasn't cut out for it, and never made good as long as I knew of him. The last time I seen him was down on the border, and he had sure grown cultus. He had quit the squaw, who was livin' with a greaser in Tucson—"

"And do you think I'm like that woman?" said Necia, in a queer, strained voice. She had listened intently to the Corporal's story, but he had purposely avoided her eyes and could not tell how she was taking it.

"No! You're different, but the army is just the same. I told you this to show you how it is out in the States. It don't apply to you, of course—"

"Of course!" agreed Necia again. "But what would happen to Lieutenant Burrell if—if—well, if he should do something like that? There are many half-breed girls, I dare say, like this other girl, or—like me."

She did not flush now as before; instead, her cheeks were pale.

"It would go a heap worse with him than it did with Captain Jefferson," said the Corporal, "for he's got more ahead of him and he comes from better stock. Why, his family is way up! They're all soldiers, and they're strong at headquarters; they're mighty proud, too, and they wouldn't stand for his doing such a thing, even if he wanted to. But he wouldn't try; he's got too much sense, and loves the army too well for that. No, sir! He'll go a long ways, that boy will, if he's let alone."

"I never thought of myself as an Indian," said Necia, dully. "In this country it's a person's heart that counts."

"That's how it ought to be," said the Corporal, heartily; "and I'm mighty sorry if I've hurt you, little girl. I'm a rough old rooster, and I never thought but what you understood all this. Up here folks look at it right, but outside it's mighty different; even yet you don't half understand."

"I'm glad I'm what I am!" cried the girl. "There's nothing in my blood to be ashamed of, and I'm white in here!" She struck her bosom fiercely. "If a man loves me he'll take me no matter what it means to him."

"Right for you," assented the other; "and if I was younger myself, I'd sure have a lot of nice things to say to you. If I'd 'a' had somebody like you I'd 'a' let liquor alone, maybe, and amounted to something, but all I'm good for now is to give advice and draw my pay." He slid down from the counter where he had been sitting. "I'm goin' to hunt up the Lieutenant and get him to let me off. Mebbe I can stake a claim and sell it."

The moment he was gone the girl's composure vanshed and she gave vent to her feelings.

"It's a lie! It's a lie!" she cried, aloud, and with her fists she beat the boards in front of her. "He loves me! I know he does!" Then she began to tremble, and sobbed: "I'm just like other girls."

She was still wrestling with herself when Gale returned, and he started at the look in her face as she approached him.

"Why did you marry my mother?" she asked. "Why? Why did you do it?"

He saw that she was in a rage, and answered, bluntly, "I didn't."

She shrank at this. "Then why didn't you? Shame! Shame! That makes me worse than I thought I was. Oh, why did you ever turn squaw-man? Why did you make me a breed?"

THE AWAKENING

"Look here! What ails you?" said the trader.

"What ails me?" she mocked. "Why, I'm neither white nor red; I'm not even a decent Indian. I'm a—a—" She shuddered. "You made me what I am. You didn't do me the justice even to marry my mother."

"Somebody's been saying things about you," said Gale, quietly, taking her by the shoulders. "Who is it? Tell me who it is."

"No, no! It's not that! Nobody has said anything to my face; they're afraid of you, I suppose, but God knows what they think and say to my back."

"I'll—" began the trader, but she interrupted him.

"I've just begun to realize what I am. I'm not respectable. I'm not like other women, and never can be. I'm a squaw—a *squaw!*"

"You're not!" he cried.

"It's a nice word, isn't it?"

"What's wrong with it?"

"No honest man can marry me. I'm a vagabond! The best I can get is my bed and board, like my mother."

"By God! Who offered you that?" Gale's face was whiter than hers now, but she disregarded him and abandoned herself to the tempest of emotion that swept her along.

"He can play with me, but nothing more, and when he is gone another one can have me, and then another and another and another—as long as I can cook and wash and work. In time my man will beat me, just like any other *squaw*, I suppose, but I can't marry; I can't be a wife to a decent man."

She was in the clutch of an hysteria that made her writhe beneath Gale's hand, choking and sobbing, until he loosed her; then she leaned exhausted against a post and wiped her eyes, for the tears were coming now.

"That's all damned rot," he said. "There's fifty good men in this camp would marry you to-morrow."

"Bah! I mean real men, not miners. I want to be a lady. I don't want to pull a hand-sled and wear moccasins all my life, and raise children for men with whiskers. I want to be loved—I want to be loved! I want to marry a gentleman."

"Burrell!" said Gale.

"No!" she flared up. "Not him nor anybody in particular, but somebody like him, some man with clean finger-nails."

He found nothing humorous or grotesque in her measure of a gentleman, for he realized that she was strung to a pitch of unreason and unnatural excitement, and that she was in terrible earnest.

"Daughter," he said, "I'm mighty sorry this knowledge has come to you, and I see it's my fault, but things are different now to what they were when I met Alluna. It wasn't the style to marry squaws where we came from, and neither of us ever thought about it much. We were happy with each other, and we've been man and wife to each other just as truly as if a priest had mumbled over us."

"But why didn't you marry her when I came? Surely you must have known what it would mean to me. It was bad enough without that."

The old man hesitated. "I'll own I was wrong," he said, finally, staring out into the sunshine with an odd expression. "It was thoughtless and wrong, dead wrong; but I've loved you better than any daughter was ever loved in this wide world, and I've worked and starved and froze and saved, and so has Alluna, so

THE AWAKENING

that you might have something to live on when I'm gone, and be different to us. It won't be long now, I guess. I've given you the best schooling of any girl on the river, and I'd have sent you out to a convent in the States, but I couldn't let you go so far away — God! I loved you too much for that — I couldn't do it, girl. I've tried, but you're all I've got, and I'm a selfish man, I reckon."

"No, no! You're not," his daughter cried, impulsively. "You're everything that's good and dear, but you've lived a different life from other men and you see things differently. It was mean of me to talk as I did." She put her arms around his neck and hugged him. "But I'm very unhappy, dad."

"Don't you aim to tell what started this?" he said, gently, caressing her with his great, hard hand as softly as a mother. But she shook her head, and he continued, "I'll take the first boat down to the Mission and marry your ma, if you want me to."

"That wouldn't do any good," said she. "We'd better leave things as they are." Then she drew away and smiled at him bravely from the door. "I'm a very bad to act this way. S'cuses?"

He nodded and she went out, but he gazed after her for a long minute, then sighed.

"Poor little girl!"

Necia was in a restless mood, and, remembering that Alluna and the children had gone berrying on the slopes behind the Indian village, she turned her way thither. All at once a fear of seeing Meade Burrell came upon her. She wanted to think this out, to find where she stood, before he had word with her. She had been led to observe herself from a strange angle, and must verify her vision, as it were. As yet she could not fully understand. What if he had changed, now that he was alone, and had had time to think? It would kill her if she saw any difference in him, and she knew she would be able to read it in his eyes.

As she went through the main street of the camp she saw Stark occupied near the water-front, where he had bought a building lot. He spoke to her as she was about to pass.

"Good-morning, Miss. Are you rested from your trip?"

She answered that she was, and would have continued on her way, but he stopped her.

"I don't want you to think that mining matter was my doing," he said. "I've got nothing against you. Your old man hasn't wasted any affection on me, and I can get along without him, all right, but I don't make trouble for girls if I can help it."

The girl believed that he meant what he said; his words rang true, and he spoke seriously. Moreover, Stark was known already in the camp as a man who did not go out of his way to make friends or to render an accounting of his deeds, so it was natural that when he made her a show of kindness Necia should treat him with less coldness than might have been expected. The man had exercised an occult influence upon her from the time she first saw him at Lee's cabin, but it was too vague for definite feeling, and she had been too strongly swayed by Poleon and her father in their attitude towards him to be conscious of it. Finding him now, however, in a gentle humor, she was drawn to him unwittingly, and felt an overweening desire to talk with him, even at the hazard of offending her own people. The encounter fitted in with her rebellious

THE AWAKENING

mood, for there were things she wished to know, things she must find out from some one who knew the world and would not be afraid to answer her questions candidly.

"I'm going to build a big dance-hall and saloon here," said Stark, showing her the stakes that he had driven. "As soon as the rush to the creek is over I'll hire a gang of men to get out a lot of house logs. I'll finish it in a week and be open for the stampede."

"Do you think this will be a big town?" she asked.

"Nobody can tell, but I'll take a chance. If it proves to be a false alarm I'll move on—I've done it before."

"You've been in a great many camps, I suppose."

He said that he had, that for twenty years he had been on the frontier, and knew it from West Texas to the Circle.

"And are they all alike?"

"Very much. The land lies different but the people are the same."

"I've never known anything except this." She swept the points of the compass with her arm. "And there is so much beyond that I want to know about— oh, I feel so ignorant! There is something now that perhaps you could tell me, you have travelled so much."

"Let's have it," said he, smiling at her seriousness.

She hesitated, at a loss for words, finally blurting out what was in her mind.

"My father is a squaw-man, Mr. Stark, and I've been raised to think that such things are customary."

"They are, in all new countries," he assured her.

"But how are they regarded when civilization comes along?"

"Well, they aren't regarded, as a rule. Squaw-men

THE BARRIER

are pretty shiftless, and people don't pay much attention to them. I guess if they weren't they wouldn't be squaw-men."

"My father isn't shiftless," she challenged, at which he remained silent, refusing to go on record. "Isn't a half-breed just as good as a white?"

"Look here," said he. "What are you driving at?"

"I'm a 'blood,'" she declared, recklessly, "and I want to know what people think of me. The men around here have never made me feel conscious of it, but—"

"You're afraid of these new people who are coming, eh? Well, don't worry about that, Miss. It wouldn't make any difference to me or to any of your friends whether you were red, white, black, or yellow."

"But it *would* make a difference with some people?" insisted the girl.

"Oh, I reckon it would with Eastern people. They look at things kind of funny, but we're not in the East."

"That's what I wanted to know. Nice people back there wouldn't tolerate a girl like me for a moment, would they? They wouldn't consider me good enough to associate with them?"

He shrugged his shoulders. "I guess you'd have a hard time breaking in among the 'bon-tonners.' But what's the use of thinking about it. This is your country and these are your people."

A morbid desire was upon her to track down this intangible racial distinction, but she saw Runnion, whom she could not bear, coming towards them, so thanked Stark hurriedly and went on her way.

"Been making friends with that squaw, eh?" remarked Runnion, casually.

"Yes," replied Stark. "She's a nice little girl, and I like her. I told her I didn't have any part in that miners' meeting affair."

"Huh! What's the matter with you? It was *all* your doing."

"I know it was, but I didn't aim it at her. I wanted that ground next to Lee's, and I wanted to throw a jolt into Old Man Gale. I couldn't let the girl stand in my way; but now that it's over, I'm willing to be friends with her."

"Me, too," said Runnion, looking after Necia as her figure diminished up the street. "By Heaven! She's as graceful as a fawn; she's white, too. Nobody would ever know she was a breed."

"She's a good girl," said Stark, musingly, in a gentle tone that Runnion had never heard before.

"Getting kind of mushy, ain't you? I thought you had passed that stage, old man."

"No, I don't like her in that way."

"Well, I do, and I'm dead sore on that soldier."

"She's not your kind," said Stark. "A bad man can't hold a good woman; he can win one easy enough, but he can't keep her. I know!"

"Nobody but a fool would want to *keep* one," Runnion replied, "specially a squaw."

"She's just woke up to the fact that she *is* a squaw and isn't as good as white. She's worried."

"I'll lay you a little eight to five that Burrell has thrown her down," chuckled Runnion.

"I never thought of that. You may be right."

"If it's true I'll shuffle up a hand for that soldier."

"If I were you I wouldn't deal it to him," said the gambler, dryly. "He may not cut to your break."

Meanwhile, Necia had passed on out of the town and

through the Indian village at the mouth of the creek, until high up on the slopes she saw Alluna and the little ones. She climbed up to them and seated herself where she could look far out over the westward valley, with the great stream flowing half a mile beneath her. She stayed there all the morning, and although the day was bright and the bushes bending with their burden of blue, she picked no berries, but fought resolutely through a dozen varying moods that mirrored themselves in her delicate face. It was her first soul struggle, but in time the buoyancy of youth and the almighty optimism of early love prevailed; she comforted herself with the fond illusion that this man was different from all others, that his regard was equal to her own, and that his love would rise above such accidental things as blood or breed or birth. And so she was in a happier frame of mind when the little company made their descent at mid-day.

As they approached the town they heard the familiar cry of "Steam-bo-o-o-at," and by the time they had reached home the little camp was noisy with the plaint of wolf-dogs. There were few men to join in the welcome to-day, every able-bodied inhabitant having disappeared into the hills, but the animals came trooping lazily to the bank, and sat down on their haunches watching the approaching steamer, in their soft eyes the sadness of a canine race of slaves. Behind them limped a sick man or two, a soldier from the barracks, and in the rear a fellow who had drifted in the week before with scurvy. It was a pitiful review that lined up to greet the tide of tenderfeet crowding towards their El Dorado, and unusual also, for as yet the sight of new faces was strange in the North.

The deserted aspect of the town puzzled the cap-

THE AWAKENING

tain of the steamer, and upon landing he made his way at once to John Gale's store, where he learned from the trader of the strike and of the stampede that had resulted. Before the recital was finished a man approached and spoke excitedly.

"Captain, my ticket reads to Dawson, but I'm getting off here. Won't you have my outfit put ashore?" He was followed by a group of fellow-passengers who made a similar request.

"This place is good enough for me," one of them said.

"Me, too," another volunteered. "This strike is new, and we've hit her just in time."

Outside a dozen men had crowded "No Creek" Lee against the wall of the store and were clamoring to hear about his find. Before the tardy ones had cleared the gang-plank the news had flashed from shore to ship, and a swarm came up the bank and into the post, firing questions and answers at each other eagerly, elbowing and fighting for a place within ear-shot of the trader or the ragged man outside.

The frenzy of a gold stampede is like the rush from a burning building, and equally easy to arouse. No statement is too wild to lack believers, no rumor too exaggerated to find takers. Within an hour the crew of the steamer was busy unloading countless tons of merchandise and baggage billed to Dawson, and tents began to show their snowy whiteness here and there. As a man saw his outfit appear he would pounce upon it, a bundle at a time, and pile it by itself, which resulted in endless disputes and much confusion; but a spirit of youth and expectancy permeated all and prevented more than angry words. Every hour the heaps of baggage grew larger and the tents more numerous.

THE BARRIER

Stark wasted no time. With money in his hands he secured a dozen men who were willing to work for hire, for there are always those who prefer the surety of ten coined dollars to the hope of a hundred. He swooped down with these helpers on his pile of merchandise that had lain beneath tarpaulins on the river-bank since the day he and Runnion landed, and by mid-afternoon a great tent had been stretched over a framework of peeled poles built on the lot where he and Necia had stood earlier in the day. Before dark his saloon was running. To be sure, there was no floor, and his polished fixtures looked strangely new and incongruous, but the town at large had assumed a similar air of incompleteness and crude immaturity, and little wonder, for it had grown threefold in half a day. Stark swiftly unpacked his gambling implements, keen to scent every advantage, and out of the handful of pale-faced jackals who follow at the heels of a healthy herd, he hired men to run them and to deal. By night Flambeau was a mining-camp.

Late in the evening the boat swung out into the river, and disclosed a strange scene of transformation to the puzzled captain of a few hours ago. The river-bank was lined with canvas shelters, illumined dully by the tent-lights within till they looked like a nest of glowworms in deep grass. A long, hoarse blast of good wishes rose from the steamer, then she sighed her way around the point above bearing forth the message that a new camp had been born.

CHAPTER X

MEADE BURRELL FINDS A PATH IN THE MOONLIGHT

"NO CREEK" LEE had come into his own at last, and was a hero, for the story of his long ill-luck was common gossip now, and men praised him for his courage. He had never been praised for anything before and was uncertain just how to take it.

"Say, are these people kiddin' me?" he inquired, confidentially, of Poleon.

"W'y? W'at you mean?"

"Well, there's a feller makin' a speech about me down by the landing."

"W'at he say?"

"It ain't nothin' to fight over. He says I'm another Dan'l Boom, leadin' the march of empire westward."

"Dat's nice, for sure."

"Certainly *sounds* good, but is it on the level?"

"Wal, I guess so," admitted Poleon.

The prospector swelled with indignation. "Then, why in hell didn't you fellers tell me long ago?"

The scanty ounce or two of gold from his claim lay in the scales at the post, where every new-comer might examine it, and, realizing that he was a never-ending source of information, they fawned on him for his tips, bribing him with newspapers, worth a dollar each, or with cigars, which he wrapped up carefully and placed in his mackinaw till every pocket of the rusty garment bulged so that he could not sit without losing them. They dwelt upon his lightest word, and stood him up beside the bar where they filled him with proofs of friendliness until he shed tears from his one good eye.

He had formed a habit of parsimony born of his years of poverty, and was so widely known as a tight man by the hundreds who had lent to him that his creditors never at any time hoped for a reckoning. And he never offered one; on the contrary, he had invariably flown into a rage when dunned, and exhibited such resentment as to discourage the practice. Now, however, the surly humor of the man began to mellow, and in gradual stages he unloosened, the process being attended by a disproportionate growth of the trader's cash receipts. Cautiously, at first he let out his wit, which was logy from long disuse, and as heavy on its feet as the Jumping Frog of Calaveras, but when they laughed at its labored leaps and sallies his confidence grew. With the regularity of a clock he planted cigars and ordered "a little more hard stuff," while his roving eye rejoiced in lachrymose profusion, its over-burden losing itself in the tangle of his careless beard. By-and-by he wandered through the town, trailed by a troop of tenderfeet, till the women marked him, whereupon he fled back to the post and hugged the bar, for he was a bashful man. When Stark's new place opened it offered him another retreat of which he availed himself for some time. But late in the evening he reappeared at Old Man Gale's store, walking a bit unsteadily, and as he mounted the flight of logs to the door he stepped once too often.

"What's become of that fourth step?" he demanded, sharply, of Poleon.

MEADE BURRELL FINDS A PATH

"Dere she is," said the Frenchman.

"I'm damned if it is. You moved it since I was here."

"I'll have 'im put back," laughed the other.

"Say! It's a grand thing to be rich, ain't it?"

"I don' know, I ain' never try it."

"Well, it is; and now that I've arrived, I'm goin' to change my ways complete. No more extravagance in mine—I'll never lend another cent."

"W'at's dat?" ejaculated Doret, in amazement.

"No more hard-luck stories and 'hurry-ups' for mine. I'm the stony-hearted jailer, I am, from now, henceforth, world 'thout end, amen! No busted miners need apply. I've been a good thing, but to-night I turn on the time-lock."

"Ba gosh! You're fonny feller," laughed Poleon, who had lent the one-eyed man much money in the past and, like others, regarded him not merely as a bad risk but as a total loss. "Mebbe you t'ink you've been a spen't'rif' all dese year."

"I've certainly blowed a lot of money on my friends," Lee acknowledged, "and they're welcome to what they've got so far, but I'm goin' to chop all them prodigal habits and put on the tin vest. I'll run the solderin'-iron up my seams so they can't get to me without a can-opener. I'm air-tight for life, I am." He fumbled in his pockets and unwrapped a gift cigar, then felt for a match. Poleon tossed one on the bar, and he reached for it twice, missing it each time.

"I guess dose new frien' of yours is mak' you purty full, M'sieu' Tin Vest."

"Nothin' of the sort. I've got a bad dose of indigestion."

"Dat's 'orrible disease! Dere's plaintee riche man die on dat seecknesse. You better lie down."

143

Doret took the hero of the day by the arm and led him to the rear of the store, where he bedded him on a pile of flour sacks, but he had hardly returned to the bar when Lee came veering out of the dimness, making for the light like a ship tacking towards a beacon.

"What kind of flour is that?" he spluttered.

"Dat's just plain w'eat flour."

"Not on your life," said the miner, with the firmness of a great conviction. "It's full of yeast powders. Why, it's r'arin' and risin' like a buckin' hoss. I'm plumb sea-sick." He laid a zigzag course for the door.

"W'ere you goin'?" asked Poleon.

"I'm goin' to get somethin' for this stomach trouble. It's fierce." He descended into the darkness boldly, and stepped off with confidence—this time too soon. Poleon heard him floundering about, his indignant voice raised irascibly, albeit with a note of triumph.

"Wha'd I tell you? You put it back while I was ashleep." Then whistling blithely, if somewhat out of tune, he steered for the new saloon to get something for his "stomach trouble."

At Stark's he found a large crowd of the new men who welcomed him heartily, plying him with countless questions, and harking to his maudlin tales of this new country which to him was old. He had followed the muddy river from Crater Lake to the Delta, searching the bars and creek-beds in a tireless quest, till he knew each stream and tributary, for he had been one of the hardy band that used to venture forth from Juneau on the spring snows, disappearing into the uncharted valley of the Yukon, to return when the river clogged and grew sluggish, and, like Gale, he had lived these

MEADE BURRELL FINDS A PATH

many years ahead of the law where each man was his own court of appeals and where crime was unknown. He had helped to build camps like Forty Mile and Circle; he knew by heart the by-laws and rules that governed every town and mining district in the country; he knew every man and child by name, but, while many of his friends had prospered, unceasing ill-luck had dogged him. Yet he had held to honesty and hard work, measuring a man by his ability to swing an axe or a shovel, and, despite his impecuniosity, regarding theft as the one crime deserving capital punishment.

"Oh, there's lots of countries worse'n this," he declared. "We may not be very han'some to the naked eye, and we may not wear our handk'chiefs in our shirt cuffs, but there ain't no widders and orphans doin' our washin', and a man can walk away from his house, stay a month, and find it there when he comes back."

"Those days are past," said Stark, who had joined in the discussion. "There's too many new people coming in for all of them to be honest."

"They'd better be," said Lee, aggressively. "We ain't got no room for stealers. Why, I had a hand in makin' the by-laws of this camp myself, 'long with John Gale, and they stip'lates that any person caught robbin' a cache is to be publicly whipped in front of the tradin'-post, then, if it's winter time, he's to be turned loose on the ice barefooted, or, if it's summer, he's to be set adrift on a log with his shirt off."

"Either one would mean certain death," said a stranger. "Frost in winter, mosquitoes in summer!"

"That's all right," another bystander declared. "A man's life depends on his grub up here, and I'd be in favor of enforcing that punishment to the letter if we caught any one thieving."

"All the same, I take no chances," said Stark. "There's too many strangers here. Just to show you how I stand, I've put Runnion on guard over my pile of stuff, and I'll be glad when it's under cover. It isn't the severity of punishment that keeps a man from going wrong, it's the certainty of it."

"Well, he'd sure get it, and get it proper in this camp," declared Lee; and at that moment, as if his words had been a challenge, the flaps of the great tent were thrust aside, and Runnion half led, half threw a man into the open space before the bar.

"Let's have a look at you," he panted. "Well, if it ain't a nigger!"

"What's up?" cried the men, crowding about the prisoner, who crouched, terror-stricken, in the trampled mud and moss, while those playing roulette and "bank" left the tables, followed by the dealers.

"He's a thief," said Runnion, mopping the sweat from his brow. "I caught him after your grub pile, Stark."

"In my cache?"

"Yes. He dropped a crate of hams when I came up on him, and tried to run, but I dropped *him*." He held his Colt in his right hand, and a trickle of blood from the negro's head showed how he had been felled.

"Why didn't you shoot?" growled Stark, angrily, at which the negro half arose and broke into excited denials of his guilt. Runnion kicked him savagely, and cursed him, while the crowd murmured approval.

"Le' me see him," said Lee, elbowing his way through the others. Fixing his one eye upon the wretch, he spoke impressively.

MEADE BURRELL FINDS A PATH

"You're the first downright thief I ever seen. Was you hungry?"

"No, he's got plenty," answered one of the tenderfeet, who had evidently arrived on the boat with the darky. "He's got a bigger outfit than I have."

The prisoner drew himself up against the bar, facing his enemies sullenly.

"Then I reckon it's a divine manifestation," said "No Creek" Lee, tearfully. "This black party is goin' to furnish an example as will elevate the moral tone of our community for a year."

"Let me take him outside," cried Stark, reaching under the bar for a weapon. His eyes were cruel, and he had the angry pallor of a dangerous man. "I'll save you a lot of trouble."

"Why not do it legal?" expostulated Lee. "It's just as certain."

"Yes! Lee is right," echoed the crowd, bent on a Roman holiday.

"What y'all aim to do?" whined the thief.

"We're goin' to try you," announced the one-eyed miner, "and if you're found guilty, as you certainly are goin' to be, you'll be flogged. After which perdicament you'll have a nice ride down-stream on a sawlog without your laundry."

"But the mosquitoes—"

"Too bad you didn't think of them before. Let's get at this, boys, and have it over with."

In far countries, where men's lives depend upon the safety of their food supply, a side of bacon may mean more than a bag of gold; therefore, protection is a strenuous necessity. And though any one of those present would have gladly fed the negro had he been needy, each of them likewise knew that unless an example were made of him no tent or cabin would be safe. The North being a gameless, forbidding country, has ever been cruel to thieves, and now it was heedless of the black man's growing terror as it set about to try him. A miners' meeting was called on the spot, and a messenger sent hurrying to the post for the book in which was recorded the laws of the men who had made the camp. The crowd was determined that this should be done legally and as prescribed by ancient custom up and down the river. So, to make itself doubly sure, it gave Runnion's evidence a hearing; then, taking lanterns, went down to the big tarpaulin-covered pile beside the river, where it found the crate of hams and the negro's tracks. There was no defence for the culprit and he offered none, being too scared by now to do more than plead. The proceedings were simple and quiet and grim, and were wellnigh over when Lieutenant Burrell walked into the tent saloon. He had been in his quarters all day, fighting a fight with himself, and in the late evening, rebelling against his cramped conditions and the war with his conscience, he had sallied out, and, drawn by the crowd in Stark's place, had entered.

A man replied to his whispered question, giving him the story, for the meeting was under Lee's domination, and the miners maintained an orderly and business-like procedure. The chairman's indigestion had vanished with his sudden assumption of responsibility, and he showed no trace of drink in his bearing. Beneath a lamp one was binding four-foot lengths of cotton tent-rope to a broomstick for a knout, while others, whom Lee had appointed, were drawing lots to see upon whom would devolve the unpleasant duty of flogging the captive. The matter-of-fact, relentless expedition of the affair shocked Burrell inexpressibly, and seeing Poleon and Gale near by, he edged towards them, thinking that they surely could not be in sympathy with this barbarous procedure.

"You don't understand, Lieutenant," said Gale, in a low voice. "This nigger is a *thief!*"

"You can't kill a man for stealing a few hams."

"It ain't so much *what* he stole; it's the idea, and it's the custom of the country."

"Whipping is enough, without the other."

"Dis stealin' she's bad biznesse," declared Poleon. "Mebbe dose ham is save some poor feller's life."

"It's mob law," said the Lieutenant, indignantly, "and I won't stand for it."

Gale turned a look of curiosity upon the officer. "How are you going to help yourself?" said he; but the young man did not wait to reply. Quickly he elbowed his way towards the centre of the scene with that air of authority and determination before which a crowd melts and men stand aside. Gale whispered to his companion:

"Keep your eye open, lad. There's going to be trouble." They stood on tiptoe, and watched eagerly.

"Gentlemen," announced Burrell, standing near the ashen-gray wretch, and facing the tentful of men, "this man is a thief, but you can't kill him!"

Stark leaned across the bar, his eyes blazing, and touched the Lieutenant on the shoulder.

"Do you mean to take a hand in *all* of my affairs?"

"This isn't your affair; it's mine," said the officer. "This is what I was sent here for, and it's my particular business. You seem to have overlooked that important fact."

"He stole my stuff, and he'll take his medicine."

THE BARRIER

"I say he won't!"

For the second time in their brief acquaintance these two men looked fair into each other's eyes. Few men had dared to look at Stark thus and live; for when a man has once shed the blood of his fellow, a mania obsesses him, a disease obtains that is incurable. There is an excitation of every sense when a hunter stands up before big game; it causes a thrill and flutter of undiscovered nerves, which nothing else can conjure up, and which once lived leaves an incessant hunger. But the biggest game of all is man, and the fiercest sensation is hate. Stark had been a killer, and his brain had been seared with the flame till the scar was ineradicable. He had lived those lurid seconds when a man gambles his life against his enemy's, and, having felt the great sensation, it could never die; yet with it all he was a cautious man, given more to brooding on his injuries and building up a quarrel than to reckless paroxysms of passion, and experience had taught him the value of a well-handled temper as well as the wisdom of knowing when to use it and put it in action. He knew intuitively that his hour with Burrell had not yet come.

The two men battled with their eyes for an opening. Lee and the others mastered their surprise at the interruption, and then began to babble until Burrell turned from the gambler and threw up his arm for silence.

"There's no use arguing," he told the mob. "You can't do it. I'll hold him till the next boat comes, then I'll send him down-river to St. Michael's."

He laid his hand upon the negro and made for the door, with face set and eyes watchful and alert, knowing that a hair's weight might shift the balance and cause these men to rive him like wolves.

MEADE BURRELL FINDS A PATH

Lee's indignation at this miscarriage of justice had him so by the throat as to strangle expostulation for a moment, till he saw the soldier actually bearing off his quarry. Then he broke into a flood of invective.

"Stop that!" he bellowed. "To hell with *your* law—we're goin' accordin' to our own." An ominous echo arose, and in the midst of it the miner, in his blind fury forgetting his exalted position, took a step too near the edge of the bar, and fell off into the body of the meeting. With him fell the dignity of the assemblage. Some one laughed; another took it up; the nervous tension broke, and a man cried:

"The soldier is right. You can't blame a dinge for stealing," and another: "Sure! Hogs and chickens are legitimate prey."

Lee was helped back to his stand, and called for order; but the crowd poked fun at him, and began moving about restlessly till some one shouted a motion to adjourn, and there arose a chorus of seconders. A few dissenting voices opposed them, but in the meantime Burrell was gone, and with him the cause of the tumult; so the meeting broke up of its own weight a moment later.

As Poleon and Gale walked home, the Frenchman said, "Dat was nervy t'ing to do."

The trader made no answer, and the other continued, "Stark is goin' for kill 'im, sure."

"It's a cinch," agreed Gale, "unless somebody gets Stark first."

When they were come to his door the trader paused, and, looking back over the glowing tents and up at the star-sprinkled heavens, remarked, as if concluding some train of thought, "If that boy has got the nerve to take a nigger thief out of a miners' meeting and hold him against this whole town, he wouldn't hesitate much at taking a white man, would he?"

"Wal," hesitated the other, "mebbe dat would depen' on de crime."

"Suppose it was—murder?"

"Ha! We ain' got no men lak' dat in Flambeau."

They said good-night, and the old man entered his house to find Alluna waiting for him, a look of worry on her stolid face.

"What's wrong?" he inquired.

"All night Necia has been weeping."

"Is she sick?" He started for the girl's door, but Alluna stopped him.

"No! It is not that kind of weeping; this comes from the heart. It is there she is sick. I went to her, but she grew angry, and said I had a black skin and could not understand; then she went out-doors and has not returned."

Gale sat down dejectedly. "Yes, she's sick in her heart, all right, and so am I, Alluna. When did she go out?"

"An hour ago."

"Where is she?"

"Out by the river-bank—I followed her in the shadows. It is best for her to stay there till she is calm."

"I know what ails her," said the father. "She's found that she's not like other girls. She's found that a white soul doesn't count with white people; *they* never go below the skin." Then he told her of the scene that morning in the store, adding that he believed she loved Lieutenant Burrell.

"Did she say so?"

"No, she denied it, now that she knows she hasn't got his kind of blood in her."

"Blood makes no difference," said the woman, stub-

MEADE BURRELL FINDS A PATH

bornly. "If he loves her, he will take her; if he does not—that is all."

Gale looked up at her, and was about to explain, when the utter impossibility of her comprehending him made him desist, and he fell moody again. At last he said, "I've got to tell her, Alluna."

"No, no!" cried the woman, aghast. "Don't tell her the truth! Nothing could be worse than that!"

But he continued, deliberately: "Love is the biggest thing in the world; it's the only thing worth while, and she has got to have a fair show at it. This has been on my mind for weeks, and I've put it away, hoping I wouldn't have to do it; but to-day I came face to face with it again, and it's up to me. She'll have to know some time, so the sooner the better."

"She would not believe you," said the woman, at which he started.

"I never thought of that. I wonder if she would doubt! I couldn't stand that."

"There is no proof, and it would mean your life. A good man's life is a great price to pay for the happiness of one girl—"

"I gave it once before," said Gale, a trifle bitterly, "and now that the game is started I've got to play the string out; but—I wonder if she would doubt—" He paused for a long moment. "Well, I'll have to risk it. However, I've got a lot of things to do first—you and the youngsters must be taken care of."

"And Stark?" said Alluna.

"Yes, and Stark."

Burrell took his prisoner to the barracks, where he placed him under guard, giving instructions to hold him at any cost, not knowing what wild and reckless humor the new citizens of Flambeau might develop during the night, for it is men who have always lived with the halter of the law tight upon their necks who run wildest when it is removed. Men grown old on the frontier adhere more closely to a rigid code than do tenderfeet who feel for the first time the liberty and license of utter unrestraint, and it was these strangers whom the soldier feared rather than men like Gale and "No Creek" Lee, who would recognize the mercy of his intervention and let the matter drop.

After he had taken every precaution he went out into the night again, and fought with himself as he had fought all that day and all the night before; in fact, ever since old Thomas had come to him after leaving Necia, and had so cunningly shaped his talk that Burrell never suspected his object until he perceived his position in such a clear light that the young man looked back upon his work with startled eyes. The Corporal had spoken garrulously of his officer's family; of their pride, and of their love for his profession; had dwelt enthusiastically upon the Lieutenant's future and the length he was sure to go, and finally drifted into the same story he had told Necia. Burrell at last sensed the meaning of the crafty old soldier's strategy and dismissed him, but not before his work had been accomplished. If a coarse-fibred, calloused old campaigner like Corporal Thomas could recognize the impossibility of a union between Necia and himself, then the young man must have been blind indeed not to have seen it for himself. The Kentuckian was a man of strong and virile passions, but he was also well balanced, and had ever followed his head rather than his heart, holding, as he did, a deep-seated contempt for weak men who laid their courses otherwise. The genera-

MEADE BURRELL FINDS A PATH

tions of discipline back of him spoke to his conscience. He had allowed himself to become attached to this girl until — yes, he knew now he loved her. If only he had not awakened her and himself with that first hot kiss; if only— But there was no going back now, no use for regrets, only the greater necessity of mapping out a course that would cause her least unhappiness. If he could have run away he would have done so gladly, but he was bound here to this camp, with no possibility of avoiding her.

When he drove his reason with firm hands he saw but one course to follow; but, when his mind went slack for a moment, the old desire to have her returned more strongly than ever, and he heard voices arguing, pleading, persuading — she was the equal of any woman in the world, they said, in mind, in purity, and in innocence. He hated himself for hesitating; he railed at his own indecision; and then, when he had justified his love and persuaded himself that he was right in seeking this union, there would rise again the picture of his people, their chagrin, and what would result from such a marriage. He knew how they would take it; he knew what his friends would say, and how he would be treated as the husband of a half-breed Indian; for in his country one drop of colored blood made a negro, and his people saw but little difference between the red and the black. It would mean his social ostracism; he would be shunned by his brother officers, and his career would be at an end. He swore aloud in the darkness that this was too great a price to pay for love, that he owed it to himself and to his dear ones at home to give up this dark-eyed maid who had bewitched him.

He had wandered far during this debate, clear past

the town, and out through the Indian village; but now that he believed he had come to an understanding with himself, he turned back towards his quarters. He knew it would be hard to give her up; but he had irrevocably decided, and his path began to unfold itself so clear and straight that he marvelled how he could have failed to see it. He was glad he had conquered, although the pain was still sharp. He felt a better man for it, and, wrapped in this complacent optimism, he passed close by the front of the trader's store, where Necia had crept to be alone with her misery.

The high moon cast a deep, wide shadow upon the store steps where the girl sat huddled, staring out into the unreal world, waiting for the night wind to blow away the fears and forebodings that would not let her sleep. It was late, and the hush of a summer midnight lay upon the distant hills. Burrell had almost passed her when he was startled by the sound of his name breathed softly; then, to his amazement, he saw her come forth like a spirit into the silver sheen.

"Necia!" he cried, "what are you doing here at this hour?" She looked up at him sadly; he saw that her cheeks were wet, and something inside him snapped and broke. Without a word he took her in his arms, meeting her lips in a long kiss, while she, trembling with the joy of his strong embrace, drew closer and closer and rested her body wearily against his.

"Little girl! little girl!" he whispered, over and over, his tone conveying every shade of sympathy, love, and understanding she had craved. He knew what had made her sad, and she knew that he knew. There was no need for words; the anguish of this long day had whetted the edge of their desire, and they were

MEADE BURRELL FINDS A PATH

too deeply, too utterly lost in the ecstasy of meeting to care for speech.

As she lay cradled in his arms, which alternately held her with the soft tenderness of a mother and crushed her with the fierce ardor of a lover, she lost herself in the bliss of a woman's surrender, and forgot all her terrifying doubts and fears. What were questions of breed or birth or color now, when she knew he loved her? Mere vapors that vanished with the first flutter of warm wings.

Nor did Meade Burrell recall his recent self-conquest or pause to reason why he should not love this little wisp of the wilderness. The barriers he had built went down in the sight and touch of his love and disappeared; his hesitation and infirmity seemed childish now—yes, more than that, cowardly. He realized all in a moment that he had been supremely selfish, that his love was a covenant, a compact, which he had entered into with her and had no right to dissolve without her consent, and, strangely enough, now that he acknowledged the bond to himself, it became very sweet and satisfying.

"Your lips cling so that I can't get free," sighed the girl, at last.

"You never shall," he whispered. But when she smiled up at him piteously, her eyes swimming, and said, "I must," he wrenched himself away and let her go.

As he went lightly towards the barracks through the far-stretching shadows, for the moon was yellow now, Meade Burrell sighed gladly to himself. Again his course ran clear and straight before him though wholly at variance with the one he had decided upon so recently. But he knew not that his vision was obscured and that the moon-madness was upon him.

157

CHAPTER XI

WHERE THE PATH LED

BY daylight next morning every man and most of the women among the new arrivals had disappeared into the hills — the women in spite of the by-laws of Lee's Creek, which discriminated against their sex. When a stampede starts it does not end with the location of one stream-bed, nor of two; every foot of valley ground for miles on every hand is preempted, in the hope that more gold will be found; each creek forms a new district, and its discoverers adopt laws to suit their whims. The women, therefore, hastened to participate in the discovery of new territory and in the shaping of its government, leaving but few of either sex to guard the tents and piles of provisions standing by the river-bank. In two days they began to return, and straggled in at intervals for a week thereafter, for many had gone far.

And now began a new era for Flambeau—an era of industry such as the frontier town had never known. The woods behind rang with the resounding discords of axes and saws and crashing timber, and new cabins appeared on every hand, rising in a day. The sluggish air was noisy with voices, and the edge of the forest receded gradually before the busy pioneers, replacing the tall timbers with little, high-banked homes of spruce and white-papered birch. From dawn till dark

WHERE THE PATH LED

arose the rhythmic rasp of men whip-sawing floor lumber to the tune of two hundred dollars per thousand; and with the second steamer came a little steam sawmill, which raised its shrill complaint within a week, punctuating the busy day with its piping whistle.

The trail along the Flambeau was dotted continuously with toiling human beasts of burden, that floundered laboriously beneath great packs of provisions and tools and other baggage, winding like an endless stream of ants through the hills to "No Creek" Lee Creek, where they re-enacted the scenes that were occurring in the town. Tents and cabins were scattered throughout the length of the valley, lumber was sawed for sluice-boxes, and the virginal breezes that had sucked through this seam in the mountains since days primeval came to smell of spruce fires and echo with the sounds of life.

A dozen tents were pitched on Lee's discovery claim, for the owner had been besieged by men who clamored to lease a part of his ground, and, yielding finally, he had allotted to each of them a hundred feet. Forthwith they set about opening their portions, for the ground was shallow, and the gold so near the surface that winter would interfere with its extraction; wherefore, they made haste. The owner oversaw them all, complacent in the certainty of a steady royalty accruing from the working of his allotments.

Every day there came into Flambeau exaggerated reports of new strikes in other spots, of strong indications and of rich prospects elsewhere. Stories grew out of nothing, until the camp took an hysterical pleasure in exciting itself and deceiving every stranger who came from north or south, for the wine of discovery was in them all, and it pleased them to distort and enlarge upon every rumor that came their way, such being the temper of new gold-fields. They knew they were lying, and that all other men were lying also, and yet they hearkened to each tale and almost deceived themselves.

Burrell sought Necia at an early day and, in presence of her father, told her that he had been approached by men who wished to lease the claims he held for her. It would prove an inexpensive way to develop her holdings, he said, and she would run no risk; moreover, it would be rapid, and insure a quick return, for a lease so near to proven territory was in great demand. After some discussion this was arranged, and Meade, as trustee, allotted her ground in tracts, as Lee had done. Poleon followed suit; but the trader chose to prospect his own claims, and to that end called in a train of stiff-backed Indian packers, moved a substantial outfit to the creek, and thereafter spent much of his time in the hills, leaving the store to Doret. He seemed anxious to get away from the camp and hide himself in the woods. Stark was almost constantly occupied at his saloon, for it was a mint, and ran day and night. Runnion was busy with the erection of a substantial structure of squared logs, larger than the trading-post, destined as a dance-hall, theatre, and gambling-house. Flambeau, the slumbrous, had indeed aroused itself, stretched its limbs, and sprung into vigorous, virile, feverish being, and the wise prophets were predicting another Dawson for it, notwithstanding that many blank spots had been found as the creek of Lee's finding bared its bedrock to the miners. These but enhanced the value of the rich finds, however, for a single stroke of good-fortune will more than offset a dozen disappointments. The truth is, the stream was very spotted, and Lee

WHERE THE PATH LED

had by chance hit upon one of the bars where the metal had lodged, while others above and below uncovered a bed-rock as barren as a clean-swept floor. In places they cross-cut from rim to rim, drove tunnels and drains and drifts, sunk shafts and opened trenches without finding a color that would ring when dropped in the pan; but that was an old, old story, and they were used to it.

During these stirring weeks of unsleeping activity Burrell saw little of Necia, for he had many things to occupy him, and she was detained much in the store, now that her father was away. When they met for a moment they were sure to be interrupted, while in and around the house Alluna seemed to be always near her. Even so, she was very happy; for she was sustained by the constant hectic excitement that was in the air and by her brief moments with Meade, which served to gladden her and make of the days one long, delicious, hopeful procession of undisturbed dreams and fancies. He was the same fond lover as on that adventurous journey up Black Bear Creek, and wooed her with a reckless fire that set her aglow. And so she hummed and laughed and dreamed the days away, her happiness matching the peace and gladness of the season.

With Burrell, on the contrary, it was a season of penance and flagellations of spirit, lightened only by the moments when he was with her, and when she made him forget all else. This damnable indecision goaded him to self-contempt; he despised himself for his weakness; his social instincts and training, his sense of duty, and the amenities of life that proud men hold dear tugged steadily, untiringly at his reason, while the little imp of impulse sat grinning wickedly, ready to pop out and upset all his high resolutions. It raised

THE BARRIER

such a tumult in his ears that he could not hear the other voices; it stirred his blood till it leaped and pounded, and then ran off with him to find this tiny brown and beaming witch who was at the bottom of it all.

No months in any clime can compare with an Arctic summer when Nature is kind, for she crowds into this short epoch all the warmth and brightness and splendor that is spread over longer periods in other lands, and every growing thing rejoices riotously in scent and color and profusion. It was on one of these heavenly days, spiced with the faintest hint of autumn, that Necia received the news of her good-fortune. One of her leasers came into the post to show her and Poleon a bag of dust. He and his partner had found the pay-streak finally, and he had come to notify her that it gave promise of being very rich, and now that its location was demonstrated, no doubt the other "laymen" would have it within a fortnight. As all of them were ready to begin sluicing as soon as the ground could be stripped, undoubtedly they would be able to take out a substantial stake before winter settled and the first frost closed them down.

She took the news quietly but with shining eyes, though her pleasure was no greater or more genuine than Poleon's, who grasped both her hands in his and shouted, gleefully:

"Bien! I'm glad! You'll be riche gal for sure now, an' wear plaintee fine dress lak' I fetch you. Jus' t'ink, you fin' gol' on your place more queecker dan your fader, an' he's good miner, too. Ha! Dat's bully!"

"Oh, Poleon! I'll be a fine lady, after all," she cried—"just as I've dreamed about! Wasn't it beautiful, that pile of yellow grains and nuggets? Dear, dear! And

WHERE THE PATH LED

part of it is mine! You know I've never had money. I wonder what it is like to be rich!"

"How I'm goin' tell you dat?"

"Oh, well, they will find it on your claims very soon."

He shook his head. "You better knock wood w'en you say dat. Mebbe I draw de blank again; nobody can't tell. I've do de sam' t'ing before, an' dose men w'at been workin' my groun' dey're gettin' purty blue."

"It's impossible. You're sure to strike it, or if you don't, you can have half of what I make—I'll be too wealthy, anyhow, so you might as well."

He laughed again, at which she suddenly remembered that he had not laughed very much of late, or else she had been too deeply absorbed in her own happiness to mark the lack of his songs and merriment.

"When you do become a Flambeau king," she continued, "what will you do with yourself? Surely you won't continue that search for your far country. It could never be so beautiful as this." She pointed to the river that never changed, and yet was never the same, and to the forests, slightly tinged with the signs of the coming season. "Just look at the mountains," she mused, in a hushed voice; "see the haze that hangs over them—the veil that God uses to cover up his treasures." She drew a deep breath. "The breeze fairly tastes with clean things, doesn't it? Do you know, I've often wanted to be an animal, to have my senses sharpened—one of those wild things with a funny, sharp, cold nose. I'd like to live in the trees and run along the branches like a squirrel, and drink in the perfume that comes on the wind, and eat the tender, growing things. The sun is bright enough and the world is good enough, but I can't feel enough. I'm incomplete."

THE BARRIER

"It's very fine," agreed the Canadian. "I don' see w'y anybody would care for livin' on dem cities w'en dere's so much nice place outside."

"Oh, but the cities must be fine also," said she, "though, of course, they can't be as lovely as this. Won't I be glad to see them!"

"Are you goin' away?" he inquired, quickly.

"Of course." Then glimpsing his downcast face, she hastened to add, "That is, when my claims turn out rich enough to afford it."

"Oh," he said, with relief. "Dat's different. I s'pose it mus' be purty dull on dem beeg town; no-w'ere to go, not'in' to see 'cept lot of houses."

"Yes," said Necia, "I've no doubt one would get tired of it soon, and long for something to do and something really worth while, but I should like to try it once, and I shall as soon as I'm rich enough. Won't you come along?"

"I don' know," he said, thoughtfully; "mebbe so I stay here, mebbe so I tak' my canoe an' go away. For long tam' I t'ink dis Flambeau she's de promis' lan' I hear callin' to me, but I don' know yet for w'ile."

"What kind of place is that land of yours, Poleon?"

"Ha! I never see 'im, but she's been cryin' to me ever since I'm little boy. It's a place w'ere I don' get too hot on de summer an' too col' on de winter; it's place w'ere birds sing an' flowers blossom an' de sun shine, an' w'ere I can sleep widout dreamin' 'bout it all de tam'."

"Why, it's the land of content—you'll never discover it by travel. I'll tell you a secret, Poleon. I've found it—yes, I have. It lies here." She laid her hand on her breast. "Father Barnum told me the story of your people, and how it lives in your blood—that hunger

WHERE THE PATH LED

to find the far places; it's what drove the voyageurs and coureur du bois from Quebec to Vancouver, and from the Mississippi to Hudson's Bay. The wanderlust was their heritage, and they pushed on and on without rest, like the salmon in the spring, but they were different in this: that they never came back to die."

"Dat's me! I never see no place yet w'at I care for die on, an' I never see no place yet w'at I care for see again 'cept dis Flambeau. I lak' it, dis one, purty good so far, but I ain' know w'en I'm goin' get tire'. Dat depen's." There was a look of great tenderness in his eyes as he bent towards her and searched her face, but she was not thinking of him, and at length he continued:

"Fader Barnum, he's goin' be here nex' Sonday for cheer up dem Injun. Constantine she's got de letter."

"Why, that's the day after to-morrow!" cried Necia. "Oh, won't I be glad to see him!"

"You don' get dem kin' of mans on de beeg cities," said Poleon. "I ain' never care for preachin' much, an' dese feller w'at all de tam' pray an' sing t'rough de nose, dey mak' me seeck. But Fader Barnum— Ba Gar! She's the swell man."

"Do you know," said Necia, wistfully, "I've always wanted him to marry me."

"You t'inkin' 'bout marry on some feller, eh?" said the other, with an odd grin. "Wal! w'y not? He'll be here all day an' night. S'pose you do it. Mos' anybody w'at ain' got some wife already will be glad for marry on you—an' mebbe some feller w'at has got wife, too! If you don' lak' dem, an' if you're goin' marry on *somebody*, you can be wife to me."

Necia laughed lightly. "I believe you *would* marry me if I wanted you to; you've done everything else I've ever asked. But you needn't be afraid; I won't take you up." In all her life this man had never spoken of love to her, and she had no hint of the dream he cherished. He had sung his songs to her and told her stories till his frank and boyish mind was like an open page to her; she knew the romance that was the very fibre of him, and loved his exaggerated chivalry, for it minded her of old tales she had read; but that he could care for her save as a friend, as a brother — such a thought had never dawned upon her.

While they were talking a boat had drawn inshore and made fast to the bank in front of them. An Indian landed and, approaching, entered into talk with the Frenchman.

By-and-by Poleon turned to the girl, and said:

"Dere's 'hondred marten-skin come in; you min' de store w'ile I mak' trade wit' dis man."

Together the two went down to the boat, leaving Necia behind, and not long after Runnion sauntered up to the store and addressed her familiarly.

"Hello, Necia! I just heard about the strike on your claim. That's fine and dandy."

She acknowledged his congratulations curtly, for although it was customary for most of the old-timers to call her by her Christian name, she resented it from this man. She chose to let it pass, however.

"I had some good news last night myself," he continued. "One of my men has hit some good dirt, and we'll know what it means in a day or so. I'll gamble we're into the money big, though, for I always was a lucky cuss. Say, where's your father?"

"He's out at the mine."

WHERE THE PATH LED

"We've used up all of our bar sugar at the saloon, and I want to buy what you've got."

"Very well, I'll get it for you."

He followed her inside, watching her graceful movements, and attempting, with his free-and-easy insolence, to make friendly advances, but, seeing that she refused to notice him, he became piqued, and grew bolder.

"Look here, Necia, you're a mighty pretty girl. I've had my eye on you ever since I landed, and the more I see of you the better I like you."

"It isn't necessary to tell me that," she replied. "The price of the sugar will be just the same."

"Yes, and you're bright, too," he declared. "That's what I like in a woman — good looks and brains. I believe in strong methods and straight talk, too; none of this serenading and moonlight mush for me. When I see a girl I like, I go and get her. That's me. I make love like a man ought to—"

"Are you making love to me?" she inquired, curiously.

"It's a little bit sudden, I know, but a man has to begin some time. I think you'd just about suit me. We'll both have money before long, and I'll be good to you."

The girl laughed derisively in his face.

"Now don't get sore. I mean business. I don't wear a blue coat and use a lot of fancy words, and then throw you down when I've had my fun, and I don't hang around and spoil your chances with other men either."

"What do you mean?"

"Well, I'm no soft-talking Southerner with gold buttons and highfalutin' ways. I don't care if you are a squaw, I'll take you—"

"Don't talk to me!" she cried, in disgust, her voice hot with anger and resentment.

But he continued, unheeding: "Now, cut out these airs and get down to cases. I mean what I say. I know you've been casting sheep's eyes at Burrell, but, Lord! he wouldn't have you, no matter how rich you get. Of course, you acted careless in going off alone with him, but I don't mind what they're saying around camp, for I've made little slips like that myself, and we'd get along—"

"I'll have you killed!" she hissed, through her clinched teeth, while her whole body vibrated with passion. "I'll call Poleon and have him shoot you!" She pointed to the river-bank a hundred yards away, where the Canadian was busy assorting skins.

But he only laughed at her show of temper, and shrugged his shoulders as he answered her, roughly:

"Understand me, I'm on the square. So think it over, and don't go up in the air like a sky-rocket."

She cried out at him to "Go—go—go!" and finally he took up his bundle, saying, as he stepped out slowly:

"All right! But I'm coming back, and you'll have to listen to me. I don't mind being called a squaw-man. You're pretty near white, and you're good enough for me. I'll treat you right—why, I'll even marry you if you're dead set on it. Sure!"

She could scarcely breathe, but checked her first inclination to call Poleon, knowing that it needed only a word from her to set that nut-brown savage at Runnion's throat. Other thoughts began to crowd her brain and to stifle her. The fellow's words had stabbed her consciousness, and done something for her that gentler means would not have accomplished; they had opened her eyes to a thing that she had forgotten—a

WHERE THE PATH LED

hideous thing that had reared its fangs once before to strike, but which her dreams of happiness had driven out of her Eden. All at once she saw the wrong that had been done her, and realized from this brute's insult that those early fears had been well grounded. It suddenly occurred to her that in all the hours she had spent with her lover, in all those unspeakably sweet and intimate hours, there had never been one word of marriage. He had looked into her eyes and vowed he could not live without her, and yet he had never said the words he should have said, the words that would bind her to him. His arms and his lips had comforted her and stilled her fears, but after all he had merely made love. A cold fear crept over the girl. She recalled the old Corporal's words of a few weeks ago, and her conversation with Stark came back to her. What if it were true—that which Runnion implied? What if he did not intend to ask her, after all? What if he had only been amusing himself? She cried out sharply at this, and when Doret staggered in beneath a great load of skins he found her in a strange excitement. When he had finished his accounting with the Indian and dismissed him, she turned an agitated face to the Frenchman.

"Poleon," she said, "I'm in trouble. Oh, I'm in such awful trouble!"

"It's dat Runnion! I seen 'im pass on de store w'ile I'm down below." His brows knit in a black scowl, and his voice slid off a pitch in tone. "W'at he say, eh?"

"No, no, it's not that. He paid me a great compliment." She laughed harshly. "Why, he asked me to marry him." The man beside her cursed at this, but she continued: "Don't blame him for liking me—

I'm the only woman for five hundred miles around—or I was until this crowd came—so how could he help himself? No, he merely showed me what a fool I've been."

"I guess you better tell me all 'bout dis t'ing," said Poleon, gravely. "You know I'm all tam' ready for help you, Necia. W'en you was little feller an' got bust your finger you run to me queeck, an' I feex it."

"Yes, I know, dear Poleon," she assented, gratefully. "You've been a brother to me, and I need you now more than I ever needed you before. I can't go to father; he wouldn't understand, or else he would understand too much, and spoil it all, his temper is so quick."

"I'm not w'at you call easy-goin' mese'f," the Canadian said, darkly, and it was plain that he was deeply agitated, which added to the girl's distress; but she began to speak rapidly, incoherently, her impulsiveness giving significance to her words, so that the man had no difficulty in following her drift. With quick insight he caught her meaning, and punctuated her broken sentences with a series of grave nods, assuring her that he knew and understood. He had always known, he had always understood, it seemed.

"Don't think I'm unwomanly, Poleon, for I'm not. I may be foolish and faithful and too trusting, but I'm not—unmaidenly. You see, I've never been like other girls—and he was so fine, so different, he made me love him—it's part of a soldier's training, I suppose. It was so sweet to be near him, and to hear him tell of himself and all the world he knows—I just let myself drift. I'm afraid—I'm afraid I listened too well, and my ears heard more than he said—my head is so full of books, you know."

WHERE THE PATH LED

"He should have know' dat, too," said Poleon.

"Yes," she flared up. "He knew I was only an Indian girl."

The only color in Doret's face lay now in his cheeks, where the sun had put it; but he smiled at her—his warm, engaging smile—and laid his great brown hand upon her shoulder softly.

"I've look' in hees eye an' I'm always t'ink he's good man. I don' never t'ink he'll mak' fun of poor little gal."

"But he has, Poleon; that's just what he has done." She came near to breaking down, and finished, pathetically, "They're telling the story on the street, so Runnion says."

"Dat's easy t'ing for feex," he said. "Runnion, she don' spread no more story lak' dat."

"I don't care what they say. I want the truth. I want to know what he means, what his intentions are. He swears he loves me, and yet he has never asked me to marry him. He has gone too far; he has made a fool of me to amuse himself, and—and I couldn't see it until to-day. He's laughing at me, Poleon, he's laughing at me now! Oh, I can't bear it!"

The Frenchman took up his wide hat from the counter and placed it carefully upon his head, but she stopped him as he moved towards the door, for she read the meaning of the glare in his eyes.

"Wait till you understand—wait, I say! He hasn't done anything yet."

"Dat's de trouble. I'm goin' mak' 'im do somet'ing."

"No, no! It isn't that; it's these doubts that are killing me—I'm not sure—"

"I hear plaintee," he said. "Dere's no tam' for monkey roun'."

THE BARRIER

"I tell you he may be honest," she declared. "He may mean to marry me, but I've got to *know*. That's why I came to you; that's what you must find out for me."

"I'm good trader, Necia," said the Canadian, after a moment. "I'll mak' bargain wit' you now. If he say yes, he'll marry you, I don' ask no more; but if he say no, you geeve 'im to me. Is it go?"

She hesitated, while he continued, musingly, "I don' see how no man on all dis worl' could lef' you go." Then to her, "Wal, is it bargain?"

"Yes," she said, the Indian blood speaking now; "but you must learn the truth, there must be no mistake—that would be terrible."

"Dere ain' goin' be no mistak'."

"If he should refuse, I—I'll marry *some* one, quick. I won't be laughed at by this camp; I won't be a joke. Oh, Poleon! I've given myself to him just as truly as if—well, he—he has taken my first kiss."

Doret smote his hands together at this and began to roll his head backward from side to side, as if in some great pain, but his lips were dry and silent. After a moment the spell left him, the fire died down, leaving only a dumb agony in its place. She came closer and continued:

"I'll never let them point at me and say, 'There goes the squaw that—he threw away.'"

"You mak' dis very hard t'ing for me," he said, wearily.

"Listen," she went on, lashing herself with pity and scorn. "You say Father Barnum will be here on Sunday. Well—I'll marry some one, I don't care who!" Then, with a sudden inspiration, she cried, "I'll marry you—you said I could be a wife to you."

WHERE THE PATH LED

He uttered a sharp cry. "You mean dat, Necia?"

"Yes," she declared. "Why not? You'll do it for my sake, won't you?"

"Would you stan' up wit' me 'longside of de pries', lovin' dat oder feller all de tam'?" he asked, queerly.

"Yes, *yes!* I'd rather it was you than anybody, but married I'll be on Sunday. I'll never let them laugh at me."

Doret held his silence for a moment, then he looked up and said, in level tones:

"It's easy t'ing for go an' ask 'im, but you mus' hear hees answer wit' your own ears—den you can't t'ink I'm lyin'. I'll fetch 'im 'ere on dis place if you feex it for hide you'se'f behin' dose post." He indicated a bundle of furs that were suspended against a pillar, and which offered ample room for concealment. "Dere's goin' be no lies to-day."

He pulled himself together and went out, with the tired gait of an old man, his great shock head bowed low. A few moments later he returned.

"I've sent li'l' Jean for 'im. You get in dere out of sight—an' wait."

CHAPTER XII

A TANGLED SKEIN

WHEN Burrell entered he wasted no time in greetings.

"I know why you sent for me, Poleon. I've heard the news, and I would have been up anyhow to congratulate her very soon. I call it pretty fine."

"Yes, dere's been beeg strike all right, an' Necia is goin' be riche gal."

"I'm as pleased as if the claim were mine, and you feel the same way, of course."

The Frenchman nodded. "I love Necia very much, lak'—well, lak' I'm broder to her." The knowledge that she was listening made him very uncomfortable—in fact, this whole affair savored more of double-dealing and treachery than anything he had ever attempted, and it went sorely against his grain, but it had presented itself as the only way to help her, and he proceeded, groping haltingly for fit expression, "Dere's t'ing I want for talk 'bout wit' you, but I'm scare' you'll t'ink I'm butt in."

"Nonsense," said Burrell. "I know you too well for that."

"You know me for good man, eh? An' you know I ain' try for bre'k up oder fellers' biznesse, never! Wal, I'm come to you now lak' wan good man to

A TANGLED SKEIN

'noder biccause I'm got bad trouble on de min', an' you mus'n't get sore."

"There's no danger, Poleon. Let's have it. If there is anything I can do, you may count on me."

"Wal," he began, nervously, clearing his throat, "it's lak' dis. Dere's feller been talk some 'bout Necia, an' it ain' nice talk neider."

"Who is he?" exclaimed the soldier, in a tone that made the girl's heart leap.

"Wait! Lemme tol' you w'at he say, den we'll talk 'bout feex 'im plaintee. He say dere's joke down on Stark's saloon dat Necia Gale is mak' fool of herse'f on you, an' dat you ain' care for marry her."

"Runnion!" cried Burrell, and started for the door. "I'll settle with him now for fair!" But Poleon blocked his way, and, observing him gravely, continued, in a tone that the other could not disregard nor mistake:

"No, M'sieu', before you pass on dat place you'll tol' me if it's true."

"True!" the Lieutenant retorted, angrily. "What business is it of yours? This concerns me."

"An' me, too! I'm w'at you call gardeen for Necia till John Gale come back, an' I'm broder of her, too. You promis' jus' now you don' get mad, an' I don' say she's Runnion neider w'at spik dose t'ing; dere's more dan 'im been talkin'. Is it true?"

His sternness offended Burrell, for the soldier was not the kind to discuss his affairs in this way, therefore he drew back scowling.

"Poleon Doret," he said, "it's not one's enemies who do him injury, it's his damned fool friends. I have learned to regard you highly because you are a brave man and an honest one, but it seems that you are a sentimental idiot."

175

"Dem is tough word," Doret replied. "But dere's reason w'y I can't tak' on no madnesse. You say I'm hones'. Wal, I'm hones' now, an' I come to you wit' fair words an' I show my han' to you—I don' hol' out no cards, M'sieu'—but I don' t'ink it is you who have play square, altogeder. I'm Necia's frien', an' I'll fight for her jus' so queecker lak' you, but I mus' know dis t'ing for sure, so if you have de good heart an' de courage of good man you'll tell me de truth. Do you have the feelin' for marry on her?"

The pause that followed was awkward for both of them, while the girl, who stood concealed near by, held her breath and buried her nails in her palms. Why did he hesitate? Would he never speak? It seemed not, for he swung between diverse emotions—anger that this outsider should question him on so intimate a matter, chagrin at the knowledge of having injured Necia, and rage, blind rage, at the thought of its becoming a bar-room topic. Gradually the conviction grew that it was not a question of idle curiosity with Doret, and the man's history recurred to him. No wonder he was interested in the girl, no wonder he wished to guard her; he had been a brother indeed, even as he said, and he could have no motive save an honorable one. It never occurred to the soldier that this Frenchman could harbor feelings akin to his own. The man was rough and foreign; his thoughts had been couched in harsher language, perhaps, than he intended; moreover, the fellow's high sense of honor was a byword—and of a sudden the desire to set himself right in this man's eyes dictated his answer.

"I am amazed at myself for listening to you," he said, at last, "and quite shocked, in fact, at my answering your questions, but perhaps I'd better, after

A TANGLED SKEIN

all. First, however, let me say that the little girl is just as pure now as she was before she knew me—"

Poleon threw up his hand. "M'sieu', dat's more closer to de insult dan w'at you call me jus' now. You don' need for spoke it."

"You're right! There's no need to tell you that. As for showing her certain attentions—well, I admit that I have, as you know, but, thank God, I can say I've been a gentleman and addressed her as I would the fairest lady I've known."

"An' you mean for marry, eh?" probed the other.

Now, no man could have answered such a direct question easily, and in this case it was especially hard for the Kentuckian. who was torn between his ungovernable desire and that decision which cold reason had thrust upon him. He wanted to say, "Yes, I'll marry her to-morrow," but something bade him pause before he sacrificed upon this altar of a youthful love his life, his hopes, his ambitions. Had he not wrestled with himself for months in thinking it all out, until his mind was weary and listless with the effort? For the great test that tries a man's soul and compels him to know himself had not yet come to Meade Burrell; wherefore, he hesitated long.

"I did not say so," he declared, at last. "It's a thing I can't well discuss, because I doubt if you could understand what I would say. This life of yours is different from mine, and it would be useless for me to explain the reason why I cannot marry her. Leaving out all question of my sentiment, there are insurmountable obstacles to such a union; but as to this talk, I think that can be stopped without annoyance to her, and as for the rest, we must trust to time to bring about a proper adjustment—"

A low, discordant sound of laughter arrested his words, and, turning, he beheld Necia standing revealed in the dimness.

"What an amusing person you are!" she said. "I've had hard work holding in all this time while you were torturing your mind and twisting the honest English language out of shape and meaning. I knew I should have to laugh sooner or later."

"What is the meaning of this?" he demanded. "Is it a joke?"

"Indeed it is," she declared, laughing afresh, "and the best I've ever enjoyed. Wasn't it funny, Poleon"—she turned gayly to the Frenchman, but he stood like one petrified—"to see him debating coolly whether he cared for me enough to face the world with me, and trying to explain to you that he was too good to marry a squaw? Oh, you were very gentlemanly about it, sir, and you wouldn't have hurt my feelings for the world!"

"Necia!"

"That's your Dixie chivalry, I suppose. Well, I've played with you long enough, Lieutenant Burrell, I'm tired of the game, and you interest me no longer."

"You—you—say you've been playing with me!" stammered the man. The bottom of things seemed suddenly to slide from under him; he was like one sinking in some hideous quagmire. He felt as if he were choking.

"Why, of course," she cried, scornfully, "just as you took me up for amusement. You were such a fine, well-dressed, immaculate mound of conceit that I couldn't resist the temptation, and you hid your condescension so poorly that I thought you ought to be taken down a peg. I knew I was a squaw, but I wanted to see if I were not like other women, after all,

A TANGLED SKEIN

and if you were not like other men." She was talking rapidly now, almost shrilly, for she had never attempted to act before, while he stood dazed and speechless, fumbling at his throat while she railed at him. "You needn't waste time debating whether I'm good enough for you, because I'm not—decidedly, I'm not your kind, and you are a joke to me."

He uttered an inarticulate cry, but she ran on unheeding, her eyes wide and glowing like coals, her lips chalk-white. "You see, it's time I stopped such foolishness, anyhow, for I'm to be married on Sunday."

"You are going to be married?" he muttered, laboriously.

"Yes, to Poleon. Why, that's been understood for years."

He whirled upon the Canadian in a fury, and his words came hot and tumbling.

"So you're in this, Doret. You're a part of this little farce. You trapped me here to make a fool of me, did you? Well, I can settle with you—"

"D-don't blame him!" cried the girl, hysterically. "It is all my doing. He had no part in it."

Burrell wheeled back to the Frenchman again. "Is this true?"

"Yes," said Doret, in a restrained voice. "Dis ain' no work of mine."

"You're a liar!" breathed the Kentuckian, now fairly wild with anger; but the other looked him squarely between the eyes and made no move.

"M'sieu'," he cried, "I'm livin' t'orty year, an' never took no nam' lak' dat before, but dere's reason here w'y I can't mak' no answer." He inclined his head towards the girl, and before Burrell could break out again he checked him.

"It's no good mak' fight wit' lesser dan two people. You've tol' me dat you are gentleman. Wal, I ain' nobody but trapper an' trader, but I don' spoil de name of no good girl, an' I don' quarrel in presence of lady, so mebbe, affer all, dere's mistak' somew'ere, an' I'm gentleman mese'f 'stead of you."

"Why, you aren't really angry, Lieutenant?" mocked Necia. "It's only the joke of an ignorant half-breed girl whose sense of humor is all out of gear. You mustn't quarrel over a *squaw!*"

She taunted him like a baited badger, for this thing was getting beyond her control and the savage instincts of the wilderness were uppermost.

"You are quite right," he replied. "I am very foolish, and the laugh is with you." His lips tried to frame a smile, but failed, and he added: "Your wit is not my kind, that is all. I beg you both to accept my congratulations on your nuptials. Undoubtedly, you will be happy together; two people with such similar ideas of humor must have much to enjoy in common." He bowed low and, turning, walked out.

The moment he was gone she cried, breathlessly:

"You must marry me, Poleon. You've got to do it now."

"Do you mean dat for sure?" he said.

"Can't you see there's nothing else for it, after this? I'll show him that he can't make me a toy to suit his convenience. I've told him I would marry you on Sunday, and I'll do it or die. Of course you don't love me, for you don't know what love is, I suppose; how—could you?" She broke down and began to catch her breath amid coughing sobs that shook her slender body, though they left her eyes dry and feverish.

A TANGLED SKEIN

"I—I'm very unhappy, b-but I'll be a good—wife to you. Oh, Poleon, if you only knew—"

He drew a long breath. When he spoke his voice had the timbre of some softly played instrument, and a tremor ran through his words.

"No! I don' know w'at kin' of love is dis, for sure. De kin' of love I know is de kin' I sing 'bout in my songs; I s'pose it's different breed to yours, an' I'm begin to see it don' live nowhere but on dem songs of mine. Dere's long tam' I waste here now—five year—but to-morrow I go again lookin' for my own countree."

"Poleon!" she cried, looking up with startled eyes. "Not to-morrow, but Sunday—we will go together."

He shook his head. "To-morrow, Necia! An' I go alone."

"Then you won't — marry me?" she asked, in a hushed and frightened voice.

"No! Dere's wan t'ing I can't do even for you, Necia, dere's wan t'ing I can't geeve, dat's all—jus' wan on all de worl'. I can't kill de li'l' god wit' de bow an' arrer. He's all dat mak' de sun shine, de birds sing, an' de leaves w'isper to me; he's de wan li'l' feller w'at mak' my life wort' livin' an' keep music in my soul. If I keel 'im dere ain' no more lef' lak' it, an' I'm never goin' fin' my lan' of content, nor sing nor laugh no more. I'm t'inkin' I would rader sing songs to 'im all alone onderneat' de stars beside my campfire, an' talk wit' 'im in my bark canoe, dan go livin' wit' you in fine house an' let 'im get col' an' die."

"But I told him I'd marry you—that I had always intended to. He'll believe I was lying," she moaned, in distress.

"Dat's too bad — but dis t'ing ain' no doin's wit' me. Dere's wan t'ing in dis worl' mus' live forever, an' dat's love—if we kill 'im den it's purty poor place for stoppin' in. I'm cut off my han' for help you, Necia, but I can't be husban' to no woman in fun."

"Your foolish head is full of romance," she burst out. "You think you're doing me a favor, but you're not. Why, there's Runnion—he wants me so much that he'd 'even marry me'!" Her wild laughter stabbed the man. "Was ever a girl in such a fix! I've been made love to ever since I was half a woman, but at thought of a priest men seem to turn pale and run like whipped dogs. I'm only good enough for a bad man and a gambler, I suppose." She sank to a seat, flung out her arms hopelessly, and, bowing her head, began to weep uncontrollably. "If—if—I only had a woman to talk to—but they are all men—all men."

Poleon waited patiently until her paroxysm of sobbing had passed, then gently raised her and led her out through the back door into the summer day, which an hour ago had been so bright and promising and was now so gray and dismal. He followed her with his eyes until she disappeared inside the log-house.

"An' dat's de end of it all," he mused. "Five year I've wait—an' jus' for dis."

Meade Burrell never knew how he gained his quarters, but when he had done so he locked his door behind him, then loosed his hold on things material. He raged about the room like a wild animal, and vented his spite on every inanimate thing that lay within reach. His voice was strange in his own ears, as was the destructive frenzy that possessed him. In time he grew quieter, as the physical energy of this brutal impulse spent itself; but there came no surcease of his mental disquiet. As yet his mind grasped but dully the fact that she was to marry another, but gradually

A TANGLED SKEIN

this thought in turn took possession of him. She would be a wife in two days. That great, roistering, brown man would fold her to himself—she would yield to him every inch of her palpitant, passionate body. The thought drove the lover frantic, and he felt that madness lay that way if he dwelt on such fancies for long. Of a sudden he realized all that she meant to him, and cursed himself anew. While he had the power to possess her he had dallied and hesitated, but now that he had no voice in it, now that she was irretrievably beyond his reach, he vowed to snatch her and hold her against the world.

As he grew calmer his reason began to dissect the scene that had taken place in the store, and he wondered whether she had been lying to him, after all. No doubt she had been engaged to the Frenchman, and had always planned to wed Poleon, for that was not out of reason; she might even have set out mischievously to amuse herself with him, but at the recollection of those rapturous hours they had spent together, he declared aloud that she had loved him, and him only. Every instinct in him shouted that she loved him, in spite of her cruel protestations.

All that afternoon he stayed locked in his room, and during those solitary hours he came to know his own soul. He saw what life meant: what part love plays in it, how dwarfed and withered all things are when pitted against it.

A man came with his supper, but he called to him to be gone. The night settled slowly, and with the darkness came such a feeling of despair and lonesomeness that Burrell lighted every lamp and candle in the place to dispel, in some measure, the gloom that had fallen upon him. There are those who believe that in passing from daylight to darkness a subtle transition occurs akin to the change from positive to negative in an electrical current, and that this intangible, untraceable atmospheric influence exerts a definite, psychical effect upon men and their modes of thought. Be this as it may, it is certain that as the night grew darker the Lieutenant's mood changed. He lost his fierce anger at the girl, and reasoned that he owed it to her to set himself right in her eyes; that in all justice to her he ought to prove his own sincerity, and assure her that whatever her own state of mind had been, she wronged him when she said he had made sport of her for his own pleasure. She might then dismiss him and proceed with her marriage, but first she must know this much of the truth at least. So he argued, insensible to the sophistry of his reasoning, which was in reality impelled by the hunger to see her and hear her voice again. He snatched his hat and bolted out, almost running in his eagerness.

An up-river steamboat was just landing as he neared the trading-post—a freighter, as he noted by her lights. In the glare at the river-bank he saw Poleon and the trader, who had evidently returned from Lee's Creek, and without accosting them he hurried on to the store. Peering in from the darkness, he saw Alluna; no doubt Necia was alone in the house behind. So he stumbled around to the back to find the window of her room aglow behind its curtain, and, receiving no answer to his knock, he entered, for it was customary at Gale's to waive ceremony. Inside the big room he paused, then stepped swiftly across and rapped at her door, falling back a pace as she came out.

Instead of speaking at once, as he had planned, to

prevent her escaping, he was struck speechless, for the vision that met his eyes was that which he had seen one blithe spring morning three months before; but to-night there was no shawl to conceal her sweetly rounded neck and shoulders, whose whiteness was startling against the black of the ball-room gown. The slim gold chain hung around her neck and her hair was piled high, as before. He noted every smallest detail as she stood there waiting for him to speak, forgetful of everything else.

She had put on the gown again to see if, perchance, there might be some mark of her blood or breed that had escaped her previous scrutiny, and, as there was no one to observe her, she had attired herself slowly, absorbed in her whimsy. Her wistful beauty dazed the young man and robbed him of the words he had rehearsed; but as she made to flee from him, with a pitiful gesture, towards her room, the fear of losing her aroused him and spurred his wit.

"Don't go away! I have something I must tell you. I've thought it over, and you've got to listen, Necia."

"I am listening," she answered, very quietly.

"Understand me, I'm not whining, and I'm willing to take my medicine. I couldn't talk or think very straight this afternoon, but you were wrong."

"Yes, I know now, I was wrong. It was most unlady-like, wasn't it? But you see, I am only a little savage."

"I don't mean that; I mean you were wrong when you said I had played with you. In the sight of God, I swear you were mistaken. You have made me love you, Necia. Can't you see?"

She made no sign.

"If you can't, I owe it to you and to myself to set

you right. I am not ashamed to acknowledge my love, and even when you are married to Poleon I want you to know that I shall love you always."

Even yet she made no sign. Was he not merely repeating the same empty words with which he had so often beguiled her? There was no word of marriage; he still considered her unworthy, beneath him. The pain of it caused the girl to wince suddenly, and her sensitive face flinched, seeing which he broke out:

"You do love me, Necia—you do; I see it in your eyes!" And he started towards her with open arms, but she shrank away from him.

"No, no! Don't touch me!" she almost screamed.

"My dear one," he breathed, "you must listen to me. You have nothing to fear, for I love you—love you—love you! You were made for me! You'll be my wife. Yes; you'll be married on Sunday, but to me, not to Poleon or any other man!"

Did she hear aright? Was he, her soldier lover, asking her, the Indian girl—?

"You do love me, don't you?" he pleaded. But still she could not speak, and he tried to read the answer in her swimming eyes.

"You mean—you want to—marry me?" she murmured, at last, hesitating shyly at the word that had come to play so momentous a part in her little world.

"Indeed I do!" he declared, with emphasis. "In spite of everything, anything. Nothing else matters."

"Nothing?"

"Nothing! I'll quit the army. I'll give up the Service, and my people, too. I'll put everything back of me, and we'll start out anew—just you and I."

"Wait a moment," she said, retreating a little from

A TANGLED SKEIN

his eager, out-stretched arms. "Why do you need to do all that?"

"Never mind why; it's as good as done. You wouldn't understand—"

"But I think I do understand now. Do I really mean all that to you?"

"Yes, and more!"

"Listen to me," said the girl, quietly. "I want you to talk slowly so I may not misunderstand. If you—marry me, must you forego all those great things you speak of—your profession, your family, your future?"

"Don't let's talk about it, Necia; I've got you, and—"

"Please answer me," she urged. "I thought I understood, but I'm afraid I don't. I thought it was my being a breed that stood in the way—"

"There's nothing in the way—"

"—that I wasn't good enough. I knew I could overcome that; I knew I could make myself grow to your level, but I didn't think my blood would fetter you and make this difference. I suppose I am putting it awkwardly, because I'm not sure that I quite understand it myself yet. Things seem different now, somehow, than they did before."

"Nonsense!" exclaimed the soldier. "If they don't bother me, Necia, why should you worry?"

"Would you really have to give up your family—your sister? Would those people you are so proud of and who are so proud of you—would they cut you off?"

"There is no question of cutting off. I have no inheritance coming; I don't want any. I don't want anything except you, dear."

"Won't you tell me?" she persisted. "You see, I am dull at these things."

"Well, what if they do?" he conceded. "You more than make it up to me — you outweigh a thousand families."

"And would your marriage to a—a—to me destroy your army career?"

"Well, it will really be much easier for both of us if I resign from the Service," he finally admitted. "In fact, I've decided to do so at once."

"No, no! You mustn't do that. To-night you think I am worth the price, but a day will come—"

He leaned forward and caught her hands in his.

"—Meade, I can't let you do it."

"I'd like to see you help yourself," he said, banteringly.

"I can and I will. You must not marry me, Meade —it's not right—it can't be." She suddenly realized what this renunciation would mean, and began to shiver. To think of losing him now, after he had come to her freely—it would be very hard! But to her, too, there had come the revelation that love means sacrifice, and she knew now that she loved her soldier too well to let her shadow darken his bright future, too well to ruin him.

"It will be over before you know it," she heard him saying, in a lame attempt at levity. "Father Barnum is an expert, and the operation won't occupy him ten minutes."

"Meade, you must listen to me now," she said, so earnestly that it sobered him. "Do you think a girl could be happy if she knew a good man had spoiled his life for her? I would rather die now than let you do such a thing. I couldn't bear to see myself a drag on you. Oh, I know it would be wonderful, this happiness of ours, for a time, and then—" She was finding it more and more difficult to continue. "A prisoner grows to hate the chains that bind him; when that day came for you, I should hate myself. No, no! Believe me, it can't be. You're not of my people, and I'm not of yours."

At that moment they heard the voices of the trader and his squaw outside, approaching the house. The girl's breath caught in her throat, she flung herself recklessly upon her lover's breast and threw her arms around his neck in an agony of farewell.

"Meade! Meade! my soldier!" she sobbed, "kiss me good-bye for the last time!"

"No," he said, roughly.

But she dragged his face down to her burning lips.

"Now you must go," she said, tearing herself away, "and, for my sake, don't see me again."

"I will! I will! I'll ask your father for you to-night."

"No, no! Don't; please don't! Wait till—till to-morrow—till I say the word! Promise me! On your love, promise!"

Her eyes held such a painful entreaty that he nodded acquiescence as the door opened and her father and Alluna entered.

CHAPTER XIII

STARK TAKES A HAND IN THE GAME

THE old man greeted the Lieutenant affably, but as his glance fell on his daughter he stopped stock-still on the threshold.

"I told you never to wear that dress again," he said, in a dry, harsh voice.

The girl made no answer, for her heart was breaking, but turned and went into her room. Burrell had an irresistible desire to tell Gale that he wanted his daughter for his wife; it would be an unwonted pleasure to startle this iron-gray old man and the shawled and shambling mummy of red, with the unwinking eyes that always reminded him of two ox-heart cherries; but he had given Necia his promise. So he descended to the exchange of ordinary topics, and inquired for news of the creek.

"Necia's ground is getting better every hour," the trader said. "Yesterday they found a sixty-dollar pan."

"Have you struck pay on yours?"

"No; Poleon and I seem to hold bad hands. Some of his laymen are quitting work. They've cross-cut in half a dozen places and can't find a color."

"But surely they haven't fully prospected his claims yet; there must be plenty of room for a pay-streak somewhere, mustn't there?"

STARK TAKES A HAND IN THE GAME

"It looks like he had drawn three blanks," said Gale, "although we can't tell for sure. They're breaking most as bad for me, too; but I've got a new hunch, and I'm running up a dreen to catch bed-rock along the left rim. I've got twenty men at work, and I'll know before long. You heard about Runnion, of course?"

"Yes; the usual story—the bad men get the good mines, and the good ones get the hungry spots. Well, I might have been one of the unfortunates if I had staked for myself; but I hardly think so, I'm pretty lucky." He laughingly bade them good-night, content with himself and at peace with the world.

Gale went to Necia's door and called her, but when she appeared he was unprepared for the tragic face with which she greeted him.

"Daughter," he said, "don't feel bad over what I said; I didn't mean to be cross with you, but—I don't like that dress."

"Were you cross with me, daddy?" she said, dully. "I didn't hear. What did you say?"

He looked at her in amazement. "Necia, little girl, what is the trouble?"

She was staring past him, and her fingers were fumbling helplessly with the lace of her gown, but she began to show signs of collapse.

"I sent him away—I—gave him up, when he wanted me—wanted me— Oh, daddy! he wants to marry me—and I sent him away."

Alluna uttered a short, satisfied exclamation, and, looking at Gale meaningly, said:

"It is good. It is good. He is a stranger."

But the man disregarded her interruption.

"He asked you to marry him in—in—in spite of who you are and what I am?"

"Yes; he is ready to give up his ambition, his army, his future, his family, everything, for me—to sacrifice it all; and so, of course, I couldn't let him. She spoke simply, as if her father would surely understand and approve her action, while in her voice was a note of inevitable resignation. "You see, I never understood what my blood would mean to him until to-night. I've been selfish and thoughtless, I guess. I just wanted him, and wanted him to take me; but now that he is mine, I love him more than I thought. He is so dear to me that I can't drag him down—I can't—I can't!" She went to the open door and stood leaning against the casing, facing the cool outer darkness, her face hidden from them, her form sagging wearily, as if the struggle had sapped her whole strength.

Alluna crept to the trader and looked up at him eagerly, whispering:

"This will end in a little while, John. She is young. She can go back to the Mission to-morrow. She will soon forget."

"Forget! Do you think she can forget?"

"Any woman can forget. Only men remember."

"It is the red blood in you—lying. You know you lie."

"It is to save your life," she said.

"I know; but it's no use." To Necia he said: "You needn't worry, little daughter." But her ears were deaf. "You needn't give him up, I say—this will end all right."

Seeing that she gave no sign of heeding, he stepped closer, and swung her about till she faced him.

"Can't you trust me this one time? You always have before, Necia. I say he'll marry you, and it will all come out right."

STARK TAKES A HAND IN THE GAME

She raised her hopeless eyes and strove gamely to meet his, then, failing, broke away, and turned back to the door. "I knew you couldn't understand. I—I—oh, God, I love him so!" With a cry like that of a wounded animal she fled out into the night, where she could give vent to her anguish unseen; for she had never wept before her father, but always crept away and hid herself until her grief was spent. Gale would have started after her, but Alluna dragged him back fiercely.

"No, no! It means your life, John. Let the secret die, and she will forget. She is so young. Time will cure her—time cures everything. Don't tell her—don't tell any one—and, above all, don't tell that soldier! He would not believe, nor would she. Even I have doubted!"

"You?"

"Yes, John. And if *I* don't believe, what is a stranger to say? No man knowing you would believe the tale—without proof. Suppose *she* doubted—have you ever thought of that? Would you not rather have her die still loving you than live and disbelieve?"

"Yes, yes! Of course, I—I've thought of that, but— Woman, you're worse than a rattlesnake!"

"Even if he knew, he might not marry her. You at least are clean, and that other man was a devil. A brave man's life is too great a price to pay for a grief that will die in a year." Alluna was speaking swiftly in her own language, her body tense, her face ablaze, and no man seeing her could ever again have called her people stolid.

"You think time will cure a love like that?" he said.

"Yes, yes!"

"That's all you know about it. Time may act that

193

way perhaps in cities and such places, but out in the hills it is different. When you've got the breath of the forest in you, I say it is different. Time—why, I've lived fifteen years in the open with a living memory. Every night I've dreamed it over, every day I've lived it through; in every camp-fire I see a face, and every wind from the south brings a voice to me. Every stormy night a girl with eyes like Necia's calls to me, and I have to follow. Every patch of moonlight shows her smiling at me, just beyond, just in the shadow's edge. Love! Time! Why, Alluna, love is the only thing in the world that never dies, and time only makes it the more enduring."

He took up the white slouch hat he had thrown down when he came in, and stepped to the door.

"Where are you going?" inquired the squaw, fearfully.

"To the barracks to give myself up!"

She flung herself at him with a great cry, and seized him about the waist.

"You never loved me, John, but I have been a good woman to you, although I knew you were always thinking of her—and had no thought of me. I have loved this girl because you loved her. I have hated your enemies because you hated them, and now I remember while you forget."

"Forget! What do you mean?"

"Stark!"

The man paused. "I did almost forget him—and after fifteen years!"

"Let us kill him to-night; then we will go to the soldier together, side by side—I am your woman. Necia will look after the little ones.

Gale stared at her, and as he gazed the red pigment

STARK TAKES A HAND IN THE GAME

underneath her skin, the straight-hanging, manelike hair, the gaudy shawl she never went without, the shapeless, skin-shod feet, the slovenly, ill-fitting garb of a mis-cast woman vanished, and he saw her as she was on a day long past, a slim, shy, silent creature, with great, watchful, trusting eyes and a soul unspoiled. No woman had ever been so loyal, so uncomplaining. He had robbed her of her people and her gods. He had shifted hither and yon at the call of his uncertain fortune, or at a sign of that lurking fear that always dogged him, and she had never left his side, never questioned, never doubted, but always served him like a slave, without asking for a part in that other love, without sharing in the caresses he had consecrated to a woman she had never seen.

"By Heaven! You're game, Alluna, but there's a limit even to what I can take from you," he said, at last. "I don't ever seem to have noticed it before, but there is. No! I've got to do this thing alone to-night, all of it, for you have no place in it, and I can't let the little girl go on like this. The sooner that soldier knows the better." He leaned down and touched her brown mouth with his grizzled lips. "Thank you, Alluna, for making a man of me when I'd nearly forgotten. Now you stay here." He knew he could count on her obedience, and so he left her. When he had gone she drew the shawl up over her face and crouched in the doorway, straining her eyes after him through the dark. In time she began to rock and sway, and then to chant, until the night moaned with the death-song of her people.

Necia had no idea whither she went; her only thought was to flee from her kin, who could not understand, to hide under cover in some solitary place, to let the darkness swallow her up, so that she might give way to her grief and be just a poor, weak woman. So, with a dull and aching heart, she wandered, bareheaded, bare-necked, half-demented, and wholly oblivious to her surroundings, without sense of her incongruous attire or of the water that squeezed up through the soggy moss at her tread and soaked her frail slippers. On she stumbled blindly through the murk like some fair creature of light cast out and banished.

The night was cloudy and a wind came sighing from the north, tossing the girl's hair and tugging at the careless folds of her dress, but she heard nothing save the devil's tattoo that rang in her head, and felt nothing beyond the pain at throat and breast, which in time became so bitter that the tears were wrung from her dry eyes, and she began to weep in a pitiful woman fashion, as if her heart would burst. The first drops cleared a way for others, and soon she was sobbing freely, alone and without solace, lost in the night.

She had not succeeded in thoroughly isolating herself, however, for a man who was steering his course by the sense of feel and the wind's direction heard her and paused. His steps were muffled in the soft footing, so that she had no warning of his presence until he was near enough to distinguish her dimly where she leaned against the log wall of a half-completed cabin.

To his question, "What's the trouble here?" she made no answer, but moved away, whereupon he detained her. "There's something wrong. Who are you, anyhow?"

"It's only Necia, Mr. Stark," said the girl, at which he advanced and took her by the arm.

"What ails you, child? What in the world are you

STARK TAKES A HAND IN THE GAME

doing here? **Come! It's only a step to my** cabin; you must come in and rest awhile, and you'll soon be all right. Why, you'll break your neck in this darkness."

She hung back, but he compelled her to go with him in spite of her unwillingness.

"Now, now," he admonished, with unusual kindliness for him; "you know you're my little friend, and I can't let you go on this way; it's scandalous. I won't stand for it. I like you too much."

In truth he had done things during these last few weeks to make her think so, having never missed an opportunity to stop and pass a word with her, at the same time showing her a queer courtesy and consideration quite foreign to his saturnine habits. She had never mentioned the fact to her father or the others, for she had developed a sort of sympathy for the man, and felt that she understood him better than they did.

He led her inside his cabin, and closed the door in the face of the night wind before he struck a light.

"I can't stand to see you cry," he repeated, as he adjusted the wick. "Now, as soon as—" He stopped in astonishment, for he had turned to behold, instead of the little half-breed girl, this slender, sorrowful stranger in her amazingly wonderful raiment.

"By—" He checked himself insensibly, and stood motionless for a long time, while she wiped her eyes and, woman-like, straightened out her gown and smoothed her hair with little feminine touches.

"I—I—hope you'll excuse me for acting this way," she smiled at him, piteously; then, observing his strange features, "Why, what is the matter, Mr. Stark; are you angry?"

His hawklike face was strained and colorless, his

black eyes fierce and eager, his body bent as if to pounce upon a victim. In truth he was now the predatory animal.

"No," he replied, as if her question carried no meaning; then, coming to himself, "No—no! of course not, but—you gave me a start. You reminded me of some one. How do you come to be dressed like that? I never knew you had such clothes?"

"Poleon brought them from Dawson; they are the first I ever had."

He shook his head in a slow, puzzled fashion.

"You look just like a white girl—I mean—I don't know what I mean." This time he roused himself fully, the effort being more like a shudder.

"So I have always thought," she said, and her eyes filled again.

"Your skin is like milk beneath your tan, and—I don't mean any disrespect, but— Well, I'm just so damned surprised! Come over here and sit down while I mix you something to put the heart back into you."

He shoved forward a big chair with a wolf-skin flung over it, into which she sank dejectedly, while he stepped to the shelves beside the Yukon stove and took down a bottle and some glasses. She glanced about with faint curiosity, but the interior of the cabin showed nothing out of the ordinary, consisting as it did of one room with a cot in the corner, upon which were tumbled blankets, and above which was a row of pegs. Opposite was a sheet-iron box-stove supported knee-high on a tin-capped framework of wood, and in the centre a table with oil-cloth cover. Around the walls were some cooking utensils, a few cases of canned goods, and clothes hanging in a row.

"I'm not fixed up very well yet," he apologized;

STARK TAKES A HAND IN THE GAME

"I've been too busy at the saloon to waste time on living quarters. But it's comfortable enough for an old roadster like me, for I've bruised around the frontier so long that I've learned there's only three things necessary to a man's comfort—warm clothes, a full stomach, and a dry place to sleep. All the rest that goes to make a man content he has inside him, and I'm not the kind to be satisfied, no matter where I am or what I have. I never was that kind, so I just don't make the attempt."

He was talking to give her leeway, and when he had concocted a weak toddy, insisted that she must drink it, which she did listlessly, while he rambled on.

"I've noticed a few things in my life, Miss Necia, and one of them is that it often does a heap of good to let out and talk things over; not that a fellow gains any real advantage from disseminating his troubles, but it serves to sort of ease his mind. Folks don't often come to me for advice or sympathy. I don't have it to give, but maybe it will help you to tell me what caused this night-marauding expedition of yours." Seeing that she hesitated, he went on: "I suppose there's a lot of reasons why you shouldn't confide in me—I don't like that old man of yours, nor any of your friends; but maybe that's why I'm interested. If any of them has upset you, I'll take particular pleasure in helping you get even."

"I don't want to get even, and there is nothing to tell," said Necia, "except a girl's troubles, and I can't talk about them." She smiled a painful, crooked smile at him.

"Your old man has been rough to you?"

"No, no! Nothing of that sort."

"Then it's that soldier?" he quizzed, shrewdly. "I

knew you cared a heap for him. Don't he love you?"

"Yes! That's the trouble; and he wants to marry me; he swears he will in spite of everything."

"See here! I don't quite follow. I thought you liked him—he's the kind most women go daffy over."

"Like him!" The girl trembled with emotion. "Like him! Why—why, I would do anything to make him happy."

"I guess I must be kind of dull," Stark said, perplexedly.

"Don't you see? I've got to give him up—I'm a squaw."

"Squaw hell! With those shoulders?"

Stark checked himself, for he found he was rejoicing in his enemy's defeat, and was in danger of betraying himself to the girl. In every encounter the young man had bested him, and these petty defeats had crystallized his antipathy to Burrell into a hatred so strong that he had begun to lie awake nights planning a systematic quarrel. For he was the kind of man who throve upon contentions: so warped in soul that when no man offered him offence he brooded over fancied wrongs and conjured up a cause for enmity, goading himself into that sour, sullen habit of mind that made him a dread and a menace to all who lacked his favor. His path was strewn from the border North with the husks of fierce brawls, and he bore the ineradicable mark of the killer, carrying always in his brain those scars that hate had seared. In his eyes forever slumbered a flame waiting to be blown to life, and when embroiled in feuds or bickerings a custom had grown upon him to fight these fights in secret many times, until of nights he would lie in solitary

STARK TAKES A HAND IN THE GAME

darkness writhing in spirit as he hounded his man to desperation, or forced him into a corner where he might slake his thirsty vengeance. After such black, sleepless hours he dragged himself from his battle-grounds of fancy, worn and weary, and the daylight discovered him more saturnine and moody, more menacing than ever.

He had brooded over his quarrel with Gale and the Lieutenant ever since their first clash, for in this place they furnished the only objects upon which his mania could work—and it was a mania, the derangement of a diseased, distorted mind. His regard for Necia was a careless whim, a rather aimless, satisfying hobby, not at all serious, entirely extraneous to his every-day life, and interesting only from its aimlessness, being as near to an unselfish and decent motive as the man had ever come. But it was not of sufficient consequence to stand out against or swerve the course of a quarrel; wherefore, he was gladdened by the news of Burrell's discomfiture.

"So you like him too much to stand in his way," he said, meditatively. "How does your father look at it?"

"He wants the Lieutenant to marry me. He says he will fix it up all right; but he doesn't understand. How could he?"

"You are doing just right," concurred the man, hypocritically, "and you'll live to be glad you stood out." Now that both his enemies desired this thing, he was set on preventing it, regardless of the girl. "How did the Lieutenant take it when you refused him?"

"He wouldn't take it at all. He only laughed and declared he would marry me, anyhow." The very thought thrilled her.

"Does he know you love him?"

The tender, sobbing laugh she gave was ample answer.

"Well, what's your plan?"

"I—I—I don't know. I am so torn and twisted with it all that I can't plan, but I have thought I—ought—to go—away."

"Good!" he said, quickly, but his acquiescence, instead of soothing her, had the contrary effect, and she burst out impulsively:

"Oh—I can't—I can't! I can't go away and never see him! I can't do it! I want to stay where he is!" She had been holding herself in stubbornly, but at last gave way with reckless abandon. "Why wasn't I born white like other girls? I've never felt like an Indian. I've always dreamed and fancied I was different, and I am, in my soul—I know I am! The white is so strong in me that it has killed the red, and I'm one of father's people. I'm not like the other two; they are brown and silent, and as cold as little toads; but I'm white and full of life, all over. *They* never see the men and women that I see in my dreams. They never have my visions of the beautiful snow-white mother, with the tender mouth and the sad eyes that always smile at me."

"You have visions of such things, eh?"

"Yes, but I came a generation late, that's all, and I've got that other woman's soul. I'm not a half-breed—I'm not me at all. I'm Merridy—Merridy! That's who I am."

Her face was turned away from him, so that she did not notice the frightful effect her words had upon Stark.

"Where did you get—that name?" His voice was

STARK TAKES A HAND IN THE GAME

pitched in a different key now. Then, after a moment, he added, "From the story I told you at the mine that night, I suppose?"

"Oh no," she answered. "I've always had it, though they call me Necia. Merridy was my father's mother. I guess I'm like her in many ways, for I often imagine she is a part of me, that her spirit is mine. It's the only way I can account for the sights I see."

"Your father's mother?" he said, mechanically. "That's queer." He seemed to be trying to shake himself free from something. "It's heredity, I suppose. You have visions of a white woman, a woman named Merridy, eh?" Suddenly his manner changed, and he spoke so roughly that she looked at him in vague alarm.

"How do you know? How do you know she was his mother?"

"He told me so— "

Stark snarled. "He lied!"

"I can show you her wedding-ring—I've always worn it." She fumbled for the chain about her neck, but it eluded her trembling fingers. "It has her name in it—'From Dan to Merridy.'"

Stark's hand darted forward and tore the thing from her shoulders, then he thrust it under the lamp and glared at the inscription, while his fingers shook so that he could barely distinguish the words. His eyes were blazing and his face livid.

Necia cried out, but he dropped the ornament and seized her fiercely, lifting her from the chair to her feet; then, with one swift, downward clutch, he laid hold of her dress at the left shoulder and ripped it half to her waist. A hoarse sound came from his throat, a cry half of amazement, half of triumph.

"Let me go! Let me go!" She struggled to free herself, but he held her in a viselike grip, while he peered closely at a blemish well down upon her back. Then he let her slip from his grasp, and, seized with terror, she staggered away from him. He was leaning heavily with both hands upon the table, his face working, his head drawn down between his shoulders, his thin lips grinning, his whole manner so terrifying that she shrank back till she brought up against the bark walls. She turned and made for the door, whereupon he straightened up and said, in a queer, commanding voice:

"Wait—don't go! I—I—you—" He licked his lips as if they were dust dry, passed an uncertain hand across his beaded brow, and, raising the water-pail beside the door to his mouth, drank heavily in great, noisy gulps.

"Let me out of here!" the girl demanded, imperiously.

"Don't be scared," he said, more quietly now. "You must excuse me. You—you gave me an awful fright. Yes—that was it. Don't worry. I didn't mean any harm."

"You hurt my shoulder," she said, almost ready to cry. "And you tore my dress," she added, angrily—"my fine dress. Are you crazy?"

"You see, it's like this, that name of Merridy and that ring—well, the whole thing was so startling, I—I went off my head. It came sudden, and I thought—I thought—it don't matter what I thought, but I'm sorry. I'll apologize—and I'll get you a new dress, a whole lot of dresses, if you like." This seemed to amuse him, and he began to laugh silently.

His first impulse had been to tell her everything, but his amazement had rendered him speechless, and

"LET ME OUT OF HERE!" THE GIRL DEMANDED, IMPERIOUSLY.

STARK TAKES A HAND IN THE GAME

now he was thankful for it. Following his discovery of her identity, he had been stricken dumb, staring at her like one demented; then, as he was about to explain, his mind suddenly grasped the significance of this revelation and the advantage it gave him over his enemies; a plan began to unfold, vague at first, its details not worked out, but a plan whereby he could by keeping silent use this knowledge to serve his vengeful ends. In an instant his vision cleared and his brain became active and alert, like that of a man brought suddenly under the stimulus of strong liquor. Care must be exercised—she must not learn too much —for if she suspected the truth she would go to her soldier lover at once, and no power on earth could hold her back. That would block the vengeance that he saw shaping in the dank recesses of his distorted brain.

First, and above all, he must get the girl away from Flambeau.

"I went clear off my head," he heard himself saying, "at that name of Merridy, that ring, and all. Why— why, I thought you might be the missing girl I told you of—you remember, that day up on Lee's Creek— so I had to see; but, dear me, I should have been more considerate—I should have explained. The trouble is I'm a nervous man, and I get impulsive streaks on me sometimes that I can't control. I'm sorry I spoiled your dress, but I'll get you another—you bet I will."

This explanation of his strange behavior seemed plausible enough to banish all personal fears from Necia's mind. Indeed, Stark had now become so gentle and apologetic in his demeanor that her woman's curiosity overcame her instinct to flee, and she ventured the question:

"So you really thought I was that other girl?"

"I did for a minute. The mother was a—a—friend of mine, and so—I lost my head. But I'm all right now, and if you'll overlook my roughness we'll go back to your troubles."

These last few moments had driven her own worries from her mind, but he was bent on recalling them, and so continued, cautiously:

"You were saying that you thought you'd go away. I think that's a good plan, and you'd be wise to do it for more reasons than one. It will give you time to think it all over and know your own mind—"

"I know my mind now, and yet—I don't want to go away."

"—and it will give Burrell a chance to prove himself. He'll either show that he has got to have you at any cost, or that you are right in your decision. If the first should happen, you can come back to him; if the last—why, it will be better for you, anyhow. As long as you stay here neither one of you can see clearly."

She was touched by his interest, and realized the force of his argument, which, strange to say, seemed to second her own thoughts; yet she hesitated.

"I want to help you—I'm going to help you—because I've got an interest in you like you were mine." Again he betrayed that strange, mirthless amusement.

"There is no place for me to go," said Necia, blankly, "except the Mission, and I have no way of getting there."

"Don't you worry. I'll furnish the means, and you'd better go to-night"—she flinched—"yes, to-night; there's no use prolonging your agony. I'll get a boat ready and send a trusty man with you. The current is swift, and if he rows well you can make it

STARK TAKES A HAND IN THE GAME

by to-morrow evening. That's only one night out, and I'll put some blankets aboard so you can wrap up and have a sleep."

"I feel as if I'd never sleep again," she sighed.

"Now, now, this will come out all right yet. I'd take you down there myself, but I've got to stay here. I've got work to do. Yes, I've sure got work of importance ahead of me."

"I must go back and get some clothes," she said, At which he would have demurred had he not seen that she could not travel in her present condition.

"Very well. But don't let anybody see you."

"Of course not."

"It's getting late, and your folks will be abed." He looked at his watch. "Midnight! Be here in an hour, and I'll have the skiff ready."

The light of sacrifice was in Necia's eyes, and her cheeks were blanched with the pallor of a great resolution. She did not stop to reason why or how she had been led to this disposal of her future, but clutched desperately at Stark's plan of rescue from her agonizing predicament.

"I'll be here in an hour," she said, simply.

He let her out, closed the door after her, and locked it; then, drawing a deep breath, he raised his clenched hands above his head, and gave a great sigh of exultation. Next he took out his six-shooter and examined it carefully. The shells did not suit him, so he filled the gun with new ones, loosened the three lower buttons of his vest, and slid the weapon inside his trousers band; then, facing the direction of Gale's trading-post, he spoke aloud.

"I was a long time coming, Gaylord, but I'm here, and I've got you where I've wanted you these fifteen years—yes, and I've got you, too, Burrell! By God, this is my night!"

His lithe body became panther-like in poise, his bearing that of the meat-eating animal, and his face set in a fierce, exultant cruelty as he blew out his light and left the cabin.

CHAPTER XIV

A MYSTERY IS UNRAVELLED

LIEUTENANT BURRELL was considerably taken aback when, a quarter of an hour after the young lover's ecstatic return to his quarters, Gale knocked at his door, for the trader's visit, coupled with the late hour and his sombre countenance, forecast new complications.

"He's here to object, but it won't go," thought the Lieutenant, as he made his visitor welcome.

It was the trader's first glimpse of the officer's quarters, and he cast a roving eye over the room, as if measuring the owner's character by his surroundings.

"I've got to have a long talk with you, Burrell," he began, with an effort. "It's liable to take me an hour or two."

"Then take this chair and be comfortable."

Meade swung his big reading-chair out beneath the hanging-lamp, and, going to the sideboard, brought back a bottle, some glasses, and a pouch of tobacco. Noting the old man's sigh of fatigue as he sat himself down heavily, he remarked, sympathetically:

"Mr. Gale, you've made a long trip to-day, and you must be tired. If this talk is to be as lengthy as you say, why not have a drink with me now, and postpone it until to-morrow?"

"I've been tired for eighteen years," the other re-

THE BARRIER

plied, "to-night I hope to get rested." He lapsed into silence, watching his host pour out two glasses of liquor, fill his pipe, and then stretch himself out contentedly, his feet resting on another chair—a picture of youthful strength, vitality, and determination. Beneath the Lieutenant's flannel shirt the long, slim muscles showed free and full, and the firm set of jaw and lip denoted a mind at rest and confident of itself. Gale found himself for a moment jealously regarding the youth and his enviable state of contentment and decision.

"Well, let's get at it," the younger man finally said.

"I suppose you'll want to interrupt and question me a heap, but I'll ask you to let me tell this story the way it comes to me, till I get it out, then we can go back and take up the queer stuff. It runs back eighteen or twenty years, and, being as it's part of a hidden life, it isn't easy to tell. You'll be the first one to hear it, and I reckon you're enough like other men to disbelieve — you're not old enough, and you haven't knocked around enough to learn that nothing is impossible, that nothing is strange enough to be unreasonable. Likewise, you'll want to know what all this has to do with you and Necia—yes, she told me about you and her, and that's why I'm here." He paused. "You really think you love her, do you?"

Burrell removed his pipe and gazed at its coal impersonally.

"I love her so well, Mr. Gale, that nothing you can say will affect me. I—I hesitated at first about asking her to be my wife, because—you'll appreciate the unusual—well, her unusual history. You see, I come from a country where mixed blood is about the only thing that can't be lived down or overlooked, and I've

A MYSTERY IS UNRAVELLED

been raised with notions of family honor and pride of race and birth, and so forth, that might seem preposterous and absurd to you. But a heap of conceits like that have been bred into me from generations back; they run in the blood of every old family in my country, and so, I'm ashamed to say, I hesitated and tried to reason myself into giving her up, but I've had my eyes opened, and I see how little those things amount to, after all. I'm going to marry Necia, Mr. Gale. I'd like to do it the day after to-morrow, Sunday, but she isn't of age yet, and if you object, we'll have to wait until November, when she turns eighteen. We'd both like your consent, of course; I'd be sorry to marry her without it; but if you refuse, we'll be forced to displease you." He looked up and met the father's gaze steadily. "Now, I'll be glad to listen as long as you care to talk, but I don't think it will do any good."

The other man's lips framed a faint smile.

"We'll see. I wish to God I'd had your decision when I was your age, this story would be different, and easier to tell." He waited a moment, then settled to his self-appointed task. "I was mining at the time up in the Mother Lode country of California, which was the frontier then, pretty much as this is now, only we had better things to eat. I came from the East, or my people did, but I was ranch-raised, and loved the hills and woods and places where you don't talk much, so I went to prospecting because it took me out where the sun was bright and I could see the wild things at play. I was one of the first men into a camp named Chandon—helped to build it, in fact, and got hold of some ground that looked real good. It was hard mining, however, and, being poor, I was still gripping my drill and hammer after the town had grown up.

THE BARRIER

"A woman came out from the East—Vermont, it was—and school-teaching was her line of business, only she hadn't been raised to it, and this was her first clatter at the game; but things had broke bad for her people, and ended in her pulling stakes and coming West all alone. Her folks died and left her up against it, I gathered from what little she told me—sort of an old story, I guess, and usual too, only for her. *She* was plumb unusual."

He seemed to ponder this a moment, and then resumed:

"It don't make any difference to you how I first saw her, and how I began to forget that anything else in the world was worth having but her. I'd lived in the woods all my life, as I said, and knew more about birds and bugs and bees than I did about women; I hadn't been broke proper, and didn't know how to act with them; but I laid out to get this girl, and I did fairly well. There's something wild in every woman that needs to be tamed, and it isn't like the wildness that runs in wood critters; you can win that over by gentleness, but you have to take it away from a woman. Every live thing that couldn't talk was my friend; but I made the mistake of courting my own kind the same way, not knowing that when two of any species mate the male must rule. I was too gentle. Even so, I reckon I'd have won out only for another man. Dan Bennett was his name — the kind that dumb animals hate, and—well, that takes his measure. His range adjoined mine, and, though I'd never seen him, I heard stories now and then—the sort of tales you can't tell to a good woman; so it worried me when I heard of his attentions to this girl. Still, I thought she'd surely find him out and recognize the kind of fellow he was;

A MYSTERY IS UNRAVELLED

but, Lord! a woman can't tell a man from a dog, and there wasn't any one to warn her. There were plenty of women who knew him, but they were the ones who flew by night, while she lived in the sunshine; and women of that kind don't make complaint, anyhow.

"This Bennett came from the town below, where he ran a saloon and a brace game or two; but being as he rode into our camp and out again in the night, and as I didn't drink nor listen to the music of the little rolling ball, why, we never met, even after he began coming to Chandon. Understand, I wasn't too good for those amusements; I just didn't happen to hanker after them, for I was living with the image of the little schoolma'am in my mind, and that destroyed what bad habits I'd formed.

"It was along in the early spring that she began to see I had notions about her, but my damned backwardness wouldn't let me speak, and, in addition, I was getting closer to ore every shot at the mine, and was holding off until I could lay both myself and my goldmine at her feet, and ask her to take the two of us, so if one didn't pan out the other might. But it seemed like I'd never get into pay. The closer I got the harder I worked, and, of course, the less I saw of her, likewise the oftener Bennett came. I reckon no man ever worked like I did—two shifts a day, eighteen hours, with six to sleep. The skin came off of my hands, and I staggered when I came out into the daylight, for the rock was hard, and I had no money to hire a helper; but I was young and strong, and the hope of her was like drink and food and sleep to me. At last I struck it, and still I waited awhile longer till I could be sure. Then I went down to my little shack and put on my other clothes. I remember I'd gone so thin that they hung loose, and my palms were so raw I had hard work handling the buttons, and got my shirt all bloody, for I'd been in the drift forty hours, without sleep and breathing powder smoke, till my knees buckled and wabbled under me. To this day the smell of stale powder smoke makes a woman of me; but that morning I sang, for I was going for my bride, and the world was brighter than it has ever been for eighteen years. The little school-house was closed, at which I remembered that the term was over. I'd been living underground for weeks and lost track of the days, so that I had to count them up on my fingers. It took me a long time, for I was pretty tired in my head; but when I'd figured it out I went on to where she was boarding.

"The woman of the place came to the door, a Scotchwoman. She had a mole on her chin, I remember, a brownish-black mole with three hairs in it. She wore an apron, too, that was kind of checkered, and three buttons were open at the neck of her dress. I recall a lot more of little things about her, though the rest of what happened is rather dreamy.

"I asked for Merridy, and she told me she'd gone away — gone with Bennett, the night before, while I was coughing blood from the powder smoke; that they were married in the front room, and that the bride looked beautiful. She had cried a bit on leaving Chandon, and—and—that was about all. I counted the buttons on the Scotchwoman's waist eight or ten times, and by-and-by she asked if I was sick. But I wasn't. She was a kind-hearted woman, and I'd been to her house a good deal, so she asked me to come in and rest. I wasn't tired, so I went away, and climbed back up to the little shack and the mine that I hated now."

The trader paused, and, reaching for the bottle,

A MYSTERY IS UNRAVELLED

poured himself out a glass of brandy, which he spilled into his throat raw, then continued:

"I turned into a kind of hermit after that, and I wasn't good to associate with. Men got so they shunned me, and I knew they told strange stories, because I heard them whisper when I went to the stores for grub once a month. I changed all over, till even my squirrels and partridges and other friends quit me; once in awhile I got out a ton or two of rock and sold it, but I never worked the mine or opened it up—I couldn't bear to go inside the drift. I tried it time and again, but the smell of its darkness drove me out; every foot of its ragged walls had left its mark on me, and my heart was torn and gouged and shivered worse than its seams and ledges. I could have sold it, but there was no place for me to go, and what did I want with money? I was shy of the world, like a crippled child that dreads the daylight, and I shrank from going out where people might see my scars; so I stayed there by myself nursing the hurt that never got any better. You see, I'd been raised among the hills and rocks, and I was like them in a way; I couldn't grow and alter and heal up.

"From time to time I heard of her, but the news, instead of gladdening me, as it would have gladdened some men, wrung out what bits of suffering were left in me, and I fairly ached for her. Nobody comes to see clearer than a woman deceived, so it didn't take her long to find out the kind of man Bennett was. He wasn't like her at all, and the reason he had courted her so hotly was just that he had had everything that rightly belongs to a man like him, and had sickened of it, so he wanted her because she was clean and pure and different; and realizing that he couldn't get her any other way, he had married her. But she was a treasure no bad man could appreciate, and so he tired quickly, even before the little one came.

"When I heard that she had borne him a daughter I wrote her a letter, which took me a month to compose, and which I tore up. One day a story came to me that made me saddle my horse to ride down and kill him—and, mind you, I was a man who made pets of little wild, trusting things. But I knew she would surely send for me when her pain became too great, so I uncinched my gear and hung it up, and waited and waited and waited. Three long, endless years I waited, almost within sound of her voice, without a word from her, without a glimpse of her, and every hour of that time went by as slowly as if I had held my breath. Then she called to me, and I went.

"I tell you, I was thankful that day for the fortune that had made me take good care of my horse, for I rode like Death on a wind-storm. It grew moonlight as I raced down the valley, and the foam from the animal's muzzle lodged on my clothes, and made me laugh and swear that the morning sun would show Dan Bennett's blood in its place. I rode through the streets of Mesa, where they lived, and past the lights of his big saloon, where I heard the sound of devil's revelry and a shrill-voiced woman singing—a woman the like of which he had tried to make my Merridy. I never skulked or sneaked in those days, and no man ever made me take back roads, so I came up to his house from the front and tied my horse to his gate-post. She heard me on the steps and opened the door.

"'You sent for me,' said I. 'Where is he?' But he had gone away to a neighboring camp, and wouldn't be back until morning, at which I felt the way a thief

A MYSTERY IS UNRAVELLED

must feel, for I'd hoped to meet him in his own house, and I wasn't the kind to go calling when the husband was out. I couldn't think very clearly, however, because of the change in her. She was so thin and worn and sad, sadder than any woman I'd ever seen, and she wasn't the girl I'd known three years before. I guess I'd changed a heap myself; anyhow, that was the first thing she spoke about, and the tears came into her eyes as she breathed:

"'Poor boy! poor boy! You took it very hard, didn't you?'

"'You sent for me,' said I. 'Which road did he take?'

"'There's nothing you can do to him,' she answered back. 'I sent for you to make sure that you still love me.'

"'Did you ever doubt it?' said I, at which she began to cry, sobbing like a woman who has worn out all emotion.

"'Can you feel the same after what I've made you suffer?' she said, and I reckon she must have read the answer in my eyes; for I never was much good at talking, and the sight of her, so changed, had taken the speech out of me, leaving nothing but aches and pains and ashes in its place. When she saw what she wished to know, she told me the story, the whole miserable story, that I'd heard enough of to suspect. Why she'd married the other man she couldn't explain herself, except that it was a woman's whim—I had stayed away and he had come the oftener—part pique and part the man's dare-devil fascination, I reckon; but a month had shown her how she really stood, and had shown him, too. Likewise, she saw the sort of man he was and the kind of life he lived. At last he got rough and cruel to her, trying every way to break her spirit; and even the baby didn't stop him—it made him worse, if anything—till he swore he'd make them both the kind he was, for her goodness seemed to rile and goad him; and, having lived with the kind of woman you have to beat, he tried it on her. Then she knew her fight was hopeless, and she sent for me.

"'He's a fiend,' she told me. 'I've stood all I can. He'll make a bad woman of me as sure as he will of the little one, if I stay on here, so I have decided to go and take her with me.'

"'Where?' said I.

"'Wherever you say,' she answered; and yet I did not understand, not till I saw the look in her eyes. Then, as it dawned on me, she broke down, for it was a terrible thing for a good woman to offer.

"'It's all for the little girl!' she cried. 'More than her life depends upon it. We must get her away from him.'

"She saw it was her only course, and went where her heart was calling."

The Lieutenant met the look of appeal in the trader's eyes, and nodded to imply his complete understanding and approval.

"We love some women for their goodness, others we love for their frailness, but there never was one who combined the two like her, and, now that I knew she loved me, I began to believe again there was a God somewhere. I'd never seen the youngster, so she led me in where it was sleeping, and I remember my boots made such a devil of a thumping on the floor that she laid her slim white finger on her lips and smiled at me. All the fingers in the world began to choke at my throat, and all the blood in me commenced to pound

A MYSTERY IS UNRAVELLED

at my heart, when I looked on that little sleeping kiddie. The tears began to roll out of my eyes, and, because they had been dry for four years, they scalded like melted metal. That was the only time I ever wept—the sight of her baby did it.

"'I love her already,' I whispered, 'and I'll spend my life making her happy and making a lady of her,' which clinched what wavering doubt the mother had, and she began to plan quickly, the fear coming on her of a sudden that our scheme might fail. I was for riding away with both of them that night, back through the streets of Mesa and up into the hills, where I'd have held them single-handed against man or God or devil, but she wouldn't hear of it.

"'We must go away,' she said, 'a long way from here, where the world won't find us and the little one can grow to womanhood without knowing. She must never learn who her father was or what her mother did. We will start all over, you and I and the baby, and forget. Do you love me well enough to do it?'

"I uttered a cry and took her in my arms, the arms that had ached for her all those years. Then I kissed her for the first time."

The old man tried to light his pipe, which had gone out, but his fingers shook so that he dropped the match; whereupon, without speaking, Burrell struck another and held it for him. The trader drew a noisy puff or two in silence and shot his host a grateful glance.

"Her plan was for me to take the youngster away that night, and for her to join us later, because pursuit was certain, and three could be traced where one might disappear; she would follow when the opportunity offered. I saw that he had instilled a terror into her, and that she feared him like death; but, as I thought it over, her scheme seemed feasible, so I agreed. I was to ride west that hour with the sleeping babe, and conceal myself at a place we selected, while she would say that the little one had wandered away and been lost in the cañon, or anything else to throw Bennett off. After a time she would join us. Well— the little girl never waked when I took her in my arms, nor when the mother broke down again and talked to me like a crazy woman. Her collapse showed the terrible strain she had been living under, and the ragged edge where her reason stood. She had been brave enough to plan coolly till the hour for giving up her baby, but when that came she was seized with a thousand dreads, and made me swear by my love for her, which was and is the holiest thing in all my life, that if anything happened I would live for the other Merridy. I begged her again to come with me, but her fears held her back. She vowed, however, that Bennett should never touch her again, and I made her swear by her love for the babe that she would die before he ever laid hands on her. It woke a savage joy in me to think I had bested him, after all.

"I never thought of what I was giving up, of the clean name I was soiling, of the mine back there that meant a fortune any time I cared to take it, for things like that don't count when a man's blood is hot, so I rode away in the yellow moonlight with a sleeping baby on my breast, where no child or woman had ever lain except for that minute before I left. She stood out from beneath the porch shadow and smiled her good-bye—the last I ever saw of her. . . .

"I travelled hard that night and swapped horses at daylight; then, leaving the wild country behind, I came into a region I didn't know, and found a Mexican

A MYSTERY IS UNRAVELLED

woman who tended the child for me, for I was close by the place where Merridy was to come. Every night I went into the village in hopes that some word had arrived, and I waited patiently for a week. Then I got the blow. I heard it from the loafers around the little post-office first, but it dazed me so I wouldn't believe it till I borrowed the paper and read the whole story, with the type dancing and leaping before me. It took some hours for it to seep in, even after that, and for years I recalled every word of the damned lie as if it had been branded on me with hot irons. They called it a shocking crime, the most brutal murder California had ever known, and in the head-lines was my name in letters that struck me between the eyes like a hammer. Mrs. Dan Bennett had been foully murdered by me, in a fit of sudden jealousy, and I had disappeared with the baby! The husband had returned unexpectedly to find her dying, so he said, but too far gone to call for help, and with barely sufficient strength to tell him who did it and how! Then the paper went on with the tale of my courting her, and her turning me down for Bennett. It told how I had gone off alone up into the hills, turning into a bear that nobody, man or child, could approach. It said I had brooded there all this time till the mania got uppermost, and so came down to wreak my vengeance. They never even did me the credit of calling me crazy; I was a fiend incarnate, a beast without soul, and a lot of things like that; and, remember, I had never harmed a living thing in all my life. However, that wasn't what hurt. What turned me into a dull, dead, suffering thing was the knowledge that she was gone. For hours I couldn't get beyond that fact. Then came the realization that Bennett had done it, for I reasoned that he had dragged a hint of the truth from her by very force of the fear he held her in — and slain her. God! — the awful rage that came over me! But there was nothing to do; I had sworn to guard the little one, so I couldn't take vengeance on him. I couldn't go back and prove my innocence, for that would give the child to him. What a night I spent! The next day I saw I had been indicted by the grand jury and was a wanted man. From a distance I watched myself become an outlaw; watched the county put a price upon my head, which Bennett doubled; watched public opinion rise to such a heat that posses began to scour the mountains. What I noted in particular was a statement in the paper that 'The sorrowing husband takes his bereavement with the quiet courage which marks a brave man'! That roused me more than the knowledge that he had made me a wolf and set my friends on my track, which I hadn't covered very well, having ridden boldly. It happened that the Mexican woman couldn't read and talked little; still, I knew they'd find me soon — it couldn't be otherwise—so I made another run for it, swearing an oath, however, before I left that I'd come back and have that gambler's heart.

"It was lucky I went, for they uncovered my sign the next day, and the country where I'd hidden blazed like a field of dry grass. They were close on my heels, and they closed in from every quarter, but, pshaw! I knew the woods like an Indian, and the wild things were my friends again, which would have made it play if I'd been alone, but a girl child of three was harder to manage. So I cowered and skulked day after day like a thief or the murderer they thought me, working always farther into the hidden places, travelling by night with the little one asleep on my bosom, by day

A MYSTERY IS UNRAVELLED

playing with her in some leafy glen, with my pursuers so close behind that for weeks I never slept; and my love for the child increased daily till it became almost an insanity.

"She was the only woman thing I had ever possessed, and it seemed like my love for the mother came back and settled on her. And she loved me, too, and trusted me. Every little smile, every clasp of her tiny, dimpled fingers showed it, and tied her to me with another knot till the fear of losing her became greater than I could bear, till it kept the chill of death in my bones and filled my veins with glacier water. I became an animal, a cowardly, quailing coyote, all through the love of a child.

"We had close squeezes many times, but I finally won, in spite of the fact that they tracked us clear to the edge of the desert, for I had hit for the state line, knowing that Nevada was a wilderness, and feeling that I'd surely lose them there. And I did. But in doing it I nearly lost Merridy. You see, the constant travel and hardship was too much for a prattling baby, and she fell sick from the heat and the dust and the thirst. I'd been going and going till I was a riding skeleton, till my arms were crooked and dead from holding her, but this new thing frightened me like those men and dogs had never done. Here was a thing I couldn't hide from nor outride, so I doubled back and came boldly into the watered country again, expecting they would take me, of course, for a runaway man with a babe in his arms isn't hard to identify, but I didn't care. I was bound for the nearest ranch or mining-camp where a woman could be found; but, as luck would have it, I went through without trying. I had gone farther from men and things, however, than I thought, and this return pursuit was a million times worse than the other, for I couldn't go fast enough to shake Death, who ran with his hand on my cantle or rode on my horse's rump. It was then I found Alluna. She was with a hunting-party of Pah-Utes, who knew nothing of me nor of the white man's affairs, and cared less; and when I saw the little squaw I rode my horse up beside her, laid the sick child in her arms, then tumbled out of the saddle. They had a harder job to pull me through than they did to save Merridy, for I'd given the baby all the water and hadn't slept or rested for many years, so it seemed.

"The little one was playing around several days before I got back my reason. Meanwhile the party had moved North, taking us with them, and, as it happened, just missing a posse who were returning from the desert.

"When I was able to get about I told Alluna that I must be going, but as I told her I watched her face, and saw the sign I wanted—the white girl had clutched at her like she had at me, and she couldn't give her up, so I made a dicker with her old man. It took all the money I had to buy that squaw, but I knew the kiddie must have a woman's care; and the three of us started out soon after, alone, and broke, and aimless—and we've been going ever since.

"That's the heart of the story, Lieutenant, and that's how I started to drift. Since then we three have never rested. I left them once in Idaho and went back to Mesa, riding all the way, mostly by night, but Bennett was gone. He'd run down mighty fast after Merridy died, so I heard, growing sullen and uglier day by day—and I reckon I was the only one who knew why—till he had a killing in his place. It

A MYSTERY IS UNRAVELLED

was unprovoked, and instead of stopping to face it out the yellow in him rose to the surface and he left before sunup, as I had left, making a clean getaway, too, for there was no such hullabaloo raised about killing a man as there was about—the other. So my trip was all for nothing.

"I was used to disappointment by now, so I took it quiet and went back to Alluna and the little one, knowing that some day we two men would meet. You see, I figured that God had framed a cold hand for me, but He would surely give me a pair before the game closed. Of course, never having seen Bennett, I was handicapped, and, added to that, he changed his name, so the search was mighty slow and blind, but I knew the day would come. And it would have come only for—this.

"There isn't much more to tell. I did what most men would have done, I reckon, because I was just average in every way. I took Alluna, and together we drifted North, along the frontier, until we landed here. Every year the little girl got more beautiful and more like her mother, and every year we two loved her more. We changed her name, of course, for I've always had the dread of the law back of me, and then the other two kiddies came along; but we were living pretty easy, the woman contented and me waiting for Bennett, till you stepped in and Necia fell in love. That's another thing I never counted on. It seems like I've always overlooked the plainest kind of facts. I've held off telling you the last few weeks, hoping you two wouldn't make it necessary, for I reckon I'm sort of a coward; but she informed me to-night that she couldn't marry you, being what she thinks she is, and knowing the blood she has in her I knew she wouldn't.

I figured it wouldn't be right to either of you to let you go it blind, and so I came in to tell you this whole thing and to give myself up."

Gale stopped, then poured himself another drink.

"To give yourself up?" echoed Burrell, vaguely. "How do you mean?" He had sat like one in a trance during the long recital, only his eyes alive.

"I'm under indictment for murder," said the trader. "I have been for fifteen years, and there's no chance in the world for me to prove my innocence."

"Have you told Necia?" the young man inquired.

"No, you'll have to do that — I never could — she might—disbelieve. What's more, you mustn't tell her yet. Wait till I give the word. It won't be long, perhaps a day. I want to go free a little while yet, for I've got some work to do."

Burrell rose to his feet and stamped the cramps from his muscles. He was deeply agitated, and his mind was groping darkly for light to lay hold of this new thing that confronted him.

"Why, yes, yes—of course—don't come until you're ready," he muttered, mechanically, as if unaware of the meaning of his words. "To be sure, I'm a policeman, am I not? I had forgotten I was a jailer, and—and all that." He said it sneeringly, and with a measure of contempt for his office; then he turned suddenly to the trader, and his voice was rich and deep-pitched with feeling.

"John Gale," he said, "you're the bravest man I ever knew, and the best." He choked a bit. "You sacrificed all that life meant when this girl was a baby, and now when she has come into womanhood you give

A MYSTERY IS UNRAVELLED

up your blood for her. By God! You are a man! I want your hand!"

In spite of himself he could not restrain the moisture that dimmed his eyes as he gripped the toil-worn palm of this great, gray hulk of a man, so aged and bent beneath the burden of his life-long, fadeless love, who, in turn, was powerfully affected by the young man's impulsive outburst of feeling and his unexpected words of praise. The old man looked up a trifle shyly.

"Then you don't doubt no part of it?"

"Certainly not."

"Somehow, I always figured nobody would believe me if ever I told the whole thing."

The soldier gazed unseeingly into the flame of his lamp, and said:

"I wonder if my love for the daughter is as great and as holy as your love for the mother. I wonder if I could give what you have given, if I had nothing but a memory to live with me." Then he inquired, irrelevantly; "But what about Bennett, Mr. Gale? You say you never found him?"

The trader answered, after a moment's hesitation, "He's still at large." At which his companion exclaimed, "I'd love to meet him in your stead!"

Gale seemed seized with a desire to speak, but, even while he hesitated, out of the silent night there came the sound of quick footsteps approaching briskly, as if the owner were in haste and knew whither he was bound. Up the steps they came lightly; then the room and the whole silence round about rang and echoed with a peremptory signal. Evidently this man rapped on the board door to awaken and alarm, for instead of his knuckles he used some hard and heavy thing like a gun-butt.

THE BARRIER

"Lieutenant Burrell! Lieutenant Burrell!" a gruff voice cried.

"Who's there?" called the young man.

"Let me in! Quick! I've got work for you to do! Open up, I say! This is Ben Stark!"

CHAPTER XV

AND A KNOT TIGHTENED

A DAY of shattered hopes is a desolate thing, but the night of such a day is desolate indeed. In all his life Poleon Doret had never sunk to such depths of despondency, for his optimistic philosophy and his buoyant faith in the goodness of life forbade it. Therefore, when darkness came it blotted out what little brightness and light and hope were left to him after Necia's stormy interview with the Lieutenant. The arrival of the freight steamer afforded him some distraction, but there was only a small consignment for the store, and that was quickly disposed of; so, leaving the other citizens of Flambeau to wrangle over their private merchandise, he went back to his solitary vigil, which finally became so unbearable that he sought to escape his thoughts, or at least to drown them for a while, amid the lights and life and laughter of Stark's saloon. Being but a child by nature, his means of distraction were primal and elementary, and he began to gamble, as usual with hard luck, for the cards had ever been unkind to him. He did not think of winnings or losings, however—he merely craved the occupation; and it was this that induced him to sit at a game in which Runnion played, although ordinarily he would not have tolerated even tacitly such a truce to his dislikes. As it was, he crouched in a corner, his hat pulled down over his brow, his swarthy face a darker hue beneath the shadow, losing steadily, only now and then showing a flash of white teeth as he saw his money go. What mattered loss to him? He had no more need of money now than Necia had of his love. He would spend the dollars he had eked and scraped and saved for her as she had spent the treasures of his heart, and now that the one had brought him no return he wished to be rid of the other, for he was shortly to go again in search of his "New Country," where no man needs gold half so much as a clean heart. It would be a long journey, far to the West and North—a journey that none of his kind had ever fared back from, and he wished to go light, as all good adventurers go.

Runnion annoyed him with his volubility, for the news of his good-fortune had fired the man with a reckless disregard for money, and he turned to gaming as the one natural recourse of his ilk. As the irony of fate would have it, he won what the Canadian lost, together with the stakes of various others who played for a time with him and then gave up, wagging their heads or swearing softly at the cards.

It was shortly after midnight that Stark came into the place. Poleon was not too absorbed in his own fortunes to fail to notice the extraordinary ferocity and exhilaration of the saloon-keeper, nor that his face was keener, his nostrils thinner, his walk more nervous, and his voice more cutting than usual when he spoke to Runnion.

"Come here."

"I'll be with you when I finish this hand," said the player, over his shoulder.

"*Come here!*" Stark snapped his command, and Runnion threw down his cards.

AND A KNOT TIGHTENED

"I'm right in the middle of a winning streak. You'll break my luck, Ben."

But the other only frowned impatiently, and, drawing the reluctant gambler aside, began to talk rapidly to him, almost within ear-shot of Poleon, who watched them, idly wondering what Stark had to say that could make Runnion start and act so queerly. Well, it was their affair. They made a bad pair to draw to. He knew that Runnion was the saloon-keeper's lieutenant and obeyed implicitly his senior's commands. He could distinguish nothing they said, nor was he at all curious until a knot of noisy men crowded up to the bar, and, forcing the two back nearer to the table where he sat, his sharp ears caught these words from Runnion's lips:

"Not with me! She'd never go with me!" and Stark's reply:

"She'll go where I send her, and with anybody I tell her to."

The Frenchman lost what followed, for a newly dealt hand required study. He scanned his cards, and tossed them face up before the dealer; then he overheard Runnion say:

"It's the only one in camp. He might sell it if you offered him enough." At this Stark called one of the men at the bar aside, and the three began to dicker.

"Not a cent less," the third man announced, loudly. "There ain't another Peterborough in town."

It was Poleon's deal now, and when he had finished both Stark and Runnion had disappeared, also the man they had accosted, which pleased the Canadian, for now that Runnion was eliminated from the game he might win a little. A steady, unvarying run of bad hands is uninteresting, and does not occupy one's mind as well as an occasional change of luck

THE BARRIER

Outside Runnion was saying again to Stark:

"She won't go with me, Ben; she don't like me. You see, I made love to her, and she got mad and wanted me killed."

"She'll never know who you are until it's too late to turn back," said the other, "and you are the only man I can trust to take her through. I *can* trust you —you owe me too much to be crooked."

"Oh, I'll act square with you! But look here, what's all this about, anyhow? Why do you want that girl? You said you didn't care for her that way; you told me so yourself. Been having a change of heart, or is it your second childhood?" He laughed disagreeably.

"It's none of your business," said the gambler. "I want her, and that's enough. All you have to do is to take her to St. Michael's and keep her there till you hear from me. She thinks she is going to the Mission, and you needn't tell her otherwise until you get her aboard a steamer; then *take* her, no matter what kind of a fight she puts up. You've got a light-rowing skiff, and you'd better keep going till you're overtaken by a down-river boat. I want her as far away from here as possible. There's going to be some hell in this camp. Now, hike, and get yourself ready."

"All right! But I ain't the safest kind of a chaperon for a good-looking girl."

Stark laid a cold hand on Runnion's shoulder, close up to his neck.

"Get that out of your mind. She belongs to me."

"You said just now—"

"Never mind what I said. She's mine, and you've got to promise to be straight with her. I've trusted you before, and if you're not on the level now, say so. It will save you a lot of trouble."

AND A KNOT TIGHTENED

"Oh! All right!" exclaimed Runnion, testily. "Only it looks mighty queer."

He melted into the darkness and Stark returned to his cabin, where he paced back and forth impatiently, smiling evilly now and then, consulting his watch at frequent intervals. A black look had begun to settle on his face, but it vanished when Necia came, and he met her with a smile.

"I was afraid you had weakened," he said. "Everything is ready and waiting. I've got the only canoe in the place, a Peterborough, and hired a good oarsman to put you through, instructing him to make as fast time as he can, and to board the first steamer that overtakes you. Too bad this freighter that just got in isn't going the other way. However, there's liable to be another any hour, and if one doesn't come along you'll find enough blankets and food in the skiff, so you needn't go ashore. You'll be there before you know it."

"You are very kind," said the girl. "I can't thank you enough." She was clothed in her simple everyday dress, and looked again the sun-colored half-breed girl with the wide, dark eyes and the twin braids of crow-black hair.

"You didn't run into anybody, eh?"

She shook her head. Then he led her out into the darkness, and they stumbled down to the river's-bank, descending to the gravelly water's edge, where rows of clumsy hand-sawed boats and poling-skiffs were chafing at their painters. The up-river steamer was just clearing.

Stark's low whistle was answered a hundred yards below, and they searched out a darker blot that proved to be a man's figure.

THE BARRIER

"Is everything ready?" he inquired, at which the shadow grunted unintelligibly. So, holding Necia by the arm, Stark helped her back to a seat in the stern.

"This man will take you through," he said. "You can trust him, all right."

The oarsman clambered in and adjusted his sweeps, then Stark laid a hand on the prow and shoved the light boat out into the current, calling softly:

"Good-bye, and good-luck."

"Good-bye, Mr. Stark. Thank you ever so much," the girl replied, too numb and worn out to say much, or to notice or care whither she was bound or who was her boatman. She had been swept along too swiftly to reason or fear for herself any more.

Half an hour later the scattered lights of the little camp winked and twinkled for the last time. Turning, she set her face forward, and, adjusting the cushions to her comfort, strained her tired eyes towards the rising and falling shadow of her boatman. She seemed borne along on a mystic river of gloom that hissed and gurgled about her, invisible but all-pervading, irresistible, monstrous, only the ceaseless, monotonous creak of the rowlocks breaking the silence.

Stark did not return to his cabin, but went back instead to his saloon, where he saw Poleon Doret still sprawling with elbows on the table, his hat pulled low above his sullen face. The owner of the place passed behind the bar and poured himself a full glass of whiskey, which he tossed off, then, without a look to right or left, went out and down towards the barracks. A light behind the drawn curtains of the officer's house told that his man was not abed, but he waited a long moment after his summons before the door was opened,

AND A KNOT TIGHTENED

during which he heard the occupant moving about and another door close in the rear. When he was allowed entrance at last he found the young man alone in a smoke-filled room with a bottle and two empty glasses on the table.

For at the sound of his voice Gale had whispered to Burrell, "Keep him out!" and the Lieutenant had decided to refuse his late visitor admittance when he lighted on the expedient of concealing the trader in the bedroom at the rear. It was only natural, he reasoned, that Gale should dislike to face a man like Stark before he had regained his composure.

"Go in there and wait till I see what he wants," he had said, and, shutting the old man in, he had gone forth to admit Stark, resenting his ill-timed intrusion and inquiring brusquely the cause of it.

Before answering, Stark entered and closed the door behind him.

"I've got some work for you, Lieutenant."

"I guess it can wait till morning," said Meade.

"No, it can't; it's got to be done to-night, right now! You represent the law, or at least you've taken every occasion to so declare yourself, and to mix in with little things that don't cut much figure; so now I've come to you with something big. It's a serious affair, and being as I'm a peaceful man I want to go by the law." His eyes mocked the words he uttered. "You're mighty prompt and determined when it comes to regulating such affairs. You seem to carry the weight of this whole community on your shoulders, so I'm here to give you some information."

Burrell ignored the taunt, and said, quietly: "It's a little late for polite conversation. Come to the point."

"I've got a criminal for you."

"What kind?"

"Murderer."

"You've had a killing in your place, eh?"

"No, I've just made a discovery. I found it all out by accident, too—pure accident. By Heaven! You can't tell me there isn't a beneficent Providence overlooking our affairs. Why, this felon has lived here among us all this time, and only for the merest chance I never would have recognized him."

"Well, well! Go on!" snapped Burrell, impatiently.

"He's a friend of yours, and a highly respected party. He's a glorious example to this whole river."

The officer started. Could it be? he wondered. Could knowledge of this affair have reached this man? He was uncomfortably aware of that presence in the back room, but he had to know the truth.

"Who is the man?"

"He's your friend. He's—" Stark paused, gloating over his enemy's suspense.

"Go on."

"He's everybody's friend. He's the shining mark of this whole country. He's the benevolent renegade, Squaw-man Gale."

"John Gale?"

"Gaylord is his name, and I was a fool not to know it sooner."

"How did you discover this?" inquired Burrell, lamely. "What proof have you?"

The disclosure had not affected the soldier as Stark expected, and his anger began to lift itself.

"That's neither here nor there; the man's a murderer; he's wanted in California, where I came from; he's been indicted, and there's a price on his head.

AND A KNOT TIGHTENED

He's hidden for fifteen years, but he'll hang as sure as I stand here."

Disclosures of a complex nature had so crowded on Burrell in the last few hours that he saw himself the centre of a most unfortunate and amazing tangle. Things were difficult enough as it was, but to have this man appear and cry for justice—this man above all others!—it was a complication quite unlooked for—a hideous mockery. He must gain time for thought. One false step might ruin all. He could not face this on the spur of the moment, so, shrugging his shoulders with an air of polite scepticism, he assumed a tone of good-natured raillery.

"Fifteen years? Murder? John Gale a murderer? Why, that's almost—pardon me if I smile—I'm getting sleepy. What proof have you?"

"Proof!" blazed the gambler. "Proof! Ask Gaylord! Proof! Why, the woman he murdered was my wife!"

It was Burrell's turn now to fall incoherent, and not only did his speech forsake him, but his thoughts went madly veering off into a wilderness where there was no trail, no light, no hope. What kind of a coil was this? What frightful bones were these he bared? This man was Bennett! This was Necia's father! This man he hated, this man who was bad, whose name was a curse throughout the length and breadth of the West, was the father of the girl he loved! His head began to whirl, then the story of the trader came back to him, and he remembered who and what the bearer of these later tidings was. He raised a pair of eyes that had become furious and bloodshot, and suddenly realized that the man before him, who persisted in saddling upon Gale this heinous crime, was the slayer of Necia's mother; for he did not doubt Gale's story for an instant. He found his fingers writhing to feel the creature's throat.

"Proof!" Stark was growling. "How much proof do you need? I've followed him for fifteen years. I've tracked him with men and dogs through woods and deserts and mining-camps. I've slept on his trail for five thousand miles, and now do you think I'm mistaken? He killed my wife, I say, and robbed me of my little girl! That's her in his house. That's her he calls Necia. She's my girl—*my girl*, do you understand?—and I'll have his life."

It was hate that animated him, and nothing more. He had no joy in the finding of his offspring, no uplifted thought of justice. The thirst for revenge, personal, violent, utter, was all that prompted this man; but Burrell had no inkling yet of the father's well-shaped plans, nor how far-reaching they were, and could barely stammer:

"So! You—you know?"

"Yes! She wears the evidence around her neck, and if that isn't enough I can furnish more—evidence enough to smother you. My name isn't Stark at all; I changed it years ago for certain reasons. I've changed it more than once, but that's my privilege and my own affair. Her name is Merridy Bennett."

"I don't suppose you know I'm going to marry her," said the Kentuckian, irrelevantly.

"No," replied the other, "I wasn't aware of the fact."

"Well, I am. I'll be your son-in-law." He said this as if it were the statement of an astonishing truth, whereat Stark grinned, a mirthless, disquieting sort of grimace, and said:

AND A KNOT TIGHTENED

"There's a lot of things for you and me to settle up first. For one thing, I want those mines of hers."

"Why?"

"Well, I'm her father, and she's not of age."

"I'll think it over."

"I'll take them, anyway, as her next of kin."

Burrell did not follow up this statement, for its truth was incontrovertible, and showed that the father's ill-will was too tangible a thing to be concealed; so he continued:

"We'll adjust that after Gale is attended to; but, meanwhile, what do you want me to do?"

"I want you to arrest the man who killed my wife. If you don't take him the miners will. I've got a following in this camp, and I'll raise a crowd in fifteen minutes—enough to hang this squaw-man, or batter down your barracks to get him. But I don't want to do that; I want to go by the law you've talked so much about; I want you to do the trick."

At last Burrell saw the gambler's deviltry. He knew Stark's reputation too well to think that he feared a meeting with Gale, for the man had lived in hope of that these fifteen years, and had shaped his life around such a meeting; but this indirect method—the Kentuckian felt a flash of reluctant admiration for a man who could mould a vengeance with such cruel hands, and, even though he came from a land of feuds, where hate is a precious thing, the cunning strength of this man's enmity dwarfed any he had ever known. Stark had planned his settlement coldly and with deliberate malice; moreover, he was strong enough to stand aside and let another take his place, and thus deny to Gale the final recourse of a hunted beast, the desperate satisfaction that the trader craved. He tied his enemy's

hands and delivered him up with his thirst unsatisfied
—to whom? He thrust a weapon into the hand of his
other enemy, and bade this other enemy use it; worse
than that, forced him to strike the man he honored—
the man he loved. Burrell never doubted that Stark
had carefully weighed the effect of this upon Necia,
and had reasoned that a girl like her could not understand a soldier's duty if it meant the blood of a parent.
If he refused to act, the gambler could break him, while
every effort he made to protect Gale would but in-
crease the other's satisfaction. There was no chance
of the trader's escape. Stark held him in his hand.
His followers would do his bidding. It was a desperate affair. Was it impossible, the Lieutenant wondered, to move this man from his purpose?

"Have you thought of Necia? She loves Gale.
What effect will this have on her?"

"Damn her! She's more his brat than mine. I
want John Gaylord!"

At this a vicious frenzy overtook Burrell, and he
thought of the man behind yonder door, whom he had
forgotten until these words woke something savage in
him. Well! Why not? These two men had stalked
each other clear into the farthest places, driven by
forces that were older than the hills. Who was he to
stand between such passions? This was ordained, it
was the course of nature, the clash of elements, and
this was a fair battle-ground, so why should he undertake to stop a thing decreed?

The gambler's words rang in his ears—"I want John
Gaylord"—and before he knew what he was doing he
had answered: "Very well. I'll give him to you," and
crossed quickly to the door of his bedroom and flung
it open. On the threshold he paused stock-still. The

AND A KNOT TIGHTENED

place was empty; a draught sucked through the open window, flirting with the curtain and telling the story of the trader's exit.

"If you're looking for your coat, it's here," he heard Stark say. "Get into it, and we'll go for him."

The Lieutenant's mind was working fast enough now, in all conscience, and he saw with clear and fateful eyes whither he was being led, at which a sudden reckless disregard for consequences seized him. He felt a blind fury at being pulled and hauled and driven by this creature, and also an unreasoning anger at Gale's defection. But it was the thought of Necia and the horrible net of evil in which this man had ensnared them both that galled him most. It was all a terrible tangle, in which the truth was hopelessly hidden, and nothing but harm could come from attempting to unravel it. There was but one solution, and that, though fundamental and effective, was not to be expected from an officer of the law. Nevertheless, he chose it, for Ben Stark was too potent a force for evil to be at large, and needed extermination as truly as if he were some dangerous beast. He determined to finish this thing here and now.

Meade went to his bureau, took his revolver from the belt where he had hung it, and came out into the other room. Stark, seeing the weapon, exclaimed:

"You don't need that; he won't resist you."

"I've decided not to take him," said Burrell.

"Decided not to take him?" shouted the other. "Have you weakened? Don't you intend to arrest that man?"

"No!" cried the soldier. "I've listened to your lies long enough; now I'm going to stop them, once for all. You're too dangerous to have around."

THE BARRIER

They faced each other silently a moment; then Stark spoke in a very quiet voice, though his eyes were glittering:

"What's the meaning of this? Are you crazy?"

"Gale was here just before you came, and told me who killed your wife. I know."

"You do?"

"I do."

"Well?"

"It's pretty late. This place is lonely. This is the simplest way."

The gambler fell to studying his antagonist, and when he did not speak Burrell continued:

"Come, brace up! I'm giving you a chance."

But Stark shook his head.

"Don't be afraid," insisted the Lieutenant. "There are no witnesses. If you get me, nobody will know, and your word is good. If not—it's much simpler than the other." Then, when the gambler still made no move, he insisted, "You wouldn't have me kill you like a rattlesnake?"

"You couldn't," said the older man. "You're not that kind—and I'm not the kind to be cheated, either. Listen! I've lived over forty years, and I never took less than was coming to me. I won't begin to-night."

"You'll get your share—"

"Bah! You don't know what I mean. I don't want you; it's him I'm after, and when I'm done with him I'll take care of you; but I won't run any risk right now. I won't take a chance on losing what I've risked so much to gain, what I've lived these fifteen years to get. You might put me away—there's the possibility—and I won't let you or any other man—or

AND A KNOT TIGHTENED

woman either, not even my girl—cheat me out of Gale. Put up your gun."

The soldier hesitated, then did as he was bidden, for this man knew him better than he knew himself.

"I ought to treat you like a mad dog, but I can't do it while your hands are up. I'm going to fight for John Gale, however, and you can't take him."

"I'll have his carcass hung to my ridge-pole before daylight."

"No."

"I say yes!" Stark turned to go, but paused at the door. "And you think you'll marry Necia, do you?"

"I know it."

"Like hell you will! Suppose you find her first."

"What do you mean? Wait—"

But his visitor was gone, leaving behind him a lover already sorely vexed, and now harassed by a new and sudden apprehension. What venom the man distilled! Could it be that he had sent Necia away? Burrell scouted the idea. She wasn't the kind to go at Stark's mere behest; and as for his forcing her, why, this was not an age of abductions! He might aim to take her, but it would require some time to establish his rights, and even then there were Gale and himself to be reckoned with. Still, this was no time for idling, and he might as well make certain, so the young man put on his coat hurriedly, knowing there was work to do. There was no telling what this night would bring forth, but first he must warn his friend, after which they would fight this thing together, not as soldier and civilian, but as man and man, not for the law, but against it. He smiled as he realized the situation. Well, he was through with the army, anyhow; his path was strange and new from this time henceforth, and led him away from all he had known, taking him among other peoples; but he did not flinch, for it led to her. Behind him was that former life; to-night he began anew.

Stark traced his way back to his cabin in a ten times fiercer mood than he had come, reviling, cursing, hating; back past the dark trading-post he went, pausing to shake his clenched fist and grind out an oath between his teeth; past the door of his own saloon, which was a-light, and whence came the sound of revelry, through the scattered houses, where he went more by feel than by sight, up to the door of his own shack. He fitted his key in the lock, but the door swung open without his aid, at which he remembered that he had only pulled it after him when he came away with Necia. He closed it behind him now, and locked it, for he had some thinking to do; then felt through his pockets for a match, and, striking it, bent over his lamp to adjust the wick. It flared up steady and strong at last, flooding the narrow place with its illumination; then he straightened up and turned towards the bed to throw off his coat, when suddenly every muscle of his body leaped with an uncontrollable spasm, as if he had uncovered a deadly serpent coiled and ready to spring. In spite of himself his lungs contracted as if with the grip of giant hands, and his breath came forth in a startled cry.

John Gale was sitting at his table, barely an arm's-length away, his gray-blue eyes fixed upon him, and the deep seams of his heavy face set as if graven in stone. His huge, knotted hands were upon the table, and between them lay a naked knife.

CHAPTER XVI

JOHN GALE'S HOUR

IT was a heathenish time of night to arouse the girl, thought Burrell, as he left the barracks, but he must allay these fears that were besetting him, he must see Necia at once. The low, drifting clouds obscured what star-glow there was in the heavens, and he stepped back to light a lantern. By its light he looked at his watch and exclaimed, then held it to his ear. Five hours had passed since he left Gale's house. Well, the call was urgent, and Necia would understand his anxiety.

A few moments later he stood above the squaw, who crouched on the trader's doorstep, wailing her death song into the night. He could not check her; she paid no heed to him, but only rocked and moaned and chanted that strange, weird song which somehow gave strength to his fears.

"What's wrong; where is Necia? Where is she?" he demanded, and at last seized her roughly, facing her to the light, but Alluna only blinked owlishly at his lantern and shook her head.

"Gone away," she finally informed him, and began to weave again in her despair, but he held her fiercely.

"Where has she gone? When did she go?" He shook her to quicken her reply.

"I don' know. I don' know. Long time she's gone now." She trailed off into Indian words he could not comprehend, so he pushed past her into the house to see for himself, and without knocking flung Necia's door open and stepped into her chamber. Before he had swept the unfamiliar room with his eyes he knew that she had indeed gone, and gone hurriedly, for the signs of disorder betrayed a reckless haste. Hanging across the back of a chair was what had once been the wondrous dress, Poleon's gift, now a damp and draggled ruin, and on the floor were two sodden satin slippers and a pair of wet silk stockings. He picked up the lace gown and saw that it was torn from shoulder to waist. What insanity had possessed the girl to rip her garment thus?

"She take her 'nother dress; the one I make las' summer," said Alluna, who had followed him in and stood staring as he stared.

"When did she go, Alluna? For God's sake, what does this mean?"

"I don' know! She come and she go, and I don' see her; mebbe three, four hour ago."

"Where's Gale? He'll know. He's gone after her, eh?"

The upward glow of the lantern heightened the young man's pallor, and again the squaw broke into her sad lament.

"John Gale—he's gone away with the knife of my father. I am afraid—I am afraid."

Burrell forced himself to speak calmly; this was no time to let his wits stampede.

"How long ago?"

"Long time."

"Did he come back here just now?"

"No; he went to the jail-house, and he would not let me follow. He don' come back no more."

JOHN GALE'S HOUR

This was confusing, and Meade cried, angrily:

"Why didn't you give the alarm? Why didn't you come to me instead of yelling your lungs out around the house?"

"He told me to wait," she said, simply.

"Go find Poleon, quick."

"He told me to wait," she repeated, stoically, and Burrell knew he was powerless to move her. He saw the image of a great terror in the woman's face. The night suddenly became heavy with the hint of unspeakable things, and he grew fearful, suspecting now that Gale had told him but a part of his story, that all the time he knew Stark's identity, and that his quarry was at hand, ready for the kill; or, if not, he had learned enough while standing behind that partition. Where was he now? Where was Necia? What part did she play in this? Stark's parting words struck Burrell again like a blow. This life-long feud was drawing swiftly to some tragic culmination, and somewhere out in the darkness those two strong, hate-filled men were settling their scores. All at once a fear for the trader's life came upon the young man, and he realized that a great bond held them together. He could not think clearly, because of the dread thing that gripped him at thought of Necia. Was he to lose her, after all? He gave up trying to think, and fled for Stark's saloon, reasoning that where one was the other must be near, and there would surely be some word of Necia. He burst through the door; a quick glance over the place showed it empty of those he sought, but, spying Poleon Doret, he dragged him outside, inquiring breathlessly:

"Have you seen Gale?"

"No."

THE BARRIER

"Have you seen Stark? Has he been about?"

"Yes, wan hour, mebbe two hour ago. W'y? W'at for you ask?"

"There's the devil to pay. Those two have come together, and Necia is gone."

"Necia gone?" the Canadian jerked out. "W'at you mean by dat? W'ere she's gone to?"

"I don't know—nobody knows. God! I'm shaking like a leaf."

"Bah! She's feel purty bad! She's go out by herse'f. Dat's all right."

"I tell you something has happened to her; there's hell to pay. I found her clothes at the house torn to ribbons and all muddy and wet."

Poleon cried out at this.

"We've got to find her and Gale, and we haven't a minute to lose. I'm afraid we're too late as it is. I wish it was daylight. Damn the darkness, anyhow! It makes it ten times harder."

His incoherence alarmed his listener more than his words.

"W'ere have you look?"

"I've been to the house, but Alluna is crazy, and says Gale has gone to kill Stark, as near as I can make out. Both of them were at my quarters to-night, and I'm afraid the squaw is right."

"But w'ere is Necia?"

"We don't know; maybe Stark has got her."

The Frenchman cursed horribly. "Have you try hees cabane?"

"No."

Without answer the Frenchman darted away, and the Lieutenant sped after him through the deserted rows of log-houses.

JOHN GALE'S HOUR

"Ha! Dere's light," snarled Doret, over his shoulder, as they neared their goal.

"Be careful," panted Burrell. "Wait! Don't knock." He forced Poleon to pause. "Let's find out who's inside. Remember, we're working blind."

He gripped his companion's arm with fingers of steel, and together they crept up to the door, but even before they had gained it they heard a voice within. It was Stark's. The walls of the house were of moss-chinked logs that deadened every sound, but the door itself was of thin, whip-sawed pine boards with ample cracks at top and bottom, and, the room being of small dimensions, they heard plainly. The Lieutenant leaned forward, then with difficulty smothered an exclamation, for he heard another voice now—the voice of John Gale. The words came to him muffled but distinct, and he raised his hand to knock, when, suddenly arrested, he seized Poleon and forced him to his knees, hissing into his ear:

"Listen! Listen! For God's sake, listen!"

For the first time in his tempestuous life Ben Stark lost the iron composure that had made his name a byword in the West, and at sight of his bitterest enemy seated in the dark of his own house waiting for him he became an ordinary, nervous, frightened man faced by a great peril. It was the utter unexpectedness of the thing that shook him, and before he could regain his balance Gale spoke:

"I've come to settle, Bennett."

"What are you doing here?" the gambler stammered.

"I was up at the soldier's place just now and heard you. I didn't want any interruptions, so I came here where we can be alone." He paused, and, when Stark

made no answer, continued, "Well, let's get at it."
But still the other made no move. "You've had all
the best of it for twenty years," Gale went on, in his
level voice, "but to-night I get even. By God! I've
lived for this."

"That shot in Lee's cabin?" recalled Stark, with the
light of a new understanding. "You knew me then?"

"Yes."

Stark took a deep breath. "What a damned fool
I've been!"

"Your devil's magic saved you that time, but it won't
stop this." The trader rose slowly with the knife in
his hand.

"You'll hang for this!" said the gambler, unsteadily,
at which Gale's face blazed.

"Ha!" exclaimed the trader, exultingly; "you can
feel it in your guts already, eh?"

With an effort Stark began to assemble his wits as
the trader continued:

"You saddled your dirty work on me, Ben Stark,
and I've carried it for fifteen years; but to-night I put
you out the way you put her out. An eye for an eye!"

"I didn't kill her," said the man.

"Don't lie. This isn't a grand jury. We're all
alone."

"I didn't kill her."

"So? The yellow is showing up at last. I knew
you were a coward, but I didn't think you'd be afraid
to own it to yourself. That thing must have lived
with you."

"Look here," said Stark, curiously, "do you really
think I killed Merridy?"

"I know it. A man who would strike a woman
would kill her—if he had the nerve."

JOHN GALE'S HOUR

Stark had now mastered himself, and smiled.

"My hate worked better than I thought. Well, well, that made it hard for you, didn't it?" he chuckled. "I supposed, of course, you knew— "

"Knew?" Gale's face showed emotion for the first time. "Knew what—?" His hands were quivering slightly.

"She killed herself."

"So help you God?"

"So help me God!"

There was a long pause.

"Why?"

"Say, it's kind of funny our standing here talking about that thing, isn't it? Well, if you want to know, I came home early that night—I guess you hadn't been gone two hours—and the surprise did it, more than anything else, I suppose—she hadn't prepared a story. I got suspicious, named you at random, and hit the nail on the head. She broke down, thought I knew more than I did, and—and then there was hell to pay."

"Go on."

"I suppose I talked bad and made threats—I was crazy over you—till she must have thought I meant to kill her, but I didn't. No. I never was quite that bad. Anyhow, she did it herself."

Gale's face was like chalk, and his voice sounded thin and dry as he said:

"You beat her, that's why she did it."

Stark made no answer.

"The papers said the room showed a struggle."

When the other still kept silent, Gale insisted:

"Didn't you?"

At this Stark flamed up defiantly.

"Well, I guess I had cause enough. No woman except her was ever untrue to me—wife or sweetheart."

"You didn't really think—?"

"Think hell! I thought so then, and I think so now. She denied it, but—"

"And you knew her so well, too. I guess you've had some bad nights yourself, Bennett, with that always on your mind—"

"I swore I'd have you—"

"—and so you put her blood on my head, and made me an outlaw." After an instant: "Why did you tell me this, anyhow?"

"It's our last talk, and I wanted you to know how well my hate worked."

"Well, I guess that's all," said Gale. So far they had watched each other with unwavering, unblinking eyes, straining at the leash and taut in every nerve. Now, however, the trader's fingers tightened on the knife-handle, and his knuckles whitened with the grip, at which Stark's right hand swept to his waist, and simultaneously Gale lunged across the table. His blade flickered in the light, and a gun spoke, once—twice—again and again. A cry arose outside the cabin, then some heavy thing crashed in through the door, bringing light with it, for with his first leap Gale had carried the lamp and the table with him, and the two had clenched in the dark.

Burrell had waited an instant too long, for the men's voices had held so steady, their words had been so vital, that the finish found him unprepared, but, thrusting the lantern into Poleon's hand, he had backed off a pace and hurled himself at the door. He had learned the knack of bunching his weight in football days, and the barrier burst and splintered before him. He fell to his knees inside, and an instant later found himself wrestling for his life between two raging beasts. The Lieutenant knew Doret must have entered too, though he could not see him, for the lantern shed a sickly gloom over the chaos. He was locked desperately with John Gale, who flung him about and handled him like a child, fighting like an old gray wolf, hoary with years and terrible in his rage. Burrell had never been so battered and harried and torn; only for the lantern's light Gale would doubtless have sheathed his weapon in his new assailant, but the more fiercely the trader struggled, the more tenaciously the soldier clung. As it was, Gale carried the Lieutenant with him and struck over his head at Stark.

Poleon had leaped into the room at Burrell's heels, to receive the impact of a heavy body hurled backward into his arms as if by some irresistible force. He seized it and tore it away from the thing that pressed after and bore down upon it with the ferocity of a wild beast. He saw Gale reach over the Lieutenant's head and swing his arm, saw the knife-blade bury itself in what he held, then saw it rip away, and felt a hot stream spurt into his face. So closely was the Canadian entangled with Stark that he fancied for an instant the weapon had wounded both of them for the trader had aimed at his enemy's neck where it joined the shoulder, but, hampered by the soldier, his blow went astray about four inches. Doret glimpsed Burrell rising from his knees, his arms about the trader's waist, and the next instant the combatants were dragged apart.

The Lieutenant wrenched the dripping blade from Gale's hand; it no longer gleamed, but was warm and slippery in his fingers. Poleon held Stark's gun, which was empty and smoking.

THE BARRIER

The fight had not lasted a minute, and yet what terrible havoc had been wrought! The gambler was drenched with his own blood, which gushed from him, black in the yellow flicker, and so plentifully that the Frenchman was befouled with it, while Gale, too, was horribly stained, but whether from his own or his enemy's veins it was hard to tell. The trader paid no heed to himself nor to the intruders, allowing Burrell to push him back against the wall, the breath wheezing in and out of his lungs, his eyes fastened on Stark.

"I got you, Bennett!" he cried, hoarsely. "Your magic is no good." His teeth showed through his grizzled muzzle like the fangs of some wild animal.

Bennett, or Stark, as the others knew him, lunged about with his captor, trying to get at his enemy, and crying curses on them all, but he was like a child in Poleon's arms. Gradually he weakened, and suddenly resistance died out of him.

"Come away from here," the Lieutenant ordered Gale.

But the old man did not hear, and gathered himself as if to resume the battle with his bare hands, whereupon the soldier, finding himself shaking like a frightened child, and growing physically weak at what he saw, doubted his ability to prevent the encounter, and repeated his command.

"Come away!" he shouted, but the words sounded foolishly flat and inane.

Then Stark spoke intelligibly for the first time.

"Arrest him! You've got to believe what I told you now, Burrell." He poured forth a stream of unspeakable profanity, smitten by the bitter knowledge of his first and only defeat. "You'll hang, Gaylord! I'll see your neck stretched, damn your heart!" To

Poleon he panted, excitedly: "I followed him for fifteen years, Doret. He killed my wife."

"Dat's damn lie!" said the Frenchman.

"No, it isn't. He's under indictment for it back in California. He shot her down in cold blood, then ran off with my kid. That's her he calls Necia. She's mine. Ain't I right, Lieutenant?"

At this final desperate effort to fix the crime upon his rival, Burrell turned on him with loathing.

"It's no use, Stark. We heard you say she killed herself. We were standing outside the door, both of us, and got it from your own lips."

Until this moment the man had stood on his own feet, but now he began to sag, seeing which, Poleon supported him to the bed, where he sank weakly, collapsing in every joint and muscle.

"It's a job," he snarled. "You put this up, you three, and came here to gang me." An unnatural shudder convulsed him as his wounds bit at him, and then he flared up viciously. "But I'll beat you all. I've got the girl! I've got her!"

"Necia!" cried Burrell, suddenly remembering, for this affray had driven all else from his mind.

Stark crouched on the edge of his bunk—a ghastly, gray, grinning thing! One weapon still remained to him, and he used it.

"Yes, I've got my daughter!"

"Where is she?" demanded the trader, hoarsely. "Where's my girl?"

The gambler chuckled; an agony seized him till he hiccoughed and strangled; then, as the spell passed, he laughed again.

"She's got you in her head, like the mother had, but I'll drive it out; I'll treat her like I did her—"

THE BARRIER

Gale uttered a terrible cry and moved upon him, but Burrell shouldered the trader aside, himself possessed by a cold fury that intensified his strength tenfold.

"Stop it, Gale! Let me attend to this. I'll make him tell!"

"Oh, will you?" mocked the girl's father.

"Where is she?"

"None of your damned business." Again he was seized with a paroxysm that left him shivering and his lips colorless. The blankets were soaked and soggy with blood, and his feet rested in a red pool.

"Ben Stark," said the tortured lover, "you're a sick man, and you'll be gone in half an hour at this rate. Won't you do one decent thing before you die?"

"Bah! I'm all right."

"I'll get you a doctor if you'll tell us where she is. If you don't—I'll—let you die. For God's sake, man, speak up!"

The wounded man strove to rise, but could not, then considered for a moment before he said:

"I sent her away."

"Where?"

"Up-river, on that freighter that left last night. She'll go out by Skagway, and I'll join her later, where I can have her to myself. She's forty miles up-river now, and getting farther every minute—oh, you can't catch her!"

The three men stared at one another blankly.

"Why did she go?" said Gale, dully.

"Because I told her who she was, and who you are; because she thinks you killed her mother; because she was glad to get away." Now that he was grown too

JOHN GALE'S HOUR

weak to inflict violent pain, the man lied malevolently, gloating over what he saw in the trader's face.

"Never mind, old man, I'll bring her back," said Burrell, and laid a comforting hand on Gale's shoulder, for the fact that she was safe, the fact of knowing something relieved him immensely; but Stark's next words plunged him into even blacker horror than the trader felt.

"You won't want her if you catch her. Runnion will see to that."

"Runnion!"

"Yes, I sent him with her."

The lover cried out in anguish, and hid his face in his hands.

"He's wanted her for a long time, so I told him to go ahead—"

None of them noticed Poleon Doret, who, upon this unnatural confession, alone seemed to retain sufficient control to doubt and to reason. He was thinking hard, straightening out certain facts, and trying to square this horrible statement with things he had seen and heard to-night. All of a sudden he uttered a great cry, and bolted out into the darkness unheeded by Gale and Burrell, who stood dazed and distraught with a fear greater than that which was growing in Stark at sight of his wounds.

The gambler looked down at his injuries, opened and closed the fingers of his hand as if to see whether he still maintained control of them, then cried out at the two helpless men:

"Well, are you going to let me bleed to death?"

It brought the soldier out of his trance.

"Why—no, no! We'll get a doctor."

But Gale touched him on the shoulder and said:

257

THE BARRIER

"He's too weak to get out. Lock him in, and let him die in the dark."

Stark cursed affrightedly, for it is a terrible thing to bleed to death in the dark, and in spite of himself the Lieutenant wavered.

"I can't do that. I promised."

"He told that lie to my girl. He gave her to that hound," said the trader, but Burrell shoved him through the door.

"No! I can't do that." And then to the wounded man he said, "I'll get a doctor, but God have mercy on your soul." He could not trust himself to talk further with this creature, nor be near him any longer, for though he had a slight knowledge of surgery, he would sooner have touched a loathsome serpent than the flesh of this monstrous man.

He pushed Gale ahead of him, and the old man went like a driven beast, for his violence had wasted itself, and he was like a person under the spell of a strong drug. At the doctor's door Burrell stopped.

"I never thought to ask you," he said, wearily; "but you must be hurt? He must have wounded you?"

"I reckon he did—I don't know." Then the man's listless voice throbbed out achingly, as he cried in despair: "She believed him, boy! She believed his lies! That's what hurts." Something like a sob caught in his throat, and he staggered away under the weight of his great bereavement.

CHAPTER XVII

THE LOVE OF POLEON DORET

TO the girl crouching at the stern of Runnion's boat it seemed as if this day and night would never end. It seemed as if the procession of natural events must have ceased, that there was no longer any time, for she had been suffering steadily for hours and hours without end, and began to wonder dreamily whether she had not skipped a day in her reckoning between the time when she first heard of the strike on her claim and this present moment. It occurred to her that she was a rich girl now in her own right, and she smiled her crooked smile, as she reflected that the thing she had longed for without hope of attainment had come with confusing swiftness, and had left her unhappier than ever. . . .

Would the day never come? She pulled the rugs up closer about her as the morning chill made her shiver. She found herself keeping mechanical count with the sound of the sweeps—they must be making good speed, she thought, and the camp must be miles behind now. Had it been earlier in the season, when the river ran full of drift, they never could have gone thus in the dark, but the water was low and the chances of collision so remote as to render blind travel safe. Even yet she could not distinguish her oarsman, except as a black bulk, for it had been a lowering night

THE BARRIER

"We're not going to get along together, Mr. Runnion—only as far as the Mission. I dare say you can tolerate me until then, can you not?" She said this bitingly.

"Stark told me to board the first boat for St. Michael's," he said, disregarding her sarcasm, "but I've made a few plans of my own the last hour or so."

"St. Michael's! Mr. Stark told you—why, that's impossible! You misunderstood him. He told you to row me to the Mission. I'm going to Father Barnum's house."

"No, you're not, and I didn't misunderstand him. He wants to get you outside, all right, but I reckon you'd rather go as Mrs. Runnion than as the sweetheart of Ben Stark."

"Are you crazy?" the girl cried. "Mr. Stark kindly offered to help me reach the Father at his Mission. I'm nothing to him, and I'm certainly not going to be anything to you. If I'd known you were going to row the boat, I should have stayed at home, because I detest you."

"You'll get over that."

"I'm not in the humor for jokes."

He rested again on his oars, and said, with deliberation:

"Stark 'kindly offered' did he? Well, whenever Ben Stark 'kindly' offers anything, I'm in on the play. He's had his eye on you for the last three months, and he wants you, but he slipped a cog when he gave me the oars. You needn't be afraid, though, I'm going to do the square thing by you. We'll stop in at the Mission and be married, and then we'll see whether we want to go to St. Michael's or not, though personally I'm for going back to Flambeau."

THE LOVE OF POLEON DORET

During the hours while he had waited for Necia to discover his identity, the man's mind had not been idle; he had determined to take what fortune tossed into his lap. Had she been the unknown, unnoticed half-breed of a month or two before, he would not have wasted thought upon priests or vows, but now that a strange fate had worked a change in her before the world, he accepted it.

The girl's beauty, her indifference, the mistaken attitude of Stark urged him, and, strongest of all, he was drawn by his cupidity, for she would be very rich, so the knowing ones said. Doubtless that was why Stark wanted her, and, being a man who acknowledged no fidelity to his kind or his Creator, Runnion determined to outwit his principal, Doret, Burrell, and all the rest. It was a chance to win much at the risk of nothing, and he was too good a gambler to let it pass.

With his brusque declaration Necia realized her position—that she was a weak, lonely girl, just come into womanhood, so cursed by good looks that men wanted her, so stained by birth that they would not take her honestly; realized that she was alone with a dissolute creature and beyond help, and for the first time in her life she felt the meaning of fear.

She saw what a frail and helpless thing she was; nothing about her was great save her soul, and that was immeasurably vexed and worried. She had just lived through a grief that had made her generous, and now she gained her first knowledge of the man-animal's gross selfishness.

"You are absolutely daft," she said. "You can't force me to marry you."

"I ain't going to force you; you'll do it willingly."

"I'll die first. I'll call the first man we see—I'll

tell Father Barnum, and he'll have you run out of the country—it would only take a word from me."

"If you haven't changed your mind when we get to his place, I'll run through without stopping; but there isn't another priest between there and St. Mike's, and by the time we get to the mouth of the river, I guess you'll say yes to most anything. However, I'd rather marry you at Holy Cross if you'll consent, and I'm pretty sure you will—when you think it over."

"We won't discuss it."

"You don't understand yet," he continued, slowly. "What will people say when they know you ran away with me."

"I'll tell them the truth."

"Huh! I'm too well known. No man on the river would ever have you after that."

"You—you—" Her voice was a-quiver with indignation and loathing, but her lips could not frame an epithet fit for him. He continued rowing for some time, then said:

"Will you marry me?"

"No! If this thing is ever known, Poleon will kill you—or father."

For a third time he rested on his oars.

"Now that we've come to threats, let me talk. I offered to marry you and do the square thing, but if you don't want to, I'll pass up the formality and take you for my squaw, the same as your father took Alluna. I guess you're no better than your mother, so your old man can't say much under the circumstances, and if he don't object, Poleon can't. Just remember, you're alone with me in the heart of a wilderness, and you've got to make a choice quick, because I'm going ashore and make some breakfast as soon as it's light

THE LOVE OF POLEON DORET

enough to choose a landing-place. If you agree to come quietly and go through with this thing like a sensible girl, I'll do what's right, but if you don't— then I'll do what's wrong, and maybe you won't be so damned anxious to tell your friends about this trip, or spread your story up and down the river. Make up your mind before I land."

The water gurgled at the bow again, and the rowlocks squeaked. Another hour and then another passed in silence before the girl noted that she no longer seemed to float through abysmal darkness, but that the river showed in muddy grayness just over the gunwale. She saw Runnion more clearly, too, and made out his hateful outlines, though for all else she beheld they might have been miles out upon a placid sea, and so imperceptible was the laggard day's approach that she could not measure the growing light. It was a desolate dawn, and showed no glorious gleams of color. There was no rose-pink glow, no merging of a thousand tints, no final burst of gleaming gold; the night merely faded away, changing to a sickly pallor that grew to ashen gray, and then dissolved the low-hung, distorted shadows a quarter of a mile inland on either hand into a forbidding row of unbroken forest backed by plain, morass, and distant hills untipped by slanting rays. Overhead a bleak ruin of clouds drifted; underneath the river ran, a bilious yellow. The whole country so far as the eye could range was unmarred by the hand of man, untracked save by the feet of the crafty forest people.

She saw Runnion gazing over his shoulder in search of a shelving beach or bar, his profile showing more debased and mean than she had ever noticed it before. They rounded a bend where the left bank crumbled before the untiring teeth of the river, forming a bristling *chevaux-de-frise* of leaning, fallen firs awash in the current. The short side of the curve, the one nearest them, protected a gravel bar that made down-stream to a dagger-like point, and towards this Runnion propelled the skiff. The girl's heart sank and she felt her limbs grow cold.

The mind of Poleon Doret worked in straight lines. Moreover, his memory was good. Stark's statement, which so upset Gale and the Lieutenant, had a somewhat different effect upon the Frenchman, for certain facts had been impressed upon his subconsciousness which did not entirely gibe with the gambler's remarks, and yet they were too dimly engraved to afford foundation for a definite theory. What he did know was this, that he doubted. Why? Because certain scraps of a disjointed conversation recurred to him, a few words which he had overheard in Stark's saloon, something about a Peterborough canoe and a woman. He knew every skiff that lay along the waterfront, and of a sudden he decided to see if this one was where it had been at dusk; for there were but two modes of egress from Flambeau, and there was but one canoe of this type. If Necia had gone up-river on the freighter, pursuit was hopeless, for no boatman could make headway against the current; but if, on the other hand, that cedar craft was gone— He ran out of Stark's house and down to the river-bank, then leaped to the shingle beneath. It was just one chance, and if he was wrong, no matter; the others would leave on the next up-river steamer; whereas, if his suspicion proved a certainty, if Stark had lied to throw them off the track, and Runnion had taken her down-

THE LOVE OF POLEON DORET

stream—well, Poleon wished no one to hinder him, for he would travel light.

The boat *was* gone! He searched the line backward, but it was not there, and his excitement grew now, likewise his haste. Still on the run, he stumbled up to the trading-post and around to the rear, where, bottom up, lay his own craft, the one he guarded jealously, a birch canoe, frail and treacherous for any but a man schooled in the ways of swift water and Indian tricks. He was very glad now that he had not told the others of his suspicions; they might have claimed the right to go, and of that he would not be cheated. He swung the shell over his shoulders, then hurried to the bank and down the steep trail like some great, misshapen turtle. He laid it carefully in the whispering current, then stripped himself with feverish haste, for the driving call of a hot pursuit was on him, and although it was the cold, raw hours of late night, he whipped off his garments until he was bare to the middle. He seized his paddle, stepped in, then knelt amidships and pushed away. The birch-bark answered him like a living thing, leaping and dancing beneath the strokes which sprung the spruce blade and boiled the water to a foam, while rippling, rising ridges stood out upon his back and arms as they rose and fell, stretched and bent and straightened.

A half-luminous, opaque glow was over the waters, but the banks quickly dropped away, until there was nothing to guide him but the suck of the current and the sight of the dim-set stars. His haste now became something crying that lashed him fiercely, for he seemed to be standing still, and so began to mutter at the crawling stream and to complain of his thews, which did not drive him fast enough, only the sound he made was more like the whine of a hound in leash or a wolf that runs with hot nostrils close to the earth.

Runnion drove his Peterborough towards the shore with powerful strokes, and ran its nose up on the gravel, rose, stretched himself, and dragged it farther out, then looked down at Necia.

"Well, what is it, yes or no? Do you want me for a husband or for a master?" She cowered in the stern, a pale, fearful creature, finally murmuring:

"You—you must give me time."

"Not another hour. Here's where you declare yourself; and remember, I don't care which you choose, only you'd better be sensible."

She cast her despairing eyes up and down the river, then at the wilderness on either shore; but it was as silent and unpeopled as if it had been created that morning. She must have time; she would temporize, pretending to yield, and then betray him to the first comer; a promise exacted under duress would not be binding.

"I'll go quietly," she said, in a faint voice.

"I knew you'd see that I'm acting square. Come! Get the cramp out of yourself while I make a pot of coffee." He held out his hand to assist her, and she accepted it, but stumbled as she rose, for she had been crouched in one position for several hours, and her limbs were stiff. He caught her and swung her ashore; then, instead of putting her feet to the ground, he pressed her to himself roughly and kissed her. She gave a stifled cry and fought him off, but he laughed and held her the closer.

"Ain't I good for one kiss? Say, this is the deuce of an engagement. Come, now—"

THE LOVE OF POLEON DORET

"No, no, no!" she gasped, writhing like a wild thing; but he crushed his lips to hers again and then let her go, whereupon she drew away from him panting, dishevelled, her eyes wide and filled with horror. She scrubbed her lips with the back of her hand, as if to erase his mark, while he reached into the canoe and brought forth an axe, a bundle of food, and a coffee-pot; then, still chuckling, he gathered a few sticks of driftwood and built a fire. She had a blind instinct to flee, and sought for a means of escape, but they were well out upon the bar that stretched a distance of three hundred feet to the wooded bank; on one side of the narrow spit was the scarcely moving, half-stagnant water of a tiny bay or eddy, on the other, the swift, gliding current tugging at the beached canoe, while the outer end of the gravelled ridge dwindled down to nothing and disappeared into the river. At sight of the canoe a thought struck her, but her face must have shown some sign of it, for the man chanced to look at the moment, and, seeing her expression, straightened himself, then gazed about searchingly. Without a word he stepped to the boat, and, seizing it, dragged it entirely out upon the bar, where her strength would not be equal to shoving it off quickly, and, not content with this, he made the painter fast, then went back to his fire. The eagerness died out of her face, but an instant later, when he turned to the clearer water of the eddy to fill the coffee-pot, she seized her chance and sped up the bar towards the bank. The shingle under foot and her noisy skirts betrayed her, and with an oath he followed. It was an unequal race, and he handled her with rough, strong hands when he overtook her.

"So! You lied to me! Well, I'm through with this

foolishness. If you'll go back on your word like this you'll 'bawl me out' before the priest, so I'll forget my promise, too, and you'll be glad of the chance to marry me."

"Let me go!" she panted. "I'll marry you. Yes, yes, I'll do it, only don't touch me now!"

He led her back to the fire, which had begun to crackle. She was so weak now that she sank upon the stones shivering.

"That's right! Sit down and behave while I make you something hot to drink. You're all in." After a time he continued, as he busied himself about his task: "Say, you ought to be glad to get me; I've got a lot of money, or I will have, and once you're Mrs. Runnion, nobody 'll ever know about this or think of you as a squaw." He talked to her while he waited for the water to boil, his assurance robbing her of hope, for she saw he was stubborn and reckless, determined to override her will as well as to conquer her body, while under his creed, the creed of his kind, a woman was made from the rib of man and for his service. He conveyed it to her plainly. He ruled horses with a hard hand, he drove his dog teams with a biting lash, and he mastered women with a similar lack of feeling or consideration.

He was still talking when the girl sprang to her feet and sent a shrill cry out over the river, but instantly he was up and upon her, his hand over her mouth, while she tore at it, screaming the name of Poleon Doret. He silenced her to a smothered, sobbing mumble, and turned to see, far out on the bosom of the great soiled river, a man in a bark canoe. The craft had just swung past the bend above, and was still a long way off—so far away, in fact, that Necia's signal had not reached it,

THE LOVE OF POLEON DORET

for its occupant held unwaveringly to the swiftest channel, his body rising and falling in the smooth, unending rhythm of a master-boatman under great haste, his arms up-flung now and then, as the paddle glinted and flashed across to the opposite side.

Runnion glanced about hurriedly, then cursed as he saw no place of concealment. The Peterborough stood out upon the bar conspicuously, as did he and the girl; but the chance remained that this man, whoever he was, would pass by, for his speed was great, the river a mile in width, and the bend sharp. Necia had cried Poleon's name, but her companion saw no resemblance to the Frenchman in this strange-looking voyager; in fact, he could not quite make out what was peculiar about the man—perhaps his eyes were not as sharp as hers—and then he saw that the boatman was naked to the waist. By now he was drawing opposite them with the speed of a hound. The girl, gagged and held by her captor's hands, struggled and moaned despairingly, and, crouching back of the boat, they might have escaped discovery in the gray morning light had it not been for the telltale fire—a tiny, crackling blaze no larger than a man's hat. It betrayed them. The dancing craft upon which their eyes were fixed whipped about, almost leaping from the water at one stroke, then came towards them, now nothing but a narrow thing, half again the width of a man's body. The current carried it down abreast of them, then past, and Runnion rose, releasing the girl, who cried out with all her might to the boatman. He made no sound in reply, but drove his canoe shoreward with quicker strokes. It was evident he would effect his landing near the lower end of the spit, for now he was within hearing distance, and driving closer every instant.

THE BARRIER

Necia heard the gambler call:

"Sheer off, Doret! You can't land here!"

She saw a gun in Runnion's hand, and a terrible, sickening fear swept over her, for he was slowly walking down the spit, keeping abreast of the canoe as it drifted. She could see exactly what would happen: no man could disembark against the will of an armed marksman, and if Poleon slackened his stroke, or stopped it to exchange his paddle for a weapon, the current would carry him past; in addition, he would have to fire from a rocking paper shell harried by a boiling current, whereas the other man stood flat upon his feet.

"Keep away or I'll fire!" threatened Runnion again; and she screamed, "Don't try it, Poleon, he'll kill you!"

At her words Runnion raised his weapon and fired. She heard the woods behind reverberate with the echoes like a sounding-board, saw the white spurt of smoke and the skitter of the bullet as it went wide. It was a long shot, and had been fired as a final warning; but Doret made no outcry, nor did he cease coming; instead, his paddle clove the water with the same steady strokes that took every ounce of effort in his body. Runnion threw open his gun and replaced the spent shell. On came the careening, crazy craft in a sidewise drift, and with it the girl saw coming a terrible tragedy. She started to run down the gravelled ridge behind her enemy, not realizing the value or moment of her action, nor knowing clearly what she would do; but as she drew near she saw Runnion raise his gun again, and, without thought of her own safety, threw herself upon him. Again his shot went wide as he strove to hurl her off, but his former taste of her strength was nothing to this, now that she fought for Poleon's life. Runnion snarled

NECIA SAW RUNNION RAISE HIS GUN, AND WITHOUT THOUGHT OF HER OWN SAFETY, THREW HERSELF UPON HIM

THE LOVE OF POLEON DORET

angrily and thrust her away, for he had waited till the canoe was close.

"Let me go, you devil!" he cried, and aimed again; but again she ran at him. This time, however, she did not pit her strength against his, but paused, and as he undertook to fire she thrust at his elbow, then dodged out of his way. Her blow was crafty and well-timed, and his shot went wild. Again he took aim, and again she destroyed it with a touch and danced out of his reach. She was nimble and light, and quickened now by a cold calculation of all that depended upon her.

Three times in all she thwarted Runnion, while the canoe drove closer every instant. On the fourth, as she dashed at him, he struck to be rid of her, cursing wickedly—struck as he would have struck at a man. Silently she crumpled up and fell, a pitiful, draggled, awkward little figure sprawled upon the rocks; but the delay proved fatal to him, for, though the canoe was close against the bank, and the huge man in it seemed to offer a mark too plain to be missed, he was too close to permit careful aim. Runnion heard him giving utterance to a strange, feral, whining sound, as if he were crying like a fighting boy; then, as the gambler raised his arm, the Canadian lifted himself up on the bottom of the canoe until he stood stretched to his full height, and leaped. As Runnion fired he sprang out and was into the water to his knees, his backward kick whirling the craft from underneath him out into the current, where the river seized it. He had risen and jumped all in one moment, launching himself at the shore like a panther. The gun roared again, but Poleon came up and on with the rush of the great, brown grizzly that no missile can stop. Run-

"He don' trouble you no more."

"He tried—he— Ugh! I—I'm glad you did it!" She broke down, trembling at her escape, until her selfishness smote her, and she was up and beside him on the instant. "Are you hurt? Oh, I never thought of that. You must be wounded!"

The Frenchman felt himself over, and looked down at his limbs for the first time. "No! I guess not," he said, at which Necia noticed his meagre attire, and simultaneously he became conscious of it. He fell away a pace, casting his eyes over the river for his canoe, which was now a speck in the distance.

"Ba gosh! I'm hell of a t'ing for lookin' at," he said. "I'm paddle hard—dat's w'y. Sacré! how I sweat!" He hitched nervously at the band of his overalls, while Necia answered:

"That's all right, Poleon." Then, without warning, her face froze with mingled repulsion and wonder. "Look! Look!" she whispered, pointing past him.

Runnion was moving slowly, crawling painfully into a sitting posture, uplifting a terribly mutilated face, dazed and half conscious, groping for possession of his wits. He saw them, and grimaced frightfully, cowering and cringing.

Poleon felt the girl's hand upon his arm, and heard her crying in a hard, sharp voice:

"He needs killing! Put him away!"

He stared down at his gentle Necia, and saw the loathing in her face and the look of strange ferocity as she met his eyes boldly.

"You don't know what he—what he did," she said, through her shut teeth. "He—" But the man waited to hear no more.

Runnion saw him coming, and scrambled frantically

THE LOVE OF POLEON DORET

to all-fours, then got on his feet and staggered down the bar. As Poleon overtook him, he cried out piteously, a shrill scream of terror, and, falling to his knees, grovelled and debased himself like a foul cripple at fear of the lash. His agony dispelled the savage taint of Alluna's aboriginal training in Necia, and the pure white blood of her ancestors cried out:

"Poleon, Poleon! Not that!" She hurried after him to where he paused above the wretch waiting for her. "You mustn't!" she said. "That would be murder, and—and—it's all over now."

The Frenchman looked at her wonderingly, not comprehending this sudden leniency.

"Let him alone; you've nearly killed him; that's enough." Whereat Runnion, broken in body and spirit, began to beg for his life.

"W'at's dat you say jus' now?" Doret asked the girl. "Was dat de truth for sure w'at you speak?"

"Yes, but you've done your work. Don't touch him again."

He hesitated, and Runnion, quick to observe it, added his entreaty to hers.

"I'm beaten, Doret. You broke me to pieces. I need help—I—I'm hurt."

"W'at you 'spec' I do wit' 'im?" the Canadian asked, and she answered:

"I suppose we'll have to take him where he can get assistance."

"Dat skiff ain' carry all t'ree of us."

"I'll stay here," groaned the frightened man. "I'll wait for a steamer to pick me up, but for God's sake don't touch me again!"

Poleon looked him over carefully, and made up his mind that the man was more injured in spirit than in

277

THE BARRIER

"How did you leave him? Is he badly injured?"

"No, I bus' it up on de face an' de rib, but she's feelin' good now. Yes. I'm leave 'im nice place for stop an' wait on de steamboat—plaintee spruce bough for set on."

She began to shudder again, and, sensitive to her every motion, he asked, solicitously, if she were sick, but she shook her head.

"I—I—was thinking what—supposing you hadn't come? Oh, Poleon! you don't know what you saved me from." She leaned forward and laid a tiny, grateful hand on the huge brown paw that rested on his oar. "I wonder if I can ever forget?"

She noted that they were running with the current, and inquired:

"Where are we going?"

"Wal, I can't pull dis boat 'gainst dat current, so I guess we pass on till I fin' my shirt, den bimebye we pick it up some steamboat an' go home."

Five miles below his quick eye detected his half-submerged "bark" lodged beneath some overhanging firs which, from the water's action, had fallen forward into the stream, and by rare good-fortune it was still upright, although awash. He towed it to the next sand-bar, where he wrung out and donned his shirt, then tipped the water from the smaller craft, and, making it fast astern of the Peterborough, set out again. Towards noon they came in sight of a little stern-wheeled craft that puffed and pattered manfully against the sweeping current, hiding behind the points and bars and following the slackest water.

"It's the Mission boat!" cried Necia. "It's the Mission boat! Father Barnum will be aboard."

She waved her arms madly and mingled her voice

THE LOVE OF POLEON DORET

with Poleon's until a black-robed figure appeared beside the pilot-house.

"Father Barnum!" she screamed, and, recognizing her, he signalled back.

Soon they were alongside, and a pair of Siwash deck-hands lifted Necia aboard, Doret following after, the painter of the Peterborough in his teeth. He dragged both canoes out of the boiling tide, and laid them bottom up on the forward deck, then climbed the narrow little stairs to find Necia in the arms of a benignant, white-haired priest, the best-beloved man on the Yukon, who broke away from the girl to greet the Frenchman, his kind face alight with astonishment.

"What is all this I hear? Slowly, Doret, slowly! My little girl is talking too furiously for these poor old wits to follow. I can't understand; I am amazed. What is this tale?

Together they told him, while his blue eyes now opened wide with wonder, now grew soft with pity, then blazed with indignation. When they had finished he laid his hand upon Doret's shoulder.

"My son, I thank God for your good body and your clean heart. You saved our Necia, and you will be rewarded. As to this—this—man Runnion, we must find him, and he must be sent out of the country; this new, clean land of ours is no place for such as he. You will be our pilot, Poleon, and guide us to the spot."

It required some pressure to persuade the Frenchman, but at last he consented; and as the afternoon drew to a close the little steamboat came squattering and wheezing up to the bar where Runnion had built his fire that morning, and a long, shrill blast summoned him from the point above. When he did not appear the priest took Poleon and his round-faced, silent crew of two and went up the bank, but they found no sign of the crippled man, only a few rags, a trampled patch of brush at the forest's edge, and—that was all. The springy moss showed no trail; the thicket gave no answer to their cries, although they spent an hour in a scattered search and sounded the steamboat's whistle again and again.

"He's try for walk it back to camp," said Doret. "Mebbe he ain' hurt so much, after all."

"You must be right," said Father Barnum. "We will keep the steamer close to this shore, so that he can hail us when we overtake him."

And so they resumed their toilsome trip; but mile after mile fell behind them, and still no voice came from the woods, no figure hailed them. Doret, inscrutable and silent, lounged against the pilot-house smoking innumerable cigarettes, which he rolled from squares of newspaper, his keen eyes apparently scanning every foot of their slow way; but when night fell, at last, and the bank faded from sight, he tossed the last butt overboard, smiled grimly into the darkness, and went below.

CHAPTER XVIII

RUNNION FINDS THE SINGING PEOPLE

"NO CREEK" LEE came into the trading-post on the following morning, and found Gale attending store as if nothing unusual had occurred.

"Say! What's this about you and Stark? I hear you had a horrible run-in, and that you split him up the back like a quail."

"We had a row," admitted the trader. "It's been a long time working out, and last night it came to a head."

"Lord—ee! And to think of Ben Stark's bein' licked! Why, the whole camp's talkin' about it! They say he emptied two six-shooters at you, but you kept a-comin', and when you did get to him you just carved your initials on him like he was a bass-wood tree. Say, John, he's a goner, sure."

"Do you mean he's—passing out?"

"Oh no! I reckon he'll get well, from what I hear, though he won't let nobody come near him except old Doc; but he's lost a battle, and that ends him. Don't you savvy? Whenever a killer quits second best, it breaks his hoodoo. Why, there's been men laying for him these twenty years, from here to the Rio Grande, and every feller he ever bested will hear of this and begin to grease his holster; then the first shave-tail desperado that meets him will spit in his eye, just to make a name for himself. No, sir! He's a spent shell. He's got to fight all his battles over again, and this time the other feller will open the ball. Oh, I've seen it happen before. You killed him last night, just as sure as if you'd hung up his hide to dry, and he knows it."

"I'm a peaceable man," said Gale, on the defensive. "I had to do it."

"I know! I know! There was witnesses—this dressmaker at the fort seen it, so I hear."

The other acquiesced silently.

"Well! Well! Ben Stark licked! I can't get over that. It must 'a' been somethin' powerful strong to make you do it, John." It was as close to a question as the miner dared come, although he was avid with curiosity, and, like the entire town, was in a fret to know what lay back of this midnight encounter, concerning which the most exaggerated rumors were rife. These stories grew the more grotesque and ridiculous the longer the truth remained hidden, for Stark could not be seen, and neither Gale nor Burrell would speak. All that the people knew was that one lay wounded to death behind the dumb walls of his cabin, and that the other had brought him down. When the old man vouchsafed no more than a nod to his question, the prospector inquired:

"Where's Poleon? I've got news for him from the creek."

"I don't know; he's gone."

"Back soon?"

"I don't know. Why?"

"His laymen have give up. They've cross-cut his ground and the pay ain't there, so they've quit work for good."

RUNNION FINDS THE SINGING PEOPLE

"He drew a blank, eh?"

"Worse'n that—three of them. The creek is spotteder than a leopard. Runnion's men, for instance, are into it bigger than a house, while Poleon's people can't raise a color. I call it tough luck—yes, worse'n tough: it's hard-biled and pickled. To them as has shall it be given, and to them as hasn't shall be took even what they 'ain't got, as the poet says. Look at Necia! She'll be richer than a cream puff. Guess I'll step around and see her."

"She's gone," said the trader, wearily, turning his haggard face from the prospector.

"Gone! Where?"

"Up-river with Runnion. They got her away from me last night."

"Sufferin' snakes!" ejaculated Lee. "So that's why!" Then he added, simply, "Let's go and git her, John."

The trader looked at him queerly.

"Maybe I won't—on the first boat! I'm eating my heart out hour by hour waiting—waiting—waiting for some kind of a craft to come, and so is Burrell."

"What's he got to do with it?" said the one-eyed miner, jealously. "Can't you and me bring her back?"

"He'll marry her! God, won't there never be a boat!"

For the hundredth time that morning he went to the door of the post and strained his eyes down-stream.

"Well, well! Them two goin' to be married," said Lee. "Stark licked, and Necia goin' to be married—all at once. I hate to see it, John; he ain't good enough; she could 'a' done a heap better. There's a lot of reg'lar men around here, and she could 'a' had her pick. Of course, always bein' broke like a dog myself, I 'ain't kept up my personal appearance like I'd ought, but I've got some new clothes now, and you wouldn't know me. I bought 'em off a tenderfoot with cold feet, but they're the goods, and you'd see a big improvement in me."

"He's a good man," said Gale. "Better than you or me, and he's all torn up over this. I never saw a man act so. When he learned about it I thought he'd go mad—he's haunted the river-bank ever since, raging about for some means of following her, and if I hadn't fairly held him he'd have set out single-handed."

"I'm still strong in the belief that Necia could have bettered her hand by stayin' out awhile longer," declared Lee, stubbornly; "but if she wants a soldier, why, we'll get one for her, only I'd rather have got her somethin' real good and pronounced in the military line—like an agitant-gen'ral or a walkin' delegate."

While they were talking Burrell came in, and "No Creek" saw that the night had affected the youth even more than it had Gale, or at least he showed the marks more plainly, for his face was drawn, his eyes were sunken as if from hunger, and his whole body seemed to have fallen away till his uniform hung upon him loose, unkempt, and careless. It was as if hope had been a thing of avoirdupois, and when taken away had caused a shrinkage. He had interrogated Stark again after getting the doctor, but the man had only cursed at him, declaring that his daughter was out of reach, where he would take care to keep her, and torturing the lover anew by linking Runnion's name with the girl's till the young man fled from the sound of the monster's voice back to his own quarters. He strove to keep the image of Runnion out of his mind, for his reason could not endure it. At such times he cried

RUNNION FINDS THE SINGING PEOPLE

aloud, cursing in a way that was utterly strange to a God-fearing man, only to break off and rush to the other extreme, praying blindly, beseechingly, for the girl's safe-keeping. At intervals an unholy impulse almost drove him to Stark's cabin to finish the work Gale had begun, to do it coldly as a matter of justice, for was he not the one who had put Necia into the hands of that ruffian? Greeting Lee mechanically, he said to Gale:

"I can't wait much longer," and sank wearily into a seat. Almost the next instant he was on his feet again, saying to the trader, as he had said it a score of times already: "Runnion comes to me, Gale! You understand he's mine, don't you?"

The old man nodded. "Yes! You can take him."

"Well, who do *I* git?" asked Lee.

"You can't come along," the trader said. "We may have to follow the hound clean to the States. Think of your mine—"

"To hell with the mine!" exploded the shaggy prospector. "I reckon I'm kind of a daddy to your gal, and I'm goin' to be in at the finish."

Back and forth paced the Lieutenant restlessly, pausing every now and then to peer down the river. Suddenly he uttered a cry, and with a bound Gale was beside him, Lee at his shoulder.

"Look! Over the point! Down yonder! I saw smoke!"

The three stared at the distant forest fringe that masked the bend of the river until their eyes ached, and the dark-green grew black and wavered indistinctly.

"You're tired, my boy," said Gale.

"Wait!"

THE BARRIER

They obeyed, and finally over the tree-tops saw a faint streamer of black.

"It is! It is!" cried the soldier. "I'm going for my war bag." And before the steamboat had hove into sight he was back with his scanty bundle of baggage, behaving like one daft, talking and laughing and running here and there. Lee watched him closely, then went behind the bar and poured out a stiff glass of whiskey, which he made Burrell drink. To Gale he whispered, a moment later:

"Keep your eye on him, John—he'll go mad at this rate."

They waited, it seemed interminably, until at last a white hull slowly rounded the point, then shaped a course across the current towards the other bank, where the water was less swift. As it came fully into sight, Gale swore aloud in despair:

"It's the Mission boat!"

"Well, what of that?" said Burrell. "We'll hire it—buy it—take it!"

"It's no use; she ain't got but three dog-power to her engines," Lee explained. "She's a down-river boat—has to run with the current to move."

"We can't use her," Gale gave in, reluctantly. "She'd only lose time for us. We've got to wait for one of the A. C. boats."

"Wait!" cried Burrell. "Good God! we've done nothing but wait, *wait*, WAIT! Let's *do* something!"

"You go back yonder and set down," commanded Lee. "We'll have a boat before long."

The arrival of the tiny Mission steamer was never of sufficient importance to draw a crowd to the river-bank, so the impatient men at the post relaxed interest in her as she came creeping up abreast of the town. It

RUNNION FINDS THE SINGING PEOPLE

was little Johnny Gale who first saw Necia and Poleon on board, for he had recognized Father Barnum's craft at a distance, and stationed himself at the bank hand-in-hand with Molly to bid the good, kind old man welcome.

The men inside the house did not hear the boy crying Necia's name, for his voice was small, and they had gone to the rear of the store.

"Understand! You leave Runnion to me," Burrell was saying. "No man shall lay hands on him except me—" His voice trailed away; he rose slowly to his feet, a strange light on his face. The others turned to see what sight had drawn his eyes. In the opening, all splendid with the golden sunlight, stood Necia and Poleon Doret, who had her by the hand—and she was smiling!

Gale uttered a great cry and went to meet them, but the soldier could move nothing save his lips, and stood dazed and disbelieving. He saw them dimly coming towards him, and heard Poleon's voice as if at a great distance, saw that the Frenchman's eyes were upon him, and that his words were directed to him.

"I bring her back to you, M'sieu'!"

Doret laid Necia's hand in that of her lover, and Burrell saw her smiling shyly up at him. Something gripped him chokingly, and he could utter no sound. There was nothing to say—she was here, safe, smiling, that was all. And the girl, beholding the glory in his eyes, understood.

Gale caught her away from him then, and buried her in his arms.

A woman came running into the store, and, seeing the group, paused at the door—a shapeless, silent, shawled figure in silhouette against the day. The

THE BARRIER

trader brought the girl to her foster-mother, who began to talk in her own tongue with a rapidity none of them had ever heard before, her voice as tender as some wild bird's song; then the two women went away together around the store into the house. Poleon had told Necia all the amazing story that had come to him that direful night, all that he had overheard, all that he knew, and much that he guessed.

The priest came into the store shortly, and the men fell upon him for information, for nothing was to be gained from Poleon, who seemed strangely fagged and weary, and who had said but little.

"Yes, yes, yes!" laughed Father Barnum. "I'll tell you all I know, of course, but first I must meet Lieutenant Burrell and take him by the hand."

The story did not lose in his telling, particularly when he came to describe the fight on the gravel bar which no man had seen, and of which Poleon had told him little; but the good priest was of a militant turn, and his blue eyes glittered and flashed like an old crusader's.

"It was a wondrous combat," he declared, with all the spirit of a spectator, "for Poleon advanced barehanded and beat him down even as the man fired into his face. It is due to the goodness and mercy of God that he was spared a single wound from this desperado —a miracle vouchsafed because of his clean heart and his righteous cause."

"But where is Runnion?" broke in Burrell.

"Nursing his injuries at some wood-cutter's camp, no doubt; but God be praised for that double spirit of generosity and forgiveness which prompted our Poleon to spare the wretch. No finer thing have I known in all my life, Doret, even though you have ever been an ungodly fellow."

RUNNION FINDS THE SINGING PEOPLE

The Frenchman moved uneasily.

"Wal, I don' know; he ain' fight so dam' hard."

"You couldn't find no trace of him?" said Lee.

"No trace whatever," Father Barnum replied; "but he will surely reach some place of refuge where we can pick him up, for the days are still mild and the woods full of berries, and, as you know, the streams overflow with salmon, which he can kill with a stick. Why, a man might live a fortnight without inconvenience!"

"I'll be on the lookout for him," said the Lieutenant, grimly. "To-night I'll send Thomas and a couple of men down the river."

When the voluble old priest had at last exhausted his narrative he requested of Burrell the privilege of a few words, and drew him apart from the others. His face was shrewdly wrinkled and warm with understanding.

"I had a long conversation with my little girl, for she is like a daughter to me, and I discovered the depth of her love for you. Do you think you are worthy of her?"

"No."

"Do you love her as much as you should?"

"As much as I can. They don't make words or numbers big enough to tell you how dear she is to me."

"Then why delay? To-morrow I leave again, and one never knows what a day may bring forth."

"But Stark?" the young man cried. "He's her father, you know; he's like a madman, and she's still under age."

"I know very little of law outside of the Church," the Father observed, "but, as I understand it, if she marries before he forbids her, the law will hold him powerless. Now, he has never made himself known to her, he has never forbidden her anything; and although my conclusion may not be correct, I believe it is, and you have a chance if you make haste. At your age, my boy, I never needed a spur."

"A spur? Good Lord! I'm from Kentucky."

"Once she is yours before God, your hold will be stronger in the eyes of men. If I am wrong, and he takes her from you—well, may some other priest rewed you two—I sha'n't!"

"Don't worry," laughed Burrell, ablaze at the thought. "You're the only preacher who'll kiss my bride, for I'm a jealous man, and all the Starks and all the fathers in the world won't get her away from me. Do you think she'll do it?"

"A woman in love will do anything."

Burrell seized the little man by the hand. "If I had known more law you needn't have given me this hint."

"I must go now to this Stark," said the Father; "he may need me. But first I shall talk with Necia. Poor child, she is in a difficult position, standing between the love of John Gale and the loyalty she owes her father. I—I fear I cannot counsel her as well as I ought, for I am very weak and human. You had better come with me; perhaps the plea of a lover may have more weight than the voice of reason." As they started towards the house, he continued, energetically: "Young man, I'm beginning to live once more. Do you know, sometimes I think I was not designed for this vocation, and, just between you and me, there was a day when—" He paused and coughed a trifle, then said, sharply, "Well, what are you waiting for?"

Together they went into the trader's house.

Back in the store there was silence after the priest and the soldier went out, which Gale broke at last:

RUNNION FINDS THE SINGING PEOPLE

"This forgiveness talk is all right, I suppose — but *I want Runnion!*"

"We'll git him, too," growled Lee, at which Poleon uttered a curt exclamation:

"No!"

"Why not?" said the miner.

"Wal," the Canadian drawled, slowly, then paused to light the cigarette he had rolled in a bit of wrapping-paper, inhaled the smoke deeply to the bottom of his lungs, held it there a moment, and blew it out through mouth and nostrils before adding, "you'll jus' be wastin' tam'!"

Gale looked up from beneath his thatch of brow, and asked, quietly:

"Why?"

"You 'member—story I tol' you wan day, two, t'ree mont' ago," Poleon remarked, with apparent evasion, "'bout Johnny Platt w'at I ketch on de Porcupine all et up by skeeter-bugs?"

"I do," answered Gale.

"Wal," — he met their eyes squarely, then drew another long breath from his cigarette — "I'm jus' hopin' nobody don' pick it up dis Runnion feller de same way. Mebbe dey fin' hees han's tie' behin' 'im wit' piece of hees shirt—"

"Good God!" cried the trader, starting to his feet. "You—you—"

"—of course, I'm jus' s'posin'. He was feel purty good w'en I lef'. He was feel so good I tak' hees coat for keepin' off dem bugs from me, biccause I lef' it my own shirt on de canoe. He's nice feller dat way; he give up easy. Ba gosh! I never see worse place for skeeters!"

Gale fell silent, and "No Creek" Lee began to swear

in little, useless, ineffective oaths, which were but two ways of showing similar emotions. Then the former stepped up and laid a big hand upon Poleon's shoulder.

"That saves us quite a trip," he said, but "No Creek" Lee continued to swear softly.

It seemed that Poleon's wish was to be gratified, for no news of the missing man came through in the days that followed. Only at a fishing village far down the river, where a few native families had staked their nets and weirs for salmon, a hunter told a strange tale to his brothers—a tale of the white man's idiosyncrasies. In sooth, they were a strange people, he observed, surpassing wise in many things, yet ignorant and childish in all others, else why should a half-naked man go wandering idly through the thickets holding a knotted rag behind his back, and that when the glades were dense and the moss-chinks filled with the singing people who lived for blood? The elders of the village nodded their heads sagely, and commended the hunter for holding aloof from the inert body, for the foolishness of this man was past belief, and—well, his people were swift and cruel in their vengeance, and sometimes doubted an Indian's word, wherefore it were best to pay no heed to their ways and say nothing. But they continued to wonder why.

Father Barnum found the three still talking in the store when he had finished an hour's counsel with Necia, so came straight to the point. It was work that delighted his soul, for he loved the girl, and had formed a strong admiration for Burrell. Two of them took his announcement quietly, the other cried out strenuous objections. It was the one-eyed miner.

RUNNION FINDS THE SINGING PEOPLE

"Right away! Not on your life! It's too onexpected. You've got to hold 'em apart for an hour, anyhow, till I get dressed." He slid down from his seat upon the counter. "What do you reckon I got all them clothes for?"

"Come as you are," urged the Father, but Lee fought his point desperately.

"I'll bust it up if you don't gimme time. What's an hour or two when they've got a life sentence comin' to 'em. Dammit, you jest ought to see them clothes!" And by very force of his vociferations he succeeded in exacting the promise of a brief stay in the proceedings before he bolted out, the rags of his yellow mackinaw flapping excitedly.

The priest returned to Necia, leaving the trader and Poleon alone.

"I s'pose it's best," said the former.

"Yes!"

"Beats the deuce, though, how things work out, don't it?"

"I'm glad for see dis day," said the Frenchman. "He's good man, an' he ain' never goin' to hurt her none." He paused. "Dere's jus' wan t'ing I want for ask it of you, John—you 'member dat day we stop on de birch grove, an' you spik 'bout her an' tol' me dose story 'bout her moder? Wal, I was dreamin' dat tam', so I'm goin' ask it you now don' never tell her w'at I said."

"Doesn't she know, my boy?"

"No; I ain' never spoke 'bout love. She t'inks I'm broder wit' her, an'—dat's w'at I am, ba Gar!" He could not hold his voice even—it broke with him; but he avoided the old man's gaze. Gale took him by the shoulders.

"There ain't nothing so cruel in the world as a gentle

THE BARRIER

woman," said he; "but she wouldn't hurt you for all the world, Poleon; only the blaze of this other thing has blinded her. She can't see nothing for the light of this new love of hers."

"I know! Dat's w'y—nobody onderstan's but you an' me—"

Gale looked out through the open door, past the sunlit river which came from a land of mystery and vanished into a valley of forgetfulness, past the forest and the hills, in his deep-set eyes the light of a wondrous love that had lived with him these many weary years, and said:

"Nobody else *can* understand but me—I know how it is. I had even a harder thing to bear, for you'll know she's happy at least, while I—" His voice trembled, but, after a pause, he continued: "They neither of them understand what you've done for them, for it was you that brought her back; but some time they'll learn how great their debt is and thank you. It 'll take them years and years, however, and when they do they'll tell their babes of you, Poleon, so that your name will never die. I loved her mother, but I don't think I could have done what you did."

"She's purty hard t'ing, for sure, but I ain' t'ink 'bout Poleon Doret none w'en I'm doin' it. No, I'm t'ink 'bout her all de tam'. She's li'l' gal, an' I'm beeg, strong feller w'at don' matter much an' w'at ain' know much—'cept singin', an' lovin' her. I'm see for sure now dat I ain' fit for her—I'm beeg, rough, fightin' feller w'at can't read, an' she's de beam of sunlight w'at blin' my eyes."

"If I was a fool I'd say you'd forget in time, but I've lived my life in the open, and I know you won't. I didn't."

RUNNION FINDS THE SINGING PEOPLE

"I don' want to forget," the brown man cried, hurriedly. "Le bon Dieu would not let me forget—it's all I've got to keep wit' me w'en I'm lookin' for my 'New Countree.'"

"You're not goin' to look for that 'New Country' any more," Gale replied.

"To-day," said the other, quietly.

"No."

"To-day! Dis affernoon! De blood in me is callin' for travel, John. I'm livin' here on dis place five year dis fall, an' dat's long tam' for voyageur. I'm hongry for hear de axe in de woods an' de moose blow at sundown. I want for see the camp-fire t'rough de brush w'en I come from trap de fox an' dem little wild fellers. I want to smell smoke in de dusk. My work she's finish here, so I'm paddle away to-day, an' I'll fin' dat place dis tam', for sure—she's over dere." He raised his long arm and pointed to the dim mountains that hid the valley of the Koyukuk, the valley that called good men and strong, year after year, and took them to itself, while in his face the trader saw the hunger of his race, the unslaked longing for the wilderness, the driving desire that led them ever North and West, and, seeing it, he knew the man would go.

"Have you heard the news from the creeks?"

"No."

"Your claims are blanks; your men have quit."

The Frenchman shook his head sadly, then smiled—a wistful little smile.

"Wal, it's better I lose dan you—or Necia; I ain' de lucky kin', dat's all; an', affer all, w'at good to me is riche gol'-mine? I ain' got no use for money—any more."

They stood in the doorway together, two rugged,

THE BARRIER

stalwart figures, different in blood and birth and every other thing, yet brothers withal, whom the ebb and flow of the far places had thrown together and now drew apart again. And they were sad, these two, for their love was deeper than comes to other people, and they knew this was farewell; so they remained thus side by side, two dumb, sorrowful men, until they were addressed by a person who hurried from the town.

He came as an apparition bearing the voice of "No Creek" Lee, the mining king, but in no other way showing sign or symbol of their old friend. Its style of face and curious outfit were utterly foreign to the miner, for he had been bearded with the robust, unkempt growth of many years, tanned to a leathery hue, and garbed perennially in the habit of a scarecrow, while this creature was shaved and clipped and curried, and the clothes it stood up in were of many startling hues. Its face was scraped so clean of whiskers as to be a pallid white, but lack of adornment ended at this point and the rest was overladen wondrously, while from the centre of the half-brown, half-white face the long, red nose of Lee ran out. Beside it rolled his lonesome eye, alive with excitement.

He came up with a strut, illumining the landscape, and inquired:

"Well, how do I look?"

"I'm darned if I know," said Gale. "But it's plumb unusual."

"These here shoes leak," said the spectacle, pulling up his baggy trousers to display his tan footgear, "because they was made for dry goin'—that's why they left the tops off; but they've got a nice, healthy color, ain't they? As a whole, it seems to me I'm sort of nifty." He revolved slowly before their admiring gaze, and while to one versed in the manners of the Far East it would have been evident that the original owner of these clothes had come from somewhere beyond the Susquehanna, and had either been a football player or had travelled with a glee club, to these three Northmen it seemed merely that here was the modish echo of a distant civilization.

"W'at's de matter on your face?" said Poleon. "You been fightin'?"

"I ain't shaved in a long time, and this here excitement has kind of shattered my nerves. I didn't have no lookin'-glass, neither, in my shack, so I had to use a lard-can cover. Does it look bad?"

"Not to my way of thinkin'," said Gale, allaying "No Creek's" anxiety. "It's more desp'rate than bad, but it sort of adds expression." At which the miner's pride burst bounds.

"I'll kindly ask you to note the shirt—ten dollars a copy, that's all! I got it from the little Jew down yonder. See them red spear-heads on the boosum? 'Flower dee Lizzies,' which means 'calla lilies' in French. Every one of 'em cost me four bits. On the level—how am I?"

"I never see no harness jus' lak it mese'f!" exclaimed Doret. "You look good 'nough for tin-horn gambler. Say, don' you wear no necktie wit' dem kin' of clothes?"

"No, sir! Not me. I'm a rude, rough miner, and I dress the part. Low-cut, blushin' shoes and straw hats I can stand for, likewise collars—they go hand-in-hand with pay-streaks; but a necktie ain't neither wore for warmth nor protection; it's a pomp and a vanity, and I'm a plain man without conceit. Now, let's proceed with the obsequies."

It was a very simple, unpretentious ceremony that took place inside the long, low house of logs, and yet it was a wonderful thing to the dark, shy maid who hearkened so breathlessly beside the man she had singled out—the clean-cut man in uniform, who stood so straight and tall, making response in a voice that had neither fear nor weakness in it. When they had done he turned and took her reverently in his arms and kissed her before them all; then she went and stood beside Gale and the red wife who was no wife, and said, simply:

"I am very happy."

The old man stooped, and for the first time in her memory pressed his lips to hers, then went out into the sunlight, where he might be alone with himself and the memory of that other Merridy, the woman who, to him, was more than all the women of the world; the woman who, each day and night, came to him, and with whom he had kept faith. The burden she had laid upon him had been heavy, but he had borne it long and uncomplainingly; and now he was very glad, for he had kept his covenant.

The first word of the wedding was borne by Father Barnum, who went alone to the cabin where the girl's father lay, entering with trepidation; for, in spite of the pleas of justice and humanity, this stony-hearted, amply hated man had certain rights which he might choose to enforce; hence, the good priest feared for the peace of his little charge, and approached the stricken man with apprehension. He was there a long time alone with Stark, and when he returned to Gale's house he would answer no questions.

"He is a strange man—a wonderfully strange man: unrepentant and wicked; but I can't tell you what he said. Have a little patience and you will soon know."

The mail boat, which had arrived an hour after the

RUNNION FINDS THE SINGING PEOPLE

Mission boat, was ready to continue its run when, just as it blew a warning blast, down the street of the camp came a procession so strange for this land that men stopped, eyed it curiously, and whispered among themselves. It was a blanketed man upon a stretcher, carried by a doctor and a priest. The face was muffled so that the idlers could not make it out; and when they inquired, they received no answer from the carriers, who pursued their course impassively down the runway to the water's edge and up the gang-plank to the deck. When the boat had gone, and the last faint cough of its towering stacks had died away, Father Barnum turned to his friends:

"He has gone away, not for a day, but for all time. He is a strange man, and some things he said I could not understand. At first I feared greatly, for when I told him what had occurred—of Necia's return and of her marriage—he became so enraged I thought he would burst open his wounds and die from his very fury; but I talked a long, long time with him, and gradually I came to know somewhat of his queer, disordered soul. He could not bring himself to face defeat in the eyes of men, or to see the knowledge of it in their bearing; therefore, he fled. He told me that he would be a hunted animal all his life; that the news of his whipping would travel ahead of him; and that his enemies would search him out to take advantage of him. This I could not grasp, but it seemed a big thing in his eyes—so big that he wept. He said the only decent thing he could or would do was to leave the daughter he had never known to that happiness he had never experienced, and wished me to tell her that she was very much like her mother, who was the best woman in the world."

CHAPTER XIX

THE CALL OF THE OREADS

THERE was mingled rejoicing and lamentation in the household of John Gale this afternoon. Molly and Johnny were in the throes of an overwhelming sorrow, the noise of which might be heard from the barracks to the Indian village. They were sparing of tears as a rule, but when they did give way to woe they published it abroad, yelling with utter abandon, their black eyes puckered up, their mouths distended into squares, from which came such a measure of sound as to rack the ears and burden the air heavily with sadness. Poleon was going away! Their own particular Poleon! Something was badly askew in the general scheme of affairs to permit of such a thing, and they manifested their grief so loudly that Burrell, who knew nothing of Doret's intention, sought them out and tried to ascertain the cause of it. They had found the French-Canadian at the river with their father, loading his canoe, and they had asked him whither he fared. When the meaning of his words struck home they looked at each other in dismay, then, bred as they were to mask emotion, they joined hands and trudged silently back up the bank with filling eyes and chins a-quiver until they gained the rear of the house. Here they sat down all forlorn, and began to weep bitterly and in an ascending crescendo.

THE CALL OF THE OREADS

"What's the matter with you tikes, anyhow?" inquired the Lieutenant. He had always filled them with a speechless awe, and at his unexpected appearance they began the slow and painful process of swallowing their grief. He was a nice man, they had both agreed long ago, and very splendid to the eye, but he was nothing like Poleon, who was one of them, only somewhat bigger.

"Come, now! Tell me all about it," the soldier insisted. "Has something happened to the three-legged puppy?"

Molly denied the occurrence of any such catastrophe.

"Then you've lost the little shiny rifle that shoots with air?" But Johnny dispelled this horrible suspicion by drawing the formidable weapon out of the grass behind him.

"Well, there isn't anything else bad enough to cause all this outlay of anguish. Can't I help you out?"

"Poleon!" they wailed, in unison.

"Exactly! What about him?"

"He's goin' away!" said Johnny.

"He's goin' away!" echoed Molly.

"Now, that's too bad, of course," the young man assented; "but think what nice things he'll bring you when he comes back."

"He ain't comin' back!" announced the heir, with the tone that conveys a sorrow unspeakable.

"He ain't comin' back!" wailed the little girl, and, being a woman, yielded again to her weakness, unashamed.

Burrell tried to extract a more detailed explanation, but this was as far as their knowledge ran. So he sought out the Canadian, and found him with Gale in

THE BARRIER

the store, a scanty pile of food and ammunition on the counter between them.

"Poleon," said he, "you're not going away?"

"Yes," said Doret. "I'm takin' li'l' trip."

"But when are you coming back?"

The man shrugged his shoulders.

"Dat's hard t'ing for tellin'. I'm res'less in my heart, so I'm goin' travel some. I ain' never pass on de back trail yet, so I 'spect I keep goin'."

"Oh, but you can't!" cried Burrell. "I—I—" He paused awkwardly, while down the breeze came the lament of the two little Gales. "Well, I feel just as they do." He motioned in the direction of the sound. "I wanted you for a friend, Doret; I hate to lose you."

"I ain' never got my satisfy yet, so I'm pass on— all de tam' pass on. Mebbe dis trip I fin' de place."

"I'm sorry—because—well, I'm a selfish sort of cuss —and—" Burrell pulled up blushingly, with a strong man's display of shame at his own emotion. "I owe all my happiness to you, old man. I can't thank you —neither of us can—we shall never live long enough for that, but you mustn't go without knowing that I feel more than I'll ever have words to say."

He was making it very hard for the Frenchman, whose heart was aching already with a dull, unending pain. Poleon had hoped to get away quietly; his heart was too heavy to let him face Necia or this man, and run the risk of their reading his secret, so a plaintive wrinkle gathered between his eyes that grew into a smile. And then, as if he were not tried sufficiently, the girl herself came flying in.

"What's this I hear?" she cried. "Alluna tells me—" She saw the telltale pile on the counter, and her face grew white. "Then it's true! Oh, Poleon!"

THE CALL OF THE OREADS

He smiled, and spoke cheerily. "Yes, I been t'inkin' 'bout dis trip long tam'."

"When are you coming back?"

"Wal, if I fin' dat new place w'at I'm lookin' for I don' never come back. You people was good frien' to me, but I'm kin' of shif'less feller, you know. Mebbe I forget all 'bout Flambeau, an' stop on my 'New Countree'—you never can tol' w'at dose Franchemans goin' do."

"It's the wander-lust," murmured Burrell to himself; "he'll never rest."

"What a child you are!" cried Necia, half angrily. "Can't you conquer that roving spirit and settle down like a man?" She laid her hand on his arm appealingly. "Haven't I told you there isn't any 'far country'? Haven't I told you that this path leads only to hardship and suffering and danger? The land you are looking for is there"—she touched his breast—"so why don't you stay in Flambeau and let us help you to find it?"

He was deeply grateful for her blindness, and yet it hurt him so that his great heart was nigh to bursting. Why couldn't she see the endless, hopeless yearning that consumed him, and know that if he stayed in sight and touch of her it would be like a living death? Perhaps, then, she would have given over urging him to do what he longed to do, and let him go on that search he knew was hopeless, and in which he had no joy. But she did not see; she would never see. He laughed aloud, for all the world as if the sun were bright and the fret for adventure were still keen in him, then, picking up his bundle, said:

"Dere's no use argue wit' Canayen man. Mebbe some day I come paddle back roun' de ben' down began to cry as she kissed her pet good-bye on its cold, wet nose.

"W'at's dis?" said Poleon, and his voice quavered, for these childish fingers tore at his heart-strings terribly.

"He's a very brave doggie," said the little girl. "He will scare de bears away!" And then she became dissolved in tears at the anguish her offering cost her.

Doret caressed her as he had her brother, then placed the puppy carefully upon the blankets in the canoe, where it wagged a grateful and amiable stump at him and regained its breath. It was the highest proof of Molly's affection for her Poleon that she kept her tear-dimmed eyes fixed upon the dog as long as it was visible.

The time had come for the last good-bye—that awkward moment when human hearts are full and spoken words are empty. Burrell gripped the Frenchman's hand. He was grateful, but he did not know.

"Good-luck and better hunting!" he said. "A heavy purse and a light heart for you always, Poleon. I have learned to love you."

"I want you to be good husban', M'sieu'. Dat's de bes' t'ing I can wish for you."

Gale spoke to him in patois, and all he said was: "May you not forget, my son."

They did not look into each other's eyes; there was no need. The old man stooped, and, taking both his children by the hand, walked slowly towards the house.

"Dis tam' I'll fin' it for sure," smiled Poleon to Necia.

Her eyes were shining through the tears, and she whispered, fervently:

"I hope so, brother. God love you—always."

It was grief at losing a playmate, a dear and well-

THE CALL OF THE OREADS

beloved companion. He knew it well, and he was glad now that he had never said a word of love to her. It added to his pain, but it lightened hers, and that had ever been his wish. He gazed on her for a long moment, taking in that blessed image which would ever live with him—in his eyes was the light of a love as pure and clean as ever any maid had seen, and in his heart a sorrow that would never cease.

"Good-bye, li'l' gal," he said, then dropped her hand and entered his canoe. With one great stroke he drove it out and into the flood, then headed away towards the mists and colors of the distant hills, where the Oreads were calling to him. He turned for one last look, and flung his paddle high; then, fearing lest they might see the tears that came at last unhindered, he began to sing:

> *"Chanté, rossignol, chanté!*
> *Toi qui à le coeur gai;*
> *Tu as le coeur à rire*
> *Mai j' l' ai-t-à pleurer.*

He sang long and lustily, keeping time to the dip of his flashing paddle and defying his bursting heart. After all, was he not a voyageur, and life but a song and a tear, and then a dream or two?

"I wish I might have known him better," sighed Meade Burrell, as he watched the receding form of the boatman.

"You would have loved him as we do," said Necia, "and you would have missed him as we will."

"I hope some time he will be happy."

"As happy as you, my soldier?"

309

Popular Copyright Books
AT MODERATE PRICES

Any of the following titles can be bought of your bookseller at the price you paid for this volume

Circle, The. By Katherine Cecil Thurston (author of "The Masquerader," "The Gambler").
Colonial Free Lance, A. By Chauncey C. Hotchkiss.
Conquest of Canaan, The. By Booth Tarkington.
Courier of Fortune, A. By Arthur W. Marchmont.
Darrow Enigma, The. By Melvin Severy.
Deliverance, The. By Ellen Glasgow.
Divine Fire, The. By May Sinclair.
Empire Builders. By Francis Lynde.
Exploits of Brigadier Gerard. By A. Conan Doyle.
Fighting Chance, The. By Robert W. Chambers.
For a Maiden Brave. By Chauncey C. Hotchkiss.

Fugitive Blacksmith, The. By Chas. D. Stewart.
God's Good Man. By Marie Corelli.
Heart's Highway, The. By Mary E. Wilkins.
Holladay Case, The. By Burton Egbert Stevenson.
Hurricane Island. By H. B. Marriott Watson.
In Defiance of the King. By Chauncey C. Hotchkiss.
Indifference of Juliet, The. By Grace S. Richmond.
Infelice. By Augusta Evans Wilson.

Lady Betty Across the Water. By C. N. and A. M. Williamson.
Lady of the Mount, The. By Frederic S. Isham.
Lane That Had No Turning, The. By Gilbert Parker.
Langford of the Three Bars. By Kate and Virgil D. **Boyles.**
Last Trail, The. By Zane Grey.
Leavenworth Case, The. By Anna Katharine Green.
Lilac Sunbonnet, The. By S. R. Crockett.
Lin McLean. By Owen Wister.
Long Night, The. By Stanley J. Weyman.
Maid at Arms, The. By Robert W. Chambers.

Popular Copyright Books
AT MODERATE PRICES

Any of the following titles can be bought of your bookseller at the price you paid for this volume

Man from Red Keg, The. By Eugene Thwing.
Marthon Mystery, The. By Burton Egbert Stevenson.
Memoirs of Sherlock Holmes. By A. Conan Doyle.
Millionaire Baby, The. By Anna Katharine Green.
Missourian, The. By Eugene P. Lyle, Jr.
Mr. Barnes, American. By A. C. Gunter.
Mr. Pratt. By Joseph C. Lincoln.
My Friend the Chauffeur. By C. N. and A. M. Williamson.
My Lady of the North. By Randall Parrish.
Mystery of June 13th. By Melvin L. Severy.
Mystery Tales. By Edgar Allan Poe.
Nancy Stair. By Elinor Macartney Lane.
Order No. 11. By Caroline Abbot Stanley.
Pam. By Bettina von Hutten.
Pam Decides. By Bettina von Hutten.
Partners of the Tide. By Joseph C. Lincoln.
Phra the Phoenician. By Edwin Lester Arnold.
President, The. By Afred Henry Lewis.
Princess Passes, The. By C. N. and A. M. Williamson.
Princess Virginia, The. By C. N. and A. M. Williamson.
Prisoners. By Mary Cholmondeley.
Private War, The. By Louis Joseph Vance.
Prodigal Son, The. By Hall Caine.

Quickening, The. By Francis Lynde.
Richard the Brazen. By Cyrus T. Brady and Edw. Peple.
Rose of the World. By Agnes and Egerton Castle.
Running Water. By A. E. W. Mason.
Sarita the Carlist. By Arthur W. Marchmont.
Seats of the Mighty, The. By Gilbert Parker.
Sir Nigel. By A. Conan Doyle.
Sir Richard Calmady. By Lucas Malet.
Speckled Bird, A. By Augusta Evans Wilson.

Popular Copyright Books
AT MODERATE PRICES

Any of the following titles can be bought of your bookseller at the price you paid for this volume

Spirit of the Border, The. By Zane Grey.
Spoilers, The. By Rex Beach.
Squire Phin. By Holman F. Day.
Stooping Lady, The. By Maurice Hewlett.
Subjection of Isabel Carnaby. By Ellen Thorneycroft Fowler.
Sunset Trail, The. By Alfred Henry Lewis.
Sword of the Old Frontier, A. By Randall Parrish.
Tales of Sherlock Holmes. By A. Conan Doyle.
That Printer of Udell's. By Harold Bell Wright.
Throwback, The. By Alfred Henry Lewis.
Trail of the Sword, The. By Gilbert Parker.
Treasure of Heaven, The. By Marie Corelli.
Two Vanrevels, The. By Booth Tarkington.
Up From Slavery. By Booker T. Washington.
Vashti. By Augusta Evans Wilson.
Viper of Milan, The (original edition). By Marjorie Bowen.
Voice of the People, The. By Ellen Glasgow.
Wheel of Life, The. By Ellen Glasgow.

When Wilderness Was King. By Randall Parrish.
Where the Trail Divides. By Will Lillibridge.
Woman in Grey, A. By Mrs. C. N. Williamson.
Woman in the Alcove, The. By Anna Katharine Green.
Younger Set, The. By Robert W. Chambers.
The Weavers. By Gilbert Parker.
The Little Brown Jug at Kildare. By Meredith Nicholson.
The Prisoners of Chance. By Randall Parrish.
My Lady of Cleve. By Percy J. Hartley.
Loaded Dice. By Ellery H. Clark.
Get Rich Quick Wallingford. By George Randolph Chester.
The Orphan. By Clarence Mulford.
A Gentleman of France. By Stanley J. Weyman.

South University Library
Richmond Campus
2151 Old Brick Road
Glen Allen, Va 23060

AUG 3 1 2012